MESSY
Sheets

D1550879

DASHAWN TAYLOR

Also by Dashawn Taylor

Kissed by the Devil II

Kissed by the Devil

From Poverty to Power Moves

MESSY Sheets ®

NEXT LEVEL PUBLISHING

Copyright © 2011 Next Level Publishing

ISBN 10: 0980015480
ISBN 13: 978-0980015485

First Next Level Publishing Co. trade paperback edition

10 9 8 7 6 5 4 3 2 1

Printed in the United States of America

For information regarding wholesale and publishing information, please contact:
info@nextlevelpublishing.com

Photographer : Sandy Porter
Model : Arekah Smith
Cover Layout and Design by: HotBookCovers.com
Editor and Book Layout: Jassi Wright {jassiwright@gmail.com}

www.nextlevelpublishing.com

Facebook.com/dashawnt
Twitter.com/dashawntaylor

This book is for my FATHER.

I know you're in the heavens somewhere shaking your head at the thought of me dedicating such a crazy project to you (*smiles*). But you always encouraged me to be creative and never shy away from my talents. So from this day forward, I promise to stay the course and show the world what it means to be TAYLOR – MADE!

Miss you, and I love you, Dad. I dedicate my career to your memory.

Michael L. Taylor

(1954-2009)

Acknowledgments

First, I have to thank GOD.

To my Mother Joanne Smith…the true ULTIMATE HUSTLER! There's no way any of this could be possible if you didn't hold us down and hold the family together for so many years. Love you always, Mom!

Thanks to my brothers, Michael Taylor, DJ Symphony and My Brother Ca$h. Much love to my little sisters, Alikah and Bria, and special love to my beautiful niece, Harmony. Also, much love to the Smith and Taylor families. You know our clan is too big to name everyone, but just know that I love you guys.

A Special thank you to the Next Level Publishing Family! Harold Williams – President (Thank you for your guidance and your strength to keep us flowing in the right direction. H…you already know…2011 and beyond belongs to us!) To Aleasha Arthur–VP of Operations & Marketing (The hardest working woman in the business. Thanks for giving NLP the proper swagger, and keeping the company shining. You are truly a blessing!)

To my industry friends. Jamise L. Dames...I'm glad you were a part of this project. Thanks for your help and dedication. To Azarel...thanks for the *Life Changing* talk when I was at my lowest because of "you know who". To Deborah Cardona... thanks for always keeping it real. And to my dude, Lee Harris... good looking on the advice. Quitting is Never an Option!

And most of all, thank you to all of the living angels who continue to hold me down. Please Support the Hustlers Always.

Kyle Newsome (Real-Hiphop.com), Shaliek Murray (Lavish Look), Bob Sumner (Laff Mobb), Carl Cole (C-Mini University), DJ Megatron (R.I.P.), Cynthia Strickland (Cee & Learn), Yvette Hayward (AALAS), Pamela Smith (Wendy Williams Show), Martinique Moore (Air It Out Show), Mother Rose (Underground Books), Michelle Edwards (The High Heel Show), Lesslie Moore (Don Diva Magazine), Olivia Fox (NAPKCC), Felicia Newsome, Shannon Phillips, Reggie Rouse (CBS Radio), Nyema Taylor, Vickie Stringer, Nikki Turner, Bum (Source Magazine), Isadora Douglas, Erick S. Gray, K'wan, Treasure E. Blue, Cynthia Anderson, Al Saadiq Banks, Brittani Williams, Shawna Grundy (G-Street Chronicles), Ox Mendez, JM Benjamin, Belinda (Hood Novels), Tanisha Malone, Black and Nobel Bookstore, Wahida Clark, Jesel Forde, Sylvia Denton, Tia Darlene Rudd, Mr. G Photography, ESharan Publishing, Omar Tyree, TLJ Bookstore, Slick Crutch, DJ Commish, Mack Mama, L-S, Marcus Oliver (MLO Entertainment), Novel Tees, Toni Ciullo, Sidi, Urban Knowledge Bookstore, Miz, Nubian Bookstore, Empire Books, Déjà vu Book Lounge ...I want to personally THANK YOU!

If you don't see your name, please blame it on my mind, not my heart! ♥

MESSY Sheets

DASHAWN TAYLOR

One

It was the dead of winter in the Tri-State area. The cold and treacherous season's constant snowfall and ice storms crippled the streets. Freezing temperatures forced many to stay indoors and avoid the hectic rat race, but not twenty-nine year old Kimi Moore. This was the perfect evening for her to be out. She navigated up the turnpike en route to her Saddle Brook, New Jersey home. The BMW X5's interior heated up by the second, closely matching her body temperature as it slowly rose in anticipation. Tonight, she carried very precious cargo in the trunk, and just the very thought of it made her more excited. She avoided every pothole, dip and divot in the highway. She wanted to make sure not to break a thing. Her mission was to get her package safely back to her home unscathed. The tricky parts were calming her heartbeat to manageable and controlling her excitement. It had been a while since Kimi felt so energized. As one of the youngest and most successful entrepreneurs in her industry, she was an overachiever. A successful businesswoman and a self proclaimed "Diva of Pleasure", Kimi had worked hard to make it to the good life. And she'd made it. With a large home, luxurious cars and a sizeable bank account, Kimi didn't want for much. And she worked nearly seventy hours some weeks to keep her business thriving to make sure she didn't.

But tonight work wasn't on her agenda. Tonight was playtime. She had been planning this evening for over a month, and her mind was ironing out every detail to make sure it was going to flow as smoothly as possible. As Kimi finally exited the highway and drove through the calm streets of Saddle Brook, her thoughts shifted to the sweet treats she was about to experience. She smiled, thinking about the package in the trunk again, and slowed down the vehicle. *Careful*, Kimi reminded herself. She carefully turned onto the long dark road leading up to the front entrance of Shady Meadows' gated community.

Kimi loved where she lived. The very affluent neighborhood was meticulously guarded, and she never had to worry about safety. There were only twenty families that lived in Shady Meadows, and, to her knowledge, she was the only homeowner who lived alone. As she approached the small guardhouse near the entrance, she prepared herself to be teased by the playful night watchman.

"Good evening, Ms. Moore." The young security guard smiled.

"Hello, Christopher," Kimi sweetly responded.

"You are looking very beautiful as always, ma'am," Christopher complimented.

Kimi glanced at the security guard's fresh face as he gawked at her. She nodded her head and smiled. "Awl, thanks Christopher. You're always so kind to me," she bashfully said.

Christopher was a cute kid, but was entirely too young for her. She was a grown woman with a grown woman's taste. And a twenty-four year old security guard who made nine dollars an hour was not going to cut it. But that didn't stop the ambitious youngster from taking a shot at the prize.

"How is everything going, Ms. Moore?" Christopher continued. "No one is bothering you are they?"

"No, not at all." Kimi giggled. "I don't let people bother me anymore. Now I just bother them."

He laughed at her joke. "Well, you know if you need me, I'm only a buzz away," he said looking inside of her car. He ran his eyes over a few shopping bags in the back seat, and then looked at Kimi. "Do you need any help with those?" He gestured to the bags.

"No, I'm fine," she replied. "Trust me, I can handle everything in this car." Her facial expression brightened on her last statement.

"Okay, ma'am," he whispered.

"I do have a question for you," Kimi said. "When are they going to fix the gates to the rear entrance?"

"I'm sorry, Ms. Moore. I really don't know what the holdup is," he replied. "Fixing those gates has been on the schedule for a few months now." His mood began to sullen with his explanation.

"Don't get me wrong, sweetie. I don't mind coming this way to say hello to you guys," Kimi continued. "The other entrance is just closer to my house."

"I understand," Christopher responded. "I will ask management about that on Monday, and see what is going on. Now, Ms. Moore, I do hope you know that we are going to miss you once the other gates are fixed."

"Awl, stop it, Christopher." Kimi laughed. "You are too funny. Have a good night, sweetie, and stay warm."

"I will try." He smiled as Kimi pulled away from the guardhouse. He reached for the side panel near his desk, then leisurely pressed the red button on the wall.

The large steel entrance gates gave way to an extravagant thirty acres of well-crafted homes and gorgeous landscapes. No matter how many times Kimi drove up the winding roads leading to her house, she couldn't help but feel like she was driving through a dream. The houses in the community seemed to be out of a storybook. New England-style homes, Bostonian-style, and Castle-style structures gracefully towered over the well-kept community lawns. Kimi felt proud as she drove slowly through the neighborhood headed to Victoria Way. She playfully winked at the street sign and chuckled. Every street was named after a famous European Queen. Each day Kimi saw *Victoria Way* reminded her that she was definitely a queen who had earned her right to live amongst the ranks of royalty. Kimi carefully turned on her street and coasted up the small hill. Her mind was still on the package in the trunk, and she reminded herself not to make any sudden maneuvers that would damage the cargo. The X5 quietly coasted down the street and approached her large home. Another rush of excitement came over her as she realized she was only minutes away from a very memorable night. She pressed the button for on garage door opener while looking around the dark street. There was only one other house on the road, and, by the looks of things, her neighbor was sound asleep. Kimi turned off the lights of the X5 as she passed her neighbor's home and continued to her house. She pulled into her driveway and disabled the house alarm from inside the SUV. The soft lights in her garage lit up as the door closed behind the vehicle. Kimi took a moment to clear her mind and sat quietly. She caressed her neck and shoulders, and enjoyed the sensation. It felt good to finally be home. She moved her hands down and found herself massaging her own thighs. Her heart fluttered for a moment, and she couldn't help but giggle. The heat from the X5 lost to the body heat coming from her, a signal that she was beyond ready for the package. Finally, she got out of the vehicle and walked to the trunk. One long look at it and she smiled again. Before she could reach down and unlock the latch, a flash of light came from just beyond the garage window. She quickly noticed that her neighbor's porch light was on. She dropped her eyebrows and investigated the area. *Did my neighbor see me?* Kimi thought. Her heart raced with a mix of emotions. She was both nervous and excited at the thought of being spotted. *Wow, did my nosey-ass neighbor actually watch me pulling into the garage?* she wondered. *What about the security guard? I wonder if he saw my package somehow and tipped everybody off.* A few more questions swirled inside of Kimi's mind as she looked through the garage window. Kimi stared at her neighbor's house for another moment and smiled. Being watched from the dark house across the street only excited her more. After a few seconds, her neighbor's porch light flickered out and the street became dark again. Kimi turned her attention back to the trunk of the X5 and took another deep breath. She carefully reached down, pulled on the latch, and proceeded with her plan to make it an unbelievable night of absolute pleasure.

TWO

About twenty miles away in Newark, New Jersey the snowfall and cold weather was just as bitter. A heavy ice storm earlier in the week had put the largest city in the state on high alert. The Mayor of Newark urged everyone to stay indoors and limit their traveling. The snowy roads and powerful winds were dreadful conditions for traveling around the city. But for thirty-one year old Marcel Harris this was no time to clam up. Serious business had to be taken care of tonight. Marcel pushed his SUV through the heavy snow and icy streets. He was only about ten minutes away from his destination, but his adrenaline made it feel like hours. Marcel looked at the clock on his dashboard and let out a frustrated gasp. Before he could dwell on the late hour, his cellphone started buzzing. He quickly picked up the phone and answered the call.

"Yea," Marcel coldly grunted.

"Where are you?" a woman questioned from the other line.

"Would you relax," he snapped. "I'm almost there. It's icy as fuck out here."

"Alright, but you don't have to curse at me," the woman responded. "Everybody's here, and we're just waiting on you."

"I'm turning down the street right now," Marcel lied. "I'll be there in two minutes."

Before the woman on the other line could say another word, Marcel hung up the phone and continued down the snowy road. By the looks of the streets, North Newark had been hit the hardest by the storm. Parked cars were still buried under mountains of snow, and the roads needed to be plowed. Five minutes later, Marcel was turning down Walnut Terrace. He drove to the biggest house located on the end of the block. There were no parking spaces in the area, so he decided to double-park in the middle of the street. He noticed a few cars in the driveway, and he sensed it was a packed house. He quickly picked up his cellphone and dialed the last caller. He put the phone to his ear and waited for the woman to pick up.

"I'm outside," Marcel announced. "Open the door for me."

Marcel didn't wait for a response. He disconnected the call and gathered his stuff. He made sure to put his cellphone and his keys in his pocket. He took another look at the large house and thought for a moment. After a few seconds, he reached down near his waist and pulled out a forty-five-caliber handgun. He flicked on the pistol's safety feature, and then carefully placed the gun under the car seat. "Damn, I hope I don't need this shit tonight," Marcel whispered under his breath. He was very diligent about protecting himself these days. He was a young entrepreneur on the rise in Newark, but his business was far from legal. While most of his family chose to work day jobs, he chose to take a shot at living the fast life. In his early twenties, he tried to become Newark's biggest drug dealer. But after being incarcerated for multiple cases, he decided to go into another line of work, and tonight was a very important night for his business. Marcel took one last look around his truck and hopped out into the brick cold. He wrapped his leather jacket tight around his body, and then carefully jogged up the driveway to the front porch. He noticed the front door was open, and Marcel walked into the house. A young sassy woman, who stood dead center in the hallway with both hands on hips, greeted him.

Twenty-four year old Tricia Daniels was a sexy woman with incredible street smarts. Standing at only five-foot-two, she was a small firecracker with a huge temper. They had been good friends for nearly three years, and their relationship was very unconventional. Outside of the crazy sex they shared, the two agreed to remain cool and never escalate their friendship. After Marcel's business started to take off, he bought a large house in North Newark and asked Tricia to live there rent-free in exchange for maintenance. Tricia agreed and never complained about the arrangement. But lately, Marcel was trying her patience with a number of late night meetings at the house. Tonight he'd called a last minute meeting to interview new workers for the business. He'd asked Tricia to prepare everything, and, reluctantly, she'd agreed. It was close to midnight when he came stumbling through the door, and the cold air he'd allowed inside only added to Tricia's frustration. She looked at Marcel as he tried to gather himself.

"So how long is this gonna take?" Tricia asked with a sharp tone.

"C'mon, stop it. I don't know how long this is gonna take," Marcel uttered.

"Don't give me that shit, Marcel," Tricia fired back. "I'm serious. It's late."

"I know," Marcel replied. He took off his jacket and gave it to Tricia. He looked around the house. "Where are they?"

"In the basement," Tricia replied.

"Is it a lot of them?" he asked.

"The last time I counted it was like nine or ten," Tricia responded.

"That's good," he said. "I'll go down there right now and get it poppin'."

Tricia watched Marcel as he walked to the mirror in

the living room and adjusted the fit of his clothes. Marcel was dressed in a slick outfit that didn't match the temperature outside. A very tight T-shirt that fit nicely around every bulging muscle of his upper body complimented his rugged True Religion jeans. Marcel took very good care of his body, and it showed. Tricia caught herself admiring Marcel's gorgeous physique as he walked toward the basement door.

"This shouldn't take too long," Marcel continued. "I shouldn't be no more than an hour."

"Okay," Tricia said. "What about when you're done? Are you gonna stay?"

There was something sensual in Tricia's request, and Marcel picked up on the vibe. He looked at his young friend and gave her a smile.

"You want me to stay?" Marcel asked with a devious expression.

"Please," Tricia whispered. "Can you?"

"I have to see," he said. "I gotta make a couple of calls and check on some things, but I'll try my best."

Tricia decided not to push the issue. She turned away from him and walked upstairs to her bedroom. Marcel took a deep breath and opened the door to the basement. He could hear the sound of people talking and laughing downstairs. A nervous boost of energy came over him. Marcel calmed himself and put on his game-face. He noticed the talking dulling to a silence as he made his way down the stairs. He walked into the enormous basement and was greeted by twelve young women staring at him. The women, scattered about the lounge area, all were admiring Marcel's beautiful house. His basement was far from an ordinary dungeon. He'd turned the bottom level into something out of a hip-hop music video. The three-room basement was plush. Flat screen televisions, leather sectionals and two poker tables were just the start of his creativity. He'd had the basement outfitted with a full dance floor, topped off with a steel pole in the middle. Because of Marcel's fetish for exotic dancers, he felt the need to install the pole just in case a dancer wanted to make him happy with a striptease.

He quickly scanned the basement and counted the women again. The ladies varied in shapes and sizes, but all were sexy. Their complexions ranged from milk chocolate to honey-brown to sweet vanilla. A smirk came to Marcel's face as the women continued to stare. He knew he was looking his best, and all the jewelry draping from his neck and wrist only added to his allure. Marcel put his hands together and smoothly fiddled with the ring on his pinky. *This is what I'm talking about*, he thought. He looked over the women one more time, and he was confident he would find his next worker somewhere in the mix.

"Good evening, ladies," Marcel slickly greeted them. "I'm sorry about the snow outside, but I didn't order this bullshit." A few of the women smiled at Marcel, and others laughed at his joke. "Some of you are coming from Jersey, and I know a couple of y'all are coming from New York, so I'll make sure not to keep you too long." Marcel walked by the women and motioned for them to follow him into the back room to the elevated dance floor. "I need y'all to line up in a single file against the wall and face me."

The women walked behind Marcel and followed his instructions. They stood by each other, and then turned to face him. Marcel walked up and down the line, inspecting the women like a military base drill instructor. He checked every feature of the women. Most of the women looked at Marcel, not knowing what to expect. They simply stayed silent and waited for him to finish with his spot check. He walked by the last girl in line and nodded his head. He was more than pleased with the women who decided to show up.

"My name is Marcel, and make no mistake about it, I run this shit." His voice was loud and dominant. All of the women froze, hanging on to his every word as he continued. "Now some of you may think you know me, and some of you may have heard about me and my company, but from this minute forward I want you to forget about everything you heard in those streets. Fuck that shit. The only person who knows exactly what I do is me, and even I don't know the full story." A few of the women giggled as Marcel continued. "One of the companies I run is a full blown escort service. The women that work for me are serious about what they do, and they get money from it. I've put bitches through a couple of colleges and even med school. When you work for me, I will make sure you get your money on time, and nobody will ever fuck with you. I only got two rules."

Marcel continued to walk up and down the line and look at the women. He made eye contact with each one of them, trying to spot any weakness. He never missed a beat as he continued to speak.

"Rule number one is to stay silent," Marcel continued. "And rule number two is to stay sexy. Never talk about my company to nobody you know. Don't tell no friends and no family about your business. Don't even tell the fuckin' dog about what you do. And when it comes to being sexy, if you work for me you betta keep that ass in the gym and stay tight. I deal with a serious clientele, and they only want the best. That's exactly what I plan to keep givin' them. Does everybody understand the rules?"

The women nodded, one at a time. Marcel looked up and down the line and decided to get a better view of the women. He walked away from them to the other side of the room. He took a moment to glance at his watch and noticed the time was getting away from him. Marcel continued to speak.

"Now let me say this straight off the rip, I definitely like this group, but, tonight, I only need one girl. I need just one bad bitch to represent my business and drive these niggas crazy. The one girl I choose gotta be off the chain and ready to work. Now I'm looking at y'all, and I see Prada bags and Fendi jackets. I see Jimmy Choo shoes over there. I see those nice ass Seven jeans that shorty got on. I'm loving the makeup right there," he said, pointing. "I see one girl right there dipped out with nice jewelry. And I see about sixty pounds of fake hair down here. This is wild. I see y'all came out to represent tonight. But a true bad bitch is not all about what's on the outside. A true bad bitch gotta have that sex appeal and lovely swagger. It's all about what she got goin' on up here." Marcel pointed to his head on his last statement. "She needs to be street-smart and bed-smart at the same time. She gotta know how to please these niggas, find out what they want, and quickly make it happen. So now I got a question for you. Which one of y'all is that bad bitch that I'm looking for?"

The women in the basement raised their hands in the air. A few of them shouted with excitement, trying to get Marcel's attention. The women saw the competition was on, and they all tried their best to outshine each other—except for one. Marcel noticed a woman to his right was not raising her hand. She held her ground and kept her arms folded. The honey-brown girl was standing with a slight attitude, and looked at the other girls with distain. The woman caught Marcel's attention, and he slowly walked over to her. Everyone turned their attention to him as he approached the young lady.

"Hey sexy, what's your name?" Marcel asked. He looked her up and down and slowly nodded his head.

"Benita," she responded.

"Benittaaaa," Marcel playfully sang her name. "Where you from, baby?"

"Philly," Benita responded.

"And you came all the way up here for this job?" Marcel asked.

12

"Yes," she whispered.

"I like that. A girl with ambition." Marcel smiled. He looked at the other girls for a moment before turning his attention back to Benita. "So why you not raising your hand? What's the matter? You don't think you're a bad bitch?"

"Actually, I don't think I'm a *bitch* at all," Benita responded with a slight attitude.

"Oh really? Is that right?" Marcel said, raising his eyebrows.

"I'm not here to be disrespected," Benita said. "If I'm going to take this job, I need to set some ground rules of my own. I'm not a bitch, and I refuse to be treated like a bitch. I am a grown woman, and I need to be respected like one. That's the bottom line. I'm not a bad bitch, so I can't raise my hand to that question. And, in all honestly, I'm nobody's bitch."

"Wow," Marcel said. He smiled at Benita for a second. He seemed to be impressed with her courage. He slowly reached into his front pocket and pulled out a large roll of money. The women in the line focused on the thick stack of cash. They watched Marcel as he peeled off five crispy one-hundred-dollar bills and gave them to Benita. He smiled at her. Benita slowly took the money, obviously shocked by his move. She folded the bills and placed them in her bra. She felt the heat from the other eyes in the room, but kept her focus on Marcel.

"Thank you," Benita said.

Marcel gave her a nod, then looked at the other women. Some of them gave him a dirty glare; obviously jealous of the attention he was giving to Benita. He made sure all of the other women were watching him when he turned his focus back to Benita.

"Now get the fuck outta my house," Marcel coldly shouted. The basement fell silent. A few of the women covered their mouth at the bitter command. Benita looked at him with a strange look. His sharp words felt like a heavy punch to her stomach.

"Excuse me?" Benita gasped. She was beyond shocked.

"You heard what the fuck I said," Marcel barked. His eyes were serious. "I'm not running no fuckin' Girl Scout meeting in here. What I'm looking for is a bad motherfucker that got her head on right. My clients are high profile businessmen, professional athletes, multi-million dollar moguls, and ballers with money. They are use to getting the best and they pay for the best. My clients can change your raggedy ass life in one month. So if they want you to be classy, you will be classy. If they want you to be a sex slave, you will be a sex slave for them. And if they want you to be a bad-bitch, then, goddammit, you betta be the baddest bitch on this planet." Marcel sharply looked at the other women in the basement. Although he was in front of Benita, Marcel was speaking to the entire group. He exhaled with frustration, and then turned back to Benita. "So I don't give a fuck if you don't want to be *nobody's bitch*. I'm not trying to save the world in here. I'm about getting money, and it's obvious that you don't have a clue what that means. So hit the bricks, and thanks for playing."

On Marcel's last words, he pointed to the second floor as a direct order to Benita. She gave him a disappointed gesture and tried to shake off his lecture, but she was clearly hurt. She gathered herself and stepped out of the line. All of the women watched Benita as she made her way to the stairs.

"And take that five-hundred dollars I gave you and buy a new attitude," Marcel yelled one last insult. "You will never get no real money with that bullshit attitude you got now." Benita headed upstairs and left the house. Marcel turned to the women and gave each one of them another onceover. "This is a serious game that we play, ladies," Marcel continued. "The stakes are very high, and the money is long. I'm not looking for somebody that's looking to play around with this shit. My clients are real people, and they wanna fuck. They have fantasies just like the rest of us. My job is to put them in front of a bad bitch that can turn their fantasies into reality. And just know that if you work with me, I will guarantee that you make six figures this year. So I'm gonna ask you again, ladies, which one of you is the baddest bitch in here?"

The ladies' hands shot to the sky like fireworks. The basement was electrified with women yelling and screaming, trying to get Marcel's undivided attention. He noticed that every woman had her hand raised, and a sly grin emerged on his face.

"That's more like it," Marcel whispered. "Now let's get down to business."

Three

"**W**hy the fuck would I steal ya money, dude? Don't get this shit twisted. I got my own money, and the only reason why I'm even here doing this is because you begged me to do this shit. Don't be tryin' to play me and say I stole your shit. I don't even get down like that!"

Twenty-eight year old Sabrina Harris found herself in a tough predicament this evening. Standing directly in front of her wearing nothing but a pair of sweatpants and a furious expression on his face was Khalil, a burly middle-aged man with an ugly reputation for beating women. Sabrina's wide eyes stared at him standing in the middle of their hotel room. He held a small pocketknife in one hand and his empty wallet in the other. For the past few minutes, he had been debating what to do with the knife while he tried to figure out where his money had gone.

Sabrina put up her hand in an effort to calm him down. "Don't do nothin' crazy, man," she nervously uttered.

She tried to keep her voice calm, yet stern. She wanted Khalil to know that if he was going to try something tonight, he was going to be in for a fight. She backed away from him and got closer to the bed. Khalil was still mentally backtracking as he tried to remember where his money was. Sabrina quickly put on her jeans and T-shirt, and then looked at Khalil, whose large body was blocking the way to the front door. She tried to figure out how to leave the hotel room without a serious alteration. She looked over to Khalil and noticed he now wore a blank expression. Sabrina didn't know if he was still thinking about the money, or if the Hennessey he'd been drinking all night was finally slowing him down.

"Did you hear what I just said?" Sabrina whispered. "I said, don't do nothing stupid. Why don't you just put down the knife?"

"What?" Khalil responded. He slowly lifted his head and looked at her. "Where the fuck is my money?" he slurred.

"I really don't know what the hell you're talking about," Sabrina repeated. She was noticeably growing anxious. "I didn't touch ya money."

"You fuckin' liar. Yes, you did!" Khalil barked.

He slammed down his empty wallet, and then looked over to Sabrina, who was now backing away from him. As Khalil got closer to her, all Sabrina could think was, *how the hell did I get here?*

Sabrina was not the typical call girl. She was a sexy woman entering her thirties and looking for a serious career change. After eight long years of trying to break into the modeling industry, she found herself on hard times and unable to handle the mounting bills. Sabrina was a very beautiful woman, and had been her whole life. Her deep chocolate skin and her curvaceous body were any man's dream, but those same attributes seemed to work against her when she entered the casting agencies. For every Tom, Dick and Harry on the streets who'd told Sabrina she was gorgeous, there were a number of agents, photographers and casting directors who'd told her she would never be successful in the modeling business. After a disappointing journey, Sabrina found out the hard way that being a dark-skinned black woman with shapely hips would only get her so far in the modeling world. She soon hung up her cat-walking shoes, deciding it was time to get real about her life and get her money woes under control.

Besides dressing like at millionaire and walking like she owned the world, Sabrina didn't have many skills. She made an attempt to work for a few businesses in the area, but the slow money only frustrated her. After a couple of years of being hired and fired from various jobs, Sabrina decided to turn to the oldest profession. Because she was so attractive, it didn't take long for Sabrina's clientele to quickly grow.

Sabrina was very independent, never wanting a man to pimp her out. She figured she could make more money and stay under the radar without someone telling her where to go and who to be with. But not having a male figure around posed a major safety problem. When things turned ugly, there was no one who could help her diffuse the drama. Tonight, she found herself in that very situation. A man who was supposed to be one of her best customers was now accusing her of stealing. She had to figure out something fast before things spun out of control. She looked Khalil straight in the eyes and tried to reason with him.

"Think about it for a minute, Khalil," she said. "Why would I steal the money you was gonna pay me with? That doesn't make any sense. Why would I do that?"

"Bitch, I had fourteen-hundred dollars in my wallet," Khalil yelled. "Where is it?" He moved closer to Sabrina with the knife blade sticking out.

"Please, Khalil. I didn't steal no money from you," Sabrina pleaded, dropping her voice. She tried again to reason with him. "Maybe you left it in the car. We can try to look in there."

"Fuck that," Khalil snapped. "Where is your purse?"

"It's right there," Sabrina said, pointing to the desk.

Khalil rushed over to the Gucci bag, placing the knife on the desk. He turned the bag upside down, and then dumped everything onto the bed. Sabrina's stuff flew everywhere. Noticing that Khalil didn't have the knife anymore, she moved closer to him, pointing at her scattered belongings. "See!" Sabrina shouted. "No money. I told you I don't have it." Sabrina grabbed her cellphone off the bed. "Listen, if we're done here, I'm gonna call a cab. You don't have to drop me off."

Khalil disregarded her last statement. He was still staring at the bed, waiting for the money to appear. But it wasn't there. Khalil looked at Sabrina and turned his attention to her jeans. "Empty your pockets, bitch," he commanded

"Khalil, I don't have your money, damn. Look," Sabrina yelled and pointed to her pants. "They're too tight for anything to fit. I'm tellin' you the truth. I don't have your money."

Khalil grew very angry on Sabrina's last statement, then rushed over to her. His face turned to pure fury. Sabrina had to make a move. Khalil barreled toward her, reaching for her pockets. His forcefulness slammed her into the desk, then he reached down near her hips and started tugging on her pants.

"Where the fuck is my money?" he yelled.

"Stop it," Sabrina screamed. "You're hurting me."

Khalil ignored her pleas and continued to violently search her jeans. Sabrina's heart pounded with terror and she grew desperate to break free from his grasp. She turned her head around and frantically looked around the desk. Her eyes zeroed in on the metal lamp near the edge of the table. Without a thought, Sabrina snatched the lamp from the desk and swung it at Khalil's head. Her awkward attempt to strike him failed. Khalil watched her the whole time, and managed to dodge the heavy lamp. Sabrina stumbled forward, almost losing her balance from swinging the too heavy lamp. He stopped for a moment, looking at Sabrina trying to gather herself. He scoffed at her lack of strength and slowly cocked back his left arm to hit her. Sabrina saw him about to clobber her from the corner of her eye, and a shot of adrenaline rushed through her. Sabrina quickly realized she had to defend herself. She mustered up the strength, swinging the heavy lamp again, backhanded this time, like a tennis racket. Khalil didn't see the lamp coming, and the impact smashed him square on the side of his chin. Sabrina yelled as the lamp split a deep gash in Khalil's face. He screamed in pain, stumbling away from her. Sabrina saw her chance to flee, then rushed toward the front door, but Khalil gave chase. Sabrina reached down to grab her bag, and the mistake proved costly. The momentary hesitation had given Khalil a chance to catch up. Before she could make it to the front door, Khalil swung at her. His heavy fist hit Sabrina hard on the back of the head, and she quickly crumbled to the carpet.

"Fuck!" Sabrina yelled in pain.

She unconsciously reached for the back of her head and quickly turned around on the floor. She noticed Khalil still coming toward her. Knowing that she wouldn't be able to make it to the front door, Sabrina crawled into the bathroom of the hotel room and slammed the door.

"What the fuck are you doin'?" Khalil yelled.

He continued to bang on the door and yell. Sabrina lay in the middle of the cold bathroom floor in pain. She tried to catch her breath and calm herself, but the fight with Khalil left her shaking in fear. She reached for her head again to check for blood. A sudden moment of relief came over Sabrina when she realized she still had a tight grip on her cellphone. She'd never let go of it. Sabrina's wheels began to turn, and she thought about her next move. She refused to call the police or hotel security. The chances of escaping arrest were sure to be slim once the details of her work were exposed. Sabrina scrolled through her phone, and thought about who could help.

"Open this fuckin' door!" Khalil yelled from just beyond the bathroom.

"Fuck you!" Sabrina fired back.

She dropped her head in her hands. The entire night was clearly getting to her. She turned her focus back to her phone. She continued to scroll through her contacts, hoping an idea would come to her. After a few moments, Sabrina scrolled to a name she hadn't called in over a year. She thought for a second and dropped her head. *This is insane*, Sabrina thought. It was a long shot, but Sabrina had to take a chance. She clicked on the contact and called the number. The phone rang and Sabrina waited silently in the bathroom for the call to connect.

*

Back in North Newark, the sound of pounding music could be heard vibrating from the basement. Tricia was upstairs watching television in her bedroom, trying hard to keep herself awake. While Marcel was still downstairs searching for his newest worker, she was trying like hell not to fall asleep. She hadn't seen him in a while, and she was hoping to convince him to spend the night with her once he was done. The hour was quickly becoming late, but he was more than worth it. As Tricia flipped through the channels, all she could think about was seducing Marcel the moment all the women in the basement left. She had a few tricks up her sleeve, and all she needed was a few minutes alone with him to persuade him to stay with her.

Tricia was still flipping though channels when the loud ring of the cordless phone on the nightstand jolted her. *What the hell?* Tricia thought. She looked at the phone, but didn't recognize the number. Her first thought was to ignore the call, but something told her to answer it. She grabbed the remote, muted the television, and answered.

"Hello."

"I need your help," a female voice hysterically whispered. "Please."

"Huh?" Tricia responded. She sat up on the edge of her bed and put the phone closer to her ear. "Who's this?" she asked.

21

"Tricia, it's me," the female uttered. "Sabrina."

"Sabrina, why you whispering?" Tricia asked.

"I'm stuck in the bathroom," she responded.

"What?" Tricia mumbled. "Is this a joke? What the hell are you doing, Sabrina? Are you drunk?"

"No, please," Sabrina pleaded. "I'm in a fucked up spot, and I need you to help me out. This is serious."

"Okay, I'm sorry," Tricia said. She sensed urgency in Sabrina's voice, and then jumped to her feet. "What's going on? What happened?"

"Not right now. I don't have a lot of time to explain," Sabrina gasped. Her voice grew more anxious with each word. "Please tell me Marcel is there with you?"

"He is, but he's in the basement working," Tricia responded.

"I need to speak with him now," Sabrina said. "Please. I'm in the middle of some serious shit." A loud banging just outside the bathroom door shook Sabrina again. She didn't know what Khalil was doing as he continued to pound on the bathroom door.

Tricia heard the banging in the background and rushed out of her bedroom. She headed downstairs to get the phone to Marcel. By the sound of things, Sabrina was in deep trouble, and she needed Tricia to act fast.

"I'm going downstairs to get him now," Tricia said.

"Hurry, please," Sabrina whispered.

Tricia rushed down to the first floor, heading for the basement. When she opened the door, she was showered by the loud music. She covered the cordless phone and rushed down the stairs. Marcel was in the back room still looking over candidates. He was narrowing down his choices to the final three when he noticed Tricia walking into the room. He dropped his eyebrows. The other women looked at Tricia and frowned.

Marcel noticed Tricia holding the phone in her hand and walked over to her. "What the fuck are you doin' down here?" he yelled.

"It's an emergency," Tricia nervously said. "It's your niece."

Marcel glanced down at the phone, then looked back at the women. He walked over to the entertainment center and turned off the music. The basement fell silent. He casually walked back to Tricia, grabbing the cordless phone from her grip. All of the women watched Marcel as he walked to the other end of the basement and put the phone to his ear.

"You got some nerve calling here, Sabrina," Marcel mumbled with an aggressive tone.

"Listen, Uncle M, this is not the time for old beef." Sabrina's voice was low and strained. The loud pounding on the bathroom door was causing her heart to race.

Marcel heard the noise in the background and stiffened his face. "What the fuck is that, Sabrina?" Marcel barked.

"I need you to come get me, Uncle M," Sabrina pleaded.

"What?" he snapped.

"I'm at the Robert Treat hotel," Sabrina continued. "I'm with this guy, and he's saying I stole money from him. He already hit me in my fuckin' head, Uncle M. Please, I need you to come get me. Now!" Sabrina's voice cracked with emotion.

A shot of anger rushed through Marcel's body. He was irritated for a few reasons tonight, but hearing that someone was putting hands on his family made him go into beast mode. He gritted his teeth in anger. "Where you at right now?" Marcel snapped.

"At the Robert Treat hotel, Uncle M," Sabrina responded.

"No, where *are* you? You still in the room with him?" Marcel questioned.

"No, I locked myself inside the bathroom," Sabrina whispered. "And he's still in the room. I really don't want to go out if he's still in there."

"Who the fuck is this dude?" Marcel asked. "Do I know him?"

"I don't think so," Sabrina said. "His name is Khalil. He's one of my customers."

"Customers?" Marcel snapped again. His voice was filled with suspicion. "What the fuck are you into, Sabrina?"

"Please, Uncle M. Not right now," she continued to plead. "Just come get me. I'm scared."

Marcel put a tighter grip on the phone, growing more furious. He looked back to Tricia and gave her a hard stare. "I'm on my way," Marcel said. "Don't come out of that bathroom until I get there. What room you in?"

"Room seven-twenty-nine," Sabrina responded.

"I'm leaving now. I'll be there in less than fifteen minutes." Marcel hung up the phone, then turned to Tricia. She knew the dark look in his eyes. He was boiling inside, and his face told the entire story.

"Send those bitches home," he mumbled, handing Tricia the cordless phone. "I'll call you later."

Tricia didn't say a word. She watched silently as Marcel turned around and headed upstairs. There were only a few things in Marcel's life that set him off. He hated when people touched his money and, especially, hated when people touched his family. With every step, he grew angrier. He grabbed his coat and headed outside. He was so irate, he never noticed the snowfall was heavier now. Marcel jumped into his truck and fired up the engine. He reached under his seat and grabbed hold of his pistol. He double checked the clip, then flicked off the safety. With his gun in his lap, he pulled away from the house and pushed through the thick storm, anxious to confront Khalil.

24

Four

Back in Shady Meadows things were heating up for an entirely different reason. Kimi Moore was still staring at her neighbor's house across the street and surveying the area. When the lights went off in front of her neighbor's house, Kimi turned her attention back to the trunk of her X5. The mood in the dark garage became more intense as her heart raced with anticipation. She was now extra ready for her package. Playfully, she knocked on the trunk and pulled on the lever. A wide smile came to her gorgeous face as the door to the hatchback opened. The sight of her cargo caused her to nibble on her bottom lip and slowly exhale. *No dents, no scratches, and no blemishes*, Kimi thought as she looked down.

Thirty-four year old Niko Stanton was comfortably huddled in the back of the trunk. The sexy man calmly looked up to Kimi's smiling face, and then returned the expression. For a man who had been cooped up in the back of the BMW for over an hour, Niko was still very relaxed. Kimi reached out her hand, bracing Niko as he pulled himself out of the tight space.

"Baby, are you okay?" she asked.

Niko climbed out of the trunk and nodded his head with a slightly exhausted expression.

"Damn, honey, how long do you think we can keep this up?" she asked as she watched Niko stretch out his arms.

"As long as we have to," Niko responded, looking at Kimi. "That wasn't too bad this time. You're getting better at avoiding those potholes."

Kimi smiled at Niko, and then kissed him on the lips. "Honey, you are so crazy. But I love it," Kimi said.

She gazed at him for a moment, and was still amazed that after a year of carrying on, the two were still very much attracted to one another. Niko was a married man, but Kimi didn't care. From the first moment she'd looked into his beautiful brown eyes she'd fallen for him. She loved everything about him. Niko's five-foot-ten frame was solid and seemed to be made just to please her. He was the type of man that took care of his body. He wasn't a heavy drinker, didn't smoke, made sure to hit the gym, and never let his routine slip. Every time Kimi embraced him, she caressed his hard shoulders and firm back, and would become instantly aroused. The attraction to him was blissful.

Because of their public lives, Kimi and Niko couldn't see enough of each other privately. He was a high profile defense attorney in Newark, and his face was always in the newspapers and on the local news channels. Niko was a homegrown celebrity throughout New Jersey, and there wasn't a day that went by when he wasn't being hounded by the local media to comment about his countless cases. When he needed to escape the hustle and bustle of the legal system, Niko would call on his beautiful friend to save him. And Kimi was more than happy to oblige.

He was also probably the biggest closet freak in New Jersey. He made a living off of keeping his composure and being cool under pressure. He was instrumental in turning some of the biggest criminals in the state into free men. But behind closed doors, Niko was totally different. He was a highly sexual person, and his brilliant mind was filled with impassioned fantasies. Niko was always the aggressor in his professional life, but when court was adjourned and the news cameras disappeared, he was thirsting for something different. He longed for a woman to come into his sexual life who would grab hold and use him at her will.

And then came Kimi. She was a highly attractive, professional woman with her own business, her own money, and her own way. Kimi was sexy and aggressive by nature. She wasn't afraid to go after something or someone she wanted. And when she and Niko met, their timing couldn't have been more perfect. She was gradually preparing herself to take her sexual fantasies to another level, and Niko was searching for a new companion to explore with. After twelve years of marriage, he and his wife were not having the same chemistry, and he found himself wandering away from home more often than before. Luckily, Kimi was no ordinary mistress for Niko. There was something special and necessary about her, and soon Niko found himself wanting to see her more often.

But being together in public was out of the question. Niko could not afford to take a chance of being spotted anywhere with her. The very rumor of adultery would not only ensure a divorce and financial disaster, but his integrity would put dozens of pending cases in jeopardy. So Niko and Kimi never checked into a hotel, went to dinner or went on vacation together. He figured the safest place where they could be alone was Kimi's home. He needed to avoid being spotted in the car with her, so he agreed to only travel in the trunk. The feeling of being willfully kidnapped by her only excited him. Every time he heard her garage door open he felt as if he was being smuggled into a fantasy. The secret life thrilled him and made their episodes much more fulfilling. Tonight, Niko's excitement was intensified. He'd told his wife he was visiting a client upstate in Elmira Corrections, and the lie bought him and Kimi an un-interrupted evening alone. The two had been planning this night for weeks, and the time had finally come to share their special evening.

Kimi embraced Niko once more, and then kissed him again. This time Niko felt something deeper in Kimi's mood. She missed him. She missed him badly. No man had ever commanded her attention like he did. His lustful presence made her uncontrollably crave him. Like a moth hopelessly drawn to a flame, his fire lured Kimi's very soul.

Kimi pulled her face away from Niko, and then looked at him for a moment. The garage fell silent.

Niko raised his eyebrows, giving her a curious expression. "What's the matter, Kimi?"

"Nothing," she softly responded. "I just want to look at you. I feel like I haven't seen you in years."

Niko didn't say a word. He gazed back into her eyes, and could see that she was growing emotional. Her eyes spoke to him in a manner that her mouth never could. She reached up to his face, placing her hand on his cheek.

"Baby?" Kimi whispered to Niko.

"Yes," he responded.

"I want to please you tonight," Kimi uttered in a very slow and seductive tone. Niko nodded his head and opened his mouth to speak, but she playfully put two fingers over his lips and smiled. "It's not a request, baby," Kimi whispered. She grabbed Niko by the hand, then led him inside of the house. The sweet aroma of scented candles she'd burned earlier relaxed him as the two made their way through the kitchen and into the living room. Kimi took Niko's jacket to make him more comfortable.

"What do you want to drink?" Kimi asked.

"Coconut Ciroc, if you got it, baby," Niko requested.

"You know I keep the Ciroc by the caseload for you, sweetie. Can you pour me a glass too?" Kimi asked. "I'm going upstairs to change. I will meet you in the playroom in five minutes, honey."

MESSY SHEETS

The playroom? Niko questioned . A wide smile came to his face when he heard those words. He loved the playroom. Whenever Kimi mentioned it, he knew he was in for an exciting night.

When Kimi had her house built she wanted it to be more marvelous than any other house she had ever seen. She'd ordered the builders to construct an additional wing on her home that was equipped with separate guest quarters and a nine-hundred-square-foot room. There were no windows in the playroom, and only those fortunate enough to be welcomed into Kimi's home-and invited to play in it-even knew the room existed.

Niko got excited about the thought again, watching as Kimi turned around and headed upstairs. He couldn't help but shake his head at the way she walked. She was so sophisticated and smooth. He turned around and made his way to the playroom, stretching out his arms to shake off the bumpy ride in the trunk as he walked down the long hall. When he entered the room, he noticed Kimi had added a few more toys to the space. A large movie screen was now stretched out across the far wall with twelve leather recliners facing the screen, and just behind the leather seats was a vintage pool table outfitted in black felt. He smiled at the custom billiard balls and cue sticks, then laughed that Kimi could be so extravagant at times. He marveled at the pool table for another moment, and then turned around and saw that she'd added a full bar into the back corner of the room. Expensive wine and shot glasses and curvy bottles of liquors were neatly stacked on the top of the cherry wood bar. He walked over and poured himself a drink. The Ciroc went down smooth and put Niko more at ease. He'd started to pour himself another glass, when Kimi entered.

"How you like it?" Kimi whispered.

Niko turned around and stared as Kimi seductively walked toward him. His heart sped and a rush of adrenaline

29

shot through his body. She was amazing. She'd changed into a fishnet, partially torn Camisette that exposed her beautiful breast. Her four inch black Stilettos helped her move sexily. She didn't hesitate a moment as she walked right up to him and embraced him. He put his arms around her and gave Kimi a deep kiss. He moved his hands down her smooth back and squeezed on her ass. Kimi deeply moaned as Niko ran his thick fingers up and down the back of her G-string. He was clearly excited. Kimi took off his shirt and tossed it to the side.

"You never answered my question, baby," Kimi moaned with passion as she kissed on Niko's bare chest.

"What question?" Niko whispered, trying to keep his concentration. Kimi licked around his nipple and softly teased him.

"I asked you how do you like it," Kimi said.

"I love it," Niko responded.

"You love *what?*" Kimi questioned as she started to move down to his belly button. "What do you love ,baby?"

"Everything," Niko gasped.

Kimi giggled at his answer, and then slowly backed away. She was now standing a few feet from him, and wore a sensual expression. She smiled at him, then looked down at herself. She wanted to give him a full view of her sexy body.

"I want to play tonight, baby," Kimi said. "Can we?"

Niko dropped his eyebrows and looked at Kimi for a moment. "Play what?"

"Just say yes, baby. Say we can play," Kimi whispered. Her smile was mischievous. She slowly reached for her G-string, pulled it down her legs and to the floor. Niko licked his lips. "So how bout it, baby. Can we play?"

"Yes, Kimi, we can play," Niko whispered.

"Good." She smiled. Kimi slowly extended her index finger and pointed to Niko's pants. "Take those off, baby. You won't need those for this game."

Niko smiled at Kimi and slowly shook his head. He loved that Kimi was in such a playful mood. He decided to play along without protest.

She watched as Niko unzipped his pants and dropped them to the floor. "And those," she added. "You won't need those either." Kimi pointed to his underwear. Niko obeyed Kimi's request and dropped his boxers. She slowly blinked her eyes as she stared at Niko's naked dick. He wasn't fully erect yet, and was still hung larger than most men she'd ever known. She walked back up to him kissed him, then grabbed him by the hand and walked him over to the pool table.

"You want to do it on here tonight?" Niko asked, pointing to the table.

"I don't know yet, that's up to George," Kimi replied.

"What?" Niko said, a slight hint of alarm in his voice. "Who the hell is George?"

"Relax, baby." Kimi giggled as she tried to put Niko's fears at ease. "You'll see in a moment."

Niko watched as Kimi turned around and bent over in front of him. She gave Niko a full view of her naked ass, and the sight caused Niko to rise. He gazed at her pretty pussy, and then began to massage himself. Kimi reached into her fishnet stockings and pulled out a small shiny object. She turned around and showed it to Niko.

"A quarter?" Niko whispered with a confused expression. "Kimi, what the hell are you up to?" Niko smiled.

"Not just any quarter," Kimi said. "This is George. This is my lucky coin. I'll tell you about that another time. But I need you to call it. Head or Tail?" Kimi asked. She bit on her bottom lip, and smiled at Niko, who continued to look confused. His boyish expression turned her on.

"Huh?" Niko grunted. "Don't you mean heads or tails?

31

With an S?" Niko asked.

"No, baby, I said it right," Kimi smiled. "Head…or… Tail?" Kimi slowly asked again and raised her left eyebrow.

Niko chuckled as the pun finally sunk in. He glanced over Kimi's sexy body one more time and licked his lips. "Tail, baby," Niko whispered.

Kimi slowly nodded her head. She grabbed the coin with both hands, and then slowly bent over the pool table. Niko walked up beside her and started to rub her back. Kimi placed the quarter on the smooth tabletop, then looked back at Niko.

"You ready?" Kimi asked.

"Let's do it," Niko replied.

He watched as Kimi stood the coin upright and plucked it as hard as she could. The impact caused the coin to spin fiercely in place. Niko smiled at the game, and then looked down at Kimi. She reached out her palm and found her way to his crotch. She kept her eyes on the coin, but kept her focus on Niko's dick. It was getting bigger in her hand. She slowly tugged on him and massaged him. Niko drifted deeply into the sensation, and dropped his palms to the edge of the pool table. He could barely keep his attention on the spinning quarter as Kimi massaged his dick. Niko moaned. Kimi felt her pussy pulsating as she anticipated how the coin would fall. Her mouth watered at the thought of the quarter landing on heads, and her pussy begged for the quarter to land on tails. She put a tighter grip on Niko and started to stroke him even harder. Niko moaned again, and his body quivered for a moment. Niko's growing dick was driving Kimi crazy. She focused on the coin and noticed that the spinning was slowing down. The suspense was drawing to a close, and Kimi's body was ready for action. She pulled Niko closer, then nibbled on her bottom lip again. The sound of the falling quarter knocked on the top of the pool table. Niko and Kimi's eyes were fixed on the coin as it finally landed on its side.

"Tail," they both whispered in unison.

Kimi smoothly turned her head around and looked at Niko. The sinful smile on her face was all he needed to see. Niko watched her as she climbed on top of the pool table and pushed the billiard balls out of her way. The sounds of the balls scattering across the table caused her to chuckle.

"Come on, baby," Kimi said as she motioned for Niko to join her.

Niko climbed on top of the table with Kimi. She turned around and got on all fours for him. She was so ready for Niko that her body trembled with anticipation. Niko got behind her. He grabbed her by the ass, then slowly kissed the center of her back. Niko was horny for Kimi and wanted her now, but he couldn't stop himself from running his tongue down the small of her back. He kept moving below until he reached the bottom of Kimi's ass. Niko kissed her hot pussy from the back, then hummed at the sweet taste of it.

"Jesus," Kimi softly moaned.

She moved her thin fingers down to her clitoris, and then began to massage it. She felt Niko's stiff tongue entering her slowly, and she dropped her head. The feeling was wonderful. Niko ran his tongue up and down her pussy until she was dripping wet. The sound of Niko's foreplay was only driving her crazier. Kimi's body moved to his rhythm, and she felt herself reaching climax. *Oh my goodness, already?* she thought . Niko sensed Kimi's body was peaking, and suddenly stopped licking her. The sudden switch threw her for a loop. She looked back just in time to see Niko getting on his knees, readying for her. Kimi never got a chance to brace herself for Niko. He rubbed the head of his dick across her wet lips and quickly entered her.

"Ow shit, Niko!" Kimi yelled as he shoved his hard dick deep inside of her tight pussy.

A rush of pleasure quickly followed the instant pain as Niko stroked Kimi like he loved her. It didn't take long for his hefty dick to hit the right spot. She quivered like she was freezing, but her body was on fire. Niko knew what was coming next, and he continued to stroke faster. Kimi screamed in pleasure as her clitoris swelled and her body became orgasmic.

"Don't stop!" Kimi yelled.

Niko got the message, loud and clear, and continued to please Kimi. He put a tighter grip on her hips and started grinding her harder. Kimi yelled Niko's name with passion. Niko felt her pussy tighten around him and moaned at the feeling. Her ass bounced up against his hips, and Niko became more excited. Kimi's legs started shaking as her orgasm started building. Kimi moaned louder and louder. She stretched her arms out onto the table as she felt Niko going deeper. She grabbed the closet thing she could and squeezed it. It was the red 3-ball. Niko smiled, watching Kimi grip the ball for dear life. He pounded her harder until her body quaked again.

"I'm coming, baby," Kimi cried out.

Her voice became higher with each moan and whimper. The heavy rush seemed to go from the back of her neck all the way down to the pit of her stomach. Niko felt her body climaxing. She bounced her ass harder and harder against him as the orgasm took over her. Niko couldn't believe how good her body felt to him. Her pussy tightened around him again, and Niko couldn't take it anymore. She was creaming all over him, and Niko felt that all-too-familiar tingle in his spine.

"Damn, baby, I'm 'bout to come too," Niko moaned.

His deep voice shook with pleasure, and Kimi felt his body shudder. Niko grabbed her by the shoulders and started stroking her uncontrollably. Kimi screamed. She felt him pushing deeper inside of her. She came again, yelling his name. Niko couldn't hold on any longer, and exploded. Kimi cried out in pain as she felt Niko thrusting deeply into her. His orgasm was powerful, and Kimi was close to tears.

"Goddamn, baby," Niko moaned. His body continued to shake and pulsate. Kimi moaned when Niko's sweaty body jerked back and forth, then collapsed on top of hers.

"Sweet Jesus, Niko," Kimi whispered. Her body fell flat onto the pool table.

The playroom fell silent. The only sound that could be heard was Niko and Kimi trying hard to catch their wind. Neither one of them wanted to ruin the moment by speaking. They both decided to lay still and soak in the sensual moment. Niko reached up, grabbed Kimi by the hand, and squeezed her palm. Kimi returned the gesture by kissing his wrist. They both cuddled on top of the pool table and rested.

Ten minutes later, Niko found himself becoming entranced by the sweet aroma of Kimi's body. With every deep breath, Niko felt himself becoming more and more sensitive to the touch of her soft skin. A flashback entered into his mind, and he started to get aroused again. Kimi felt Niko's manhood rising behind her, and moaned. She slowly reached for the quarter on the pool table and showed it to Niko. He smiled. Kimi spun the quarter on the smooth tabletop and both of them watched in anticipation. Kimi ran her tongue across her teeth, then smiled. She felt her body warming with excitement as she watched the coin spin right in front of her. The quarter softly knocked on the table as it slowed down and landed on its side. Kimi looked at Niko, who was smiling at the coin.

"Round two, baby?" Niko asked.

"Hell yes," Kimi whispered. "Round two."

*F*ive

Marcel sped down the icy streets like it was drier out than the middle of July. He barely flinched at the snowy conditions as he made his way downtown to the hotel. Sabrina's shaky voice replayed in his mind like a scene from a horror movie. The only thing he envision was some greasy man putting his hands on Sabrina. Marcel was over protective when it came to the women in his life. And because of his business, Marcel took extra pride in checking men who physically abused women, especially women who were close to him. Marcel never hesitated to punish someone for violating his circle.

Although Marcel and Sabrina were blood related, they were not as close these days as they used to be. Sabrina was Marcel's only niece. And despite being only four years apart in age, Sabrina respected Marcel like a father figure. Since their school days, Marcel had always looked out for his niece. He'd taught her many rules of survival and growing up in Newark. As they got older and moved into their twenties, he taken Sabrina under his wing and helped her with her modeling career. He made sure she had money in her pocket every week to do what she needed to do. He bought Sabrina everything she asked for, from expensive outfits to overpriced shoes. Marcel knew his niece was beautiful, and she could make it big one day with the right support. But once Marcel got arrested and sent to prison, he couldn't help Sabrina anymore.

Their relationship turned sour once Sabrina approached her uncle about working for him. Marcel never wanted to get her involved in his sex business, but Sabrina needed the money. Marcel went against his better judgment and allowed her to take on some of his clients. Everything went smooth for the first six months of their arrangement. Sabrina was making good money, and Marcel made sure she got paid on time and was safe. But things got out of control when Marcel's biggest client claimed that he was missing money from his bedroom. The client kicked Sabrina out of his house, and the heat came down heavy on Marcel. He approached his niece about it, and a huge argument resulted. The two went their separate ways, and they didn't speak for nearly a year. Tonight was the first time Marcel had heard his niece's voice since their huge fight. And, despite the fact that he was still upset with Sabrina, he was not going to turn his back on his niece in her time of need.

Marcel pulled up to the Robert Treat Hotel, and pushed all of his disagreements with Sabrina to the back burner. He thought for a moment and turned his attention to the man hitting her in the hotel room. He had never heard the name Khalil before. Marcel had a good idea of who the real gangsters were in Newark, and Khalil's name was not on the list. Nevertheless, Marcel didn't want to take a chance. He grabbed his gun, and then tucked it tightly in his waist. He took one last look around the streets, and then jumped out of the truck. The bitter cold wind engulfed Marcel, but he couldn't feel a thing. Anger heated his body to boiling point. Getting Sabrina safely out of the hotel room was the only thing on his mind as he stomped through the snow, and then quickly made his way into the hotel lobby.

Back upstairs in Room 729, Khalil continued to pound on the bathroom door and yell at Sabrina. His heavy fist seemed to shake the entire bathroom, but Sabrina refused to open the door.

"You only making it worse on yourself," Khalil yelled.

"Fuck you," Sabrina whispered under her breath.

She was too tired and edgy to yell anymore. She had been stuck in the bathroom for over twenty minutes, and she was growing more nervous by the second. She couldn't believe Khalil was still knocking. He refused to leave the room until he found out what happened to his money. He had been pacing back and forth around the small hotel room, trying to locate the cash. He was sure Sabrina had it, but he couldn't find it in her Gucci. He checked his empty wallet again, and then slammed it down to the carpet.

"Shit!" he yelled in frustration.

Khalil was tired of playing games with Sabrina. He turned his attention to the pocketknife on the desk. He took another long sip of Hennessy, then grabbed the knife. He rushed over to the bathroom door and shoved the blade into the keyhole. The sound of the twisting doorknob made Sabrina jump to her feet. She could hear Khalil wrestling with the lock and trying to break it with the stiff blade. Her heart dropped to the floor when she saw the doorknob twisting and turning. He was getting closer to breaking in. Sabrina grabbed the knob with both hands, trying to stop him from entering the bathroom. He shoved the knife deeper into the keyhole until he heard a stark clicking sound. The lock was broken. Khalil's mood grew more aggressive when the doorknob twisted with ease. Sabrina put her weight against the bathroom door and tried to stop Khalil, but he was too strong. He pushed the door with his shoulder, and then violently barged into the tight bathroom. Sabrina backed up against the wall. Khalil took one look at her face and went into attack mode. He smacked Sabrina across the jaw and threw her to the floor. Sabrina yelled in agony. The hit dazed her.

Khalil grabbed her by the shoulders and gave her a death stare. "Now where the fuck is my money?" he yelled.

"Please stop!" Sabrina shouted at the top of her lungs.

Her piercing voice startled him for a moment. He looked at her again and was about to smack her once more when a loud knocking came from the door of the hotel room. Khalil froze. The knocking escalated into a loud banging, and Khalil looked down at Sabrina. He pointed his finger directly in her face.

"Don't say a fuckin' word," he threatened. He stood up, and then cautiously ran out of the bathroom. "Who's there?" he shouted as he approached the door.

"Hotel security!" a stern voice reported from the hallway.

Khalil peered through the peephole, but couldn't make out the face.

"We good in here," Khalil yelled through the door.

"There was a noise complaint for this floor," the voice shouted.

"Yea, I heard the noise too. It's probably the people next door," Khalil lied. "We good in here."

"Sir, if you don't open the door, I'll have to call the police to come up here," the voice continued. "I need to make sure that everything is okay in there."

Khalil looked around the disheveled hotel room. The last thing he needed was the Newark Police knocking on the door. He looked in the bathroom and noticed Sabrina struggling to pick herself up off the floor. Khalil needed to get rid of the security guard right away so he could get back to his business. He decided to poke his head out of the door to put the security guard at ease. Without a thought, Khalil twisted the knob and slowly eased open the door.

"I told you, sir," Khalil said peeking through the crack. "We are fine in here."

Before Khalil could finish his sentence, the heavy door came smashing against his face. The shock and the brutality of the impact threw Khalil's body backward. An angry man came busting through the door, and Khalil realized he was not hotel security. It was Marcel. He was brandishing a jet-black pistol in his hand, and wearing a depraved expression on his face. Khalil tried to get back to his feet, but Marcel was all over him. He rushed over to Khalil, smashing him in the head with the gun. Khalil yelled like an opera singer as the solid metal rocked his skull. Marcel didn't stop thumping Khalil until he lay half conscious on the bloody carpet.

"Oh my God," a voice yelled.

Marcel turned around just in time to see Sabrina standing near the entrance to the bathroom. She was nursing a small cut on her face. Marcel saw her wide eyes staring at him in horror. When he noticed the blood on her white T-shirt, he grew irate again. He turned his focus back to Khalil, and then started kicking him hard in the stomach.

"You put your fuckin' hands on the wrong girl, nigga," Marcel shouted. He showed Khalil no remorse, continuing to pound him. Khalil could barely defend himself.

"Stop it, Uncle M! You're gonna kill him," Sabrina shouted. The sight of the violence was too much for her. She wanted it to end. Her uncle ignored her and continued swinging at Khalil.

"Please stop it!" Sabrina yelled again.

Her strained voice froze Marcel. He stood up and looked down at his victim with hatred. Khalil was curled up into a tight ball, aching from the punishment. Marcel was still furious and his temper was flaring. He looked back at his niece again. Her terrified expression calmed him.

"You alright?" Marcel asked, focusing in on her bloody lip.

"Yea," Sabrina mumbled.

"Get your shit together, and get the hell outta here,"

he ordered.

Sabrina didn't hesitate for another second. She walked over to the bed, and then put all of her belongings back into her Gucci Bag. She grabbed the rest of her clothes and threw them over her shoulder.

"Who paid for the room?" Marcel asked.

"He did," Sabrina responded, pointing to Khalil.

"With a credit card?"

"No, cash."

Marcel looked down at Khalil again, then tightened his jaw. He was so angry he could barely see straight. He turned back to his niece, who was grabbing the last of her things. He tossed her the keys to his vehicle.

"Wait for me outside," Marcel continued. "My truck is parked right out front."

Sabrina took the keys and didn't say a word to her uncle. The scary look in Marcel's eyes terrified her. She looked down at Khalil and imagined what his fate would soon be.

"Hurry up!" Marcel yelled at her.

He watched Sabrina as she turned around and headed out the door. The minute his niece was out of sight, Marcel kicked Khalil again in the stomach, then pointed the gun at him.

"Chill, man," Khalil groaned. "I didn't know she was your lady."

"That's not my girl. That's family, nigga," Marcel coldly replied.

"Come on, my dude. Please don't do this," Khalil cried out. "I'm sorry."

His loud pleading didn't faze Marcel. Khalil's apologies only made him angrier. Marcel moved closer to Khalil with gun raised. The look in his eyes grew even darker. Khalil put his arms up and covered his face, fearing the inevitable was only seconds away. Marcel took a hard look at Khalil's forearm, and then dropped his gun.

"Yo!" Marcel yelled.

Khalil didn't budge.

"Yo, nigga! Look at me!" Marcel yelled again.

Khalil slowly lowered his arm, and his terrified eyes peered at his attacker.

"Look at my face," Marcel said. Khalil reluctantly glanced at him. "Do you know me?" Marcel asked.

"Huh...what?" Khalil stuttered

"Nigga...do you know me?" Marcel slowly repeated.

Khalil looked at Marcel for a second. "Nah fam, I don't know you," Khalil mumbled.

"Where you bid at?" Marcel questioned.

"Huh?" Khalil mumbled.

"What the fuck, am I speaking' Chinese?" Marcel shouted. "I said, where the fuck did you bid at?"

"Bayside prison."

"How long you been home?"

"Twenty-three months."

Marcel let out a lung full of air. He was clearly frustrated. Khalil didn't know what to think. Marcel looked around the room, and then turned back to Khalil.

"That's how you got that ink?" Marcel questioned referring to a large tattoo on Khalil's forearm. "You got that when you was in Bayside?"

"Yea," Khalil answered. "About four years ago."

Marcel thought for a moment, glaring at Khalil. He tried to remember his face, but Khalil didn't look familiar to him. "So you know my cousin, Boogie, from Hillside then?" Marcel asked.

"I know Boogie," Khalil answered as he slowly

nodded his head. "We both was in Bayside at the same time."

"No bullshit?" Marcel uttered. He gave Khalil a long and suspicious look. "You must be tight with him if he let you get that ink on your arm," Marcel said.

"We are tight. But Boogie is not from Hillside," Khalil mumbled. "Boogie is from Newark."

Marcel rubbed his chin with the back of his hand and nodded his head. He'd tried to trip up Khalil, but it was clear that Khalil was being honest with him. Marcel lifted his sleeve, showing Khalil that he had the same jailhouse-tattoo on his arm.

"You a lucky motherfucker ," Marcel said and gave him a harsh stare. He knelt down next to Khalil. "I'm gonna give you a pass this time on the strength of my cousin, Boogie. But you better stay the fuck away from Sabrina. You hear me?"

"Yes," Khalil nervously mumbled.

"And you damn sure better remember my face," Marcel continued. "The next time you see it, you better go the other way. You feel me?"

Khalil was too nervous to speak. Marcel rose to his feet and looked around the room one last time. Khalil kept a strict eye on Marcel and watched him as he tucked the gun. A thick silence fell between the two as Marcel stared at Khalil. Neither one of them said a word. After a moment, Marcel turned around and smoothly walked out of the room. He left Khalil bruised and shaking on the floor and contemplating just how close he came to witnessing his own demise.

*S*ix

"*K*imi, I really don't know what it is about you. But you drive me crazy every time I come over here." Niko's words barely squeezed out of his exhausted body. He was still trying to catch his breath after another passionate sex session. The two had made love in Kimi's playroom for hours, then decided to make their way up to her bedroom, where things escalated more. Kimi looked over to Niko's worn out face and smiled. She covered her naked body with her platinum silk sheets and giggled at his expression.

"Damn, you must be an alien or something. Is that what it is?" Kimi asked with a sexy tone, admiring Niko's body.

"Baby, I was going to ask you the same thing," he responded and took a deep breath. "You're like the goddamn Energizer bunny tonight. I think we just set a record for the most screams in one night."

"My screams or yours?" Kimi asked with a smirk.

"Shit, I couldn't even hear you screaming over my loud ass," Niko laughed at himself and shook his head.

The chemistry between Niko and Kimi was only getting better with time. He turned over on his back, and Kimi calmly placed her head on his chest. The sound of his heartbeat made her feel alive. He brought something different to her life that she had never known before. His affection and calm demeanor settled her. She felt more comfortable around him, and free to be herself. With the stresses of her company constantly weighing down on her, it felt good to let go and just be free whenever she was in his presence. Kimi wrapped her arm around Niko's stomach and squeezed him. She was overjoyed to be laying next to her good friend tonight.

"You know I hate you, right?" Kimi whispered.

"Not as much as I hate you," Niko smoothly responded.

A girlish smile came to Kimi's face. She loved it when her friend played along with her. Because Niko was a married man, Kimi told herself that she would never fall in love with him, and tried to keep her emotions in check.

Despite being tough as nails when it came to the business world, being around Niko turned Kimi into another person. Her heart would turn soft as butter when she was around him. And before she knew it, Kimi found herself falling hard for him. Kimi was undeniably in love with Niko, but she was too scared to let him know how she felt. She didn't want her emotions to ruin what they had. She always wondered if he felt the same about her, but she never had the heart to ask. Tonight she was tempted to check his pulse on the subject of love, but before she could ask him the big question, Niko sparked up a conversation out of the blue.

"So are you excited about your presentation tomorrow?" Niko asked.

"I don't think excited is the word," Kimi reluctantly responded. "I'm more ready to get it over with than anything. I have been preparing for this for so long, and I'm just ready to get it out of my mind."

"So I will take that as a yes," Niko joked.

"Yes baby," Kimi said with a chuckle. "I'm ready. We are expecting a lot of buyers tomorrow, so I hope we can get a few new contracts and, possibly, someone to buy the company."

"I still can't believe you are selling your company, Kimi," Niko said.

"Me neither. But it is definitely time to move on," Kimi continued. "I am so ready to start my magazine, baby. I know it will be a success. But there is no way I can concentrate on two businesses at one time. So I figured, I can make this happen by the end of the month, then start my magazine by summer."

"I think it's a wonderful concept, and I'm sure you will do good," Niko said. "They will love you, baby. Trust me."

"Thanks, sweetie," Kimi whispered. Niko's choice of words made her smile. "I hope so. This idea can really bring in a lot of money for my company. I do believe this is going to be a great year."

"I agree," Niko added.

"What about the firm?" Kimi asked. "How are things going up there? I read up on that Marquez story you told me about. Crazy stuff."

"Business is good at the law firm," Niko said. "Another day will always bring yet another asshole to me who's breaking the law."

"Damn, I never looked at it like that," Kimi said. "But you're right. People are so crazy these days. What do you think the outcome of this Marquez case will be?"

"I hope he walks," Niko boasted. "The lead prosecutor is pressing too hard to get a conviction. She's trying to set an example out of Marquez, but it's not going to work. She's making a lot of rookie mistakes."

"Wow," Kimi whispered.

"Wow, is right," Niko continued. "But, I can tell you this, those Marquez boys are savages. They are carjacking people like crazy around Newark. I know you don't go down to Newark a lot, but when you do go, please stay away from Bergen Avenue, South Orange Avenue, and don't even think about riding through Avon Avenue."

"Damn, those streets bring back a lot of memories," Kimi said.

"I'm serious, baby," Niko said. "It's scary down there now. Three women were already carjacked this month, and one of them got killed out there trying to fight back. So just be careful when you are out there. Okay?"

"Okay, I will," Kimi whispered. She thought about Niko's words for a moment. "Baby, can I ask you something?" Kimi whispered.

"Sure," Niko replied.

"Do you ever think about me when we're not together?"

"Of course I do," Niko quickly responded.

"Okay, let me rephrase the question," Kimi continued. "Do you ever think about me in a non-sexual way when we are not together?"

"You know I do," Niko mumbled.

Kimi sat up on the bed, then turned to Niko. She looked at him straight in the eyes.

"I'm serious, baby," Kimi said.

"I'm serious too. I thought I just answered your question," Niko said. A quiet moment fell between the two. Niko dropped his eyebrows, deciding to break the awkward silence. "What's going on in your head, Kimi?"

"Just you," she replied. "I really want you to know that you stay on my mind and I worry about you."

"Worry about what?" Niko questioned.

"I don't know. A lot of things. You work around a lot of dangerous people, and, sometimes, I worry if you're okay or not," she continued. "I know we're just friends and you don't belong to me. I can live with that, but that still doesn't change the fact that I care about you, baby. Seriously." Niko didn't say a word. Kimi continued speaking. "I just want you to know that I really appreciate you, and I don't know what they hell I would do if something was to happen to you."

"I hear you ,baby," Niko calmly said.

"I know you hear me, but do you believe me, Niko?" She gave him a playful attitude.

Niko sat up, and then grabbed Kimi by the back of her head. He pulled her face close to his, and then gave her a deep kiss. She grabbed his shoulders, almost melting in his grip.

"What about now?" he asked. "Do you think I believe you now?"

Kimi nodded her head and gave Niko another kiss. She started moaning heavily and caressing his back. He moved closer and started kissing on her neck. Kimi moaned when Niko moved to her ear.

"You know what would make me very happy?" Niko whispered. His voice gave her the chills.

"What's that, baby?" she moaned. She squeezed his back with anticipation as her heart started racing again.

"Are you going to do it for me, baby?" Niko asked.

"Anything for you, Niko," she moaned again. "Just ask me."

"Okay," Niko whispered. He gave her a quick kiss on the lips, and then pulled away from her. He reached for the silk sheets, pulled them up to his neck, and got comfortable on the bed. "Can you turn off the lights and set the alarm for tomorrow. I'm taking my ass to sleep now."

"Goddammit, Niko," she shouted. She watched him lay back down on the king size bed. Kimi grabbed a pillow and playfully hit him on the head. "I thought we were going for round four."

"Round four? Hell no!" Niko blurted. "We only

got a few hours of sleep to get, and I know you have your presentation tomorrow. We both need some rest."

"You're right," Kimi said. She stood up and headed to the other side of the room. She checked her clock and made sure her alarm was set for 7:00 A.M. She flicked off the light and got back in the bed.

"Goodnight, sweetie," she whispered. She curled up behind Niko and hugged his warm body. Niko grabbed her arm and slowly drifted into a deep sleep. The two lay hugged up with each other for the rest of the evening.

$\mathcal{S}$even

Back in Newark there was a dead silence inside of Marcel's truck as he recklessly navigated the snowy downtown streets. The violent episode with Khalil was still flashing in his mind. He was still hyped from the fight earlier, and every wild turn he made proved his adrenaline was still pumping. He looked over to Sabrina, who was sitting quietly on the passenger seat, tending to the ugly bruises on her face.

Sabrina could sense her uncle's temper was still flaring as she looked over to him. "Are you alright?" she whispered, breaking the silence.

"What do you think?" he snapped.

"Listen, I know you pissed off about tonight, but I didn't have nobody else to call," she said.

"Nobody?" Marcel questioned. His voice was thick with frustration.

"No. I didn't have nobody else to call."

"Where's your boyfriend at?" Marcel asked. "You probably stay with some nigga, sittin' in the cut somewhere."

"I don't have a boyfriend," Sabrina responded. "I'm serious. I really didn't have nobody else to call. That's why I hit you up."

"You're never gonna change, Sabrina." Marcel shook his head and concentrated on the road.

MESSY SHEETS

"What the hell is that suppose to mean?"

"You know exactly what that means. You still a fuckin' liar," Marcel barked at his niece.

"Come on, Uncle M," Sabrina continued. "Why you always so hard on a bitch? Why are you talking to me like that? I thought we was family."

"We are family, that's why I know when you're lying," he said. "And what the fuck are you still doing out here dealing with these animals? You don't work no more?"

"No, I quit that job a while ago."

"So you stopped working to come out here and fuck around with these street niggas for money?" Marcel questioned. "Come on, Sabrina, I thought you was done with the dumb shit. You askin' for trouble by doing this shit."

"Look at my face, Uncle M," Sabrina said pointing to the bruise on her cheek. "You think I asked for this type of shit to come into my life. I had no clue that Khalil was going to act the way he did tonight-"

"Get the fuck out of here with that Oprah bullshit, girl," Marcel shouted, cutting her off. "You probably deserved that shit!"

"Fuck you, nigga," Sabrina shouted. She was offended by her uncle's words.

"No, fuck you!" Marcel yelled at his niece. He abruptly pulled the truck over to the side of the road, then stared at Sabrina, who was clearly shocked by his move. "You can pull that sympathy shit with those stupid ass clowns out there, but I know you for real, Sabrina. You always been a liar, and I know you lying now."

"Whatever, Uncle M. Can you just drive the car?" she nervously whispered.

"Where's the money?" Marcel snapped.

"What money?" Sabrina fired back.

51

"Don't play stupid," Marcel responded. "The money you stole from that dude. And don't say you didn't take it because I'm not a fucking idiot. I know you got it. There is no way y'all go from fucking each other to fighting each other. Something had to go wrong. He came there with that money, and you took it."

Sabrina didn't say a word. She gave her uncle an exhausted look as he continued to scold her.

"I been playing in these streets too long, and I know how these niggas think," Marcel continued. "There's no way he's gonna risk going back to prison over you if he didn't know for a fact that you had his money. So I'm gonna ask you one last time, where is the money? And if try to play me and lie to me again, I swear I'll kick ya ass out in this snow and make you walk home."

There was a cold silence in the truck. Marcel never blinked an eye as he stared at his niece's face with intensity. She dropped her head for a moment and let out a gasp.

"Don't be mad at me, Uncle M," Sabrina whispered.

Marcel dropped his eyebrows as he watched his niece reach for her Gucci Bag. She turned it upside down and unzipped a small compartment on the bottom of the bag. She pulled out the money and showed it to her uncle.

"Un-fucking believable," Marcel barked. "Like I said, you will never fuckin' change."

"You don't understand, Uncle M. I'm sorry. But I had to take it," Sabrina pleaded.

"What?" he yelled. "How the fuck does somebody *have* to steal money from a customer? Where the fuck do they do that at?"

"No, listen, Uncle M. Seriously. Just hear me out," Sabrina pleaded. "I'm in some big trouble ." Sabrina looked away from her uncle.

Marcel noticed a more serious expression was coming to her face.

Sabrina raised a small piece of tissue to her cheek and continued to wipe the blood away. She turned back to her uncle and gave him a worried look. "I need to tell you something, and you have to believe me. Okay?"

"What is it?" Marcel sternly responded.

"I know this is gonna sound crazy, but promise me that you'll hear me out?" Sabrina nervously asked.

"Spit it out," Marcel barked. "I'm listening."

"Okay, I know you told me to get out the game a while ago when you went to prison. And I did," Sabrina continued. "I went back to work for a minute, but that shit was really moving too slow. So I started fucking around for money."

"Okay. I figured out that part," Marcel said. He was growing impatient with his niece.

"Right, so you know I got back into the hustle." Sabrina dropped her head and continued to come clean. "About three years ago, I started fucking with Gary Banks."

"Gary Banks?" Marcel asked with a twisted expression. "The Mayor of Newark?"

"Yes," Sabrina quickly responded. "But he wasn't the mayor when I met him. Gary was just a councilman. Anyway, he was one of my biggest clients back then. Seriously, Uncle M. You wouldn't believe the type of money he was paying me to fuck around with him. When he went on those trips out of state, Gary was paying for me to meet him at the hotels and hang out. It was crazy."

Marcel turned away from his niece. He knew she was notorious for concocting extravagant stories about her life.

Sabrina realized she was losing her uncle's attention and yelled at him. "Uncle M, I'm not lying to you," she shouted. "I'm keeping it real. Gary Banks is a fuckin' animal, and I can prove it."

Something in his niece's words made him turn around and glance at her. Her face was serious. For the first time tonight, Marcel couldn't see a legitimate reason not to believe her. He turned his body toward his niece.

"Okay," Marcel uttered. "So what the fuck does Gary Banks have to do with all of this shit?"

"This is what I'm tryin' to explain to you now," Sabrina continued. "Right before Gary started running for mayor, he asked me to come over to his house. Now, any other day, he would send a car for me, but this time something told me to drive myself over there. Anyway, everything was basically the same as usual. I got there after twelve, we fucked for about an hour, and that was it. I jumped in the shower and got dressed."

Sabrina paused for a moment and shook her head. Marcel could tell that her mind was flashing back to something dark. Sabrina took a deep breath and continued speaking.

"Right before I was about to leave, he got a call about some emergency downtown," Sabrina continued. "So Gary starts running around, getting dressed, grabbing his stuff, and telling me not to leave. He kept saying that he wanted me to stay and wait for him to come back. I really didn't see a problem with staying as long as he was gonna pay me for my time. So Gary dropped a half-stack in my lap and told me I could keep it if I waited for him to come back. So that's exactly what I did. When he left, I got comfortable in his bedroom and went to sleep. I woke up like three o'clock in the morning, but he was still gone. I didn't wanna leave and lose out on that five hundred dollars, so I stayed there. But I was bored. So I decided to pop in a DVD and wait for him to come back."

Sabrina took another pause and looked out the

window. She thought back to that night at Gary's house and closed her eyes. Marcel noticed his niece getting emotional and decided to keep quiet as Sabrina continued.

"I don't know what possessed me to dig though his DVDs looking for a movie that night, but I did." Sabrina's voice dropped. "I couldn't find a good movie, so I kept digging. Gary had a million DVDs in his collection, but I had seen them all. So I kept looking. I was in his shit for almost twenty minutes digging for something good. After a while, I didn't even know what I was looking for. I was just digging. And then...I found it." Sabrina slowly turned to her uncle and just stared at him. Her eyes were distant.

"Found what?" Marcel sharply asked.

"I found an all white DVD at the bottom of the pile," Sabrina mumbled. "It wasn't no writing on the DVD. No sticker on it, nothing. Just blank. So I popped it in thinking it was a nasty movie or something. But, Uncle M, it wasn't no porno flick. It was something crazier." Sabrina leaned up against the passenger side window and put her hand on her head. "I really fucked up for real. I gotta get out of here."

"Sabrina, what are you talking about?" Marcel asked. "I'm not following."

"The mayor was on the video, Uncle M," Sabrina nervously confessed. I saw it with my own two eyes. It was Gary on there. He's a real fucking animal."

"What, Sabrina?" Marcel uttered. His eyes became wide with interest. "What the hell was he doing on the video?"

"He was….um…damn, Uncle M," Sabrina stuttered for a second and bobbed her head. Her hands were slightly shaking as she tried to say the words. "Gary was on there…. umm. He was….damn. I can't even say it. You just gotta see it for yourself."

"Hold up, you got the DVD?" Marcel asked.

"Fuck yea, I got it," Sabrina quickly responded. "I had to take the DVD from his house. It was too sick."

"And you still have it after all this time?"

"I been holding on to it for the last couple of years," Sabrina responded. "I didn't think he would know that I had it. But then some strange shit started happening to me. That's why I gotta get out of Newark. I was getting death threats at my apartment so I moved out, and, now, I'm getting shit coming to my email. It's crazy, Uncle M, I'm telling you. The threats are getting worse every day, and I been seeing people follow me out the blue. That's why I had to take the money from Khalil tonight. I had been saving up to get the fuck out of here."

Marcel shook his head toward Sabrina. He didn't know how to respond. He watched as his niece gathered her thoughts. After a few quiet moments in the car, Marcel decided to find out more about the video.

"So where's the DVD now?" Marcel asked.

"Back at the hotel," she responded.

"The Robert Treat?"

"No, it's at the Howard Johnson over on Route One and Nine," Sabrina said. "I been living in that hotel all month. I'm scared to live anywhere else, Uncle M."

"What the fuck, Sabrina?" Marcel barked. "You been living in a goddamn hotel room?" Sabrina closed her mouth and nodded her head toward her uncle. "Why didn't you call me and tell me you was living in some damn room, Sabrina?" Marcel asked.

"I thought you was still mad at me," she responded.

"I am still mad at you," Marcel snapped. "But we still family. I don't want you living at the fuckin' Howard Johnson. Goddamn, that is not the move at all."

Marcel sat back in his seat and thought for a moment. Sabrina was clearly going through a lot more than he'd ever imagined. He put the truck back in gear, and then continued to drive through the snow. Sabrina sat quietly on the passenger side as her uncle sped through the rough weather. She was trying to shake the horrid images of the video and calm her nerves.

Marcel's mind was also on the DVD. He was trying to image what could be on the video that would have his niece running scared. By the time Marcel pulled his truck into the parking lot of the Howard Johnson, his curiosity was in full swing. He pulled up to the front lobby of the hotel and parked the truck.

"How much stuff you got in your room, Sabrina?" Marcel asked.

"What do you mean?" Sabrina whispered.

"I'm not gonna let you spend another night in a damn hotel room," Marcel stated. "You're coming with me. So hurry up, and get your shit. You can stay at my crib until we figure this shit out."

Sabrina looked over to Marcel. "Are you sure ,Uncle M?" Sabrina calmly asked. "I know your friend Tricia is staying with you. Are you sure she's gonna be cool with that?"

"It's my house, Sabrina," Marcel said with a stiff tone. "She's gonna be cool with it when I tell her to be cool with it. So don't worry about that. Just hurry up, and get your shit before I change my mind."

Sabrina gave her uncle a humbling look and smiled for the first time tonight. She was beyond grateful that Marcel would open up his house to her. She reached over and gave Marcel a quick hug. The emotional night was clearly having an effect on her.

"Thank you, Uncle M," Sabrina uttered. "Give me fifteen minutes, and I will pack all of my shit. Thank you so much."

Marcel didn't say a word. He slowly nodded toward his niece and watched her as she jumped out of the truck, and then went into the hotel. He reached for his phone and dialed his friend Tricia. He was surprised when she picked up on the first ring.

"Is everything alright, baby?" Tricia yelled through the phone. "What happened?"

"Everything's cool," Marcel calmly responded. "Listen, I'll be there in about a half hour. I need to get the first floor guest room together for me. My niece is going to be staying there for a while." There was a silence on the phone. Tricia didn't say a word. "Hello? Did you hear what I said?" Marcel barked.

"Yea, baby," Tricia mumbled. "I heard you. You want me to clean it up now?"

"Yup," Marcel responded. He disregarded the late hour, continuing to bark orders to his friend. "Just make it happen for me, okay?"

"Okay ,baby. You know I will do whatever you ask me to," Tricia said. "Are you staying here tonight?"

"Yes. I'll be there tonight," Marcel responded.

"Good," Tricia whispered. "You sound a little tense . Can I help you relax later?"

A small grin came to Marcel's face. He quickly decoded Tricia's message, and then licked his lips in anticipation. "Hell yes," Marcel said. "After tonight, I could use some calming down."

"Okay ,baby. I'll take care of that room   for you," Tricia said. "I will see you when you get here."

"Cool. See you in a minute," Marcel responded.

"Bye ,baby," Tricia said.

Marcel hung up the phone and looked out the window. His mood was finally easing from the drama filled night. He felt good knowing that his niece would be safe living at his house until he figured out what her next move would be. His attention shifted back and forth to the thoughts of the video his niece spoke about. *What the hell was Gary Banks into? And is he really sending death threats to my niece?* Marcel's mind continued to fire off questions about the mayor. Marcel knew his answers would come soon enough. He calmly sat back in his leather seat and waited patiently for his niece to return with her things.

Eight

An hour later, Marcel was pulling up to his house back in North Newark. He looked over to Sabrina's exhausted face and saw she was still awake but clearly out of it. The last bit of energy she had was spent packing Marcel's truck with all of her clothes and belongings from the hotel room.

Sabrina looked up to Marcel's house and felt relieved. She was ready to hit a soft bed and say goodnight to this unforgettable evening. "Though I've never been inside, I can't believe you still got this place," she whispered.

"Four years now," Marcel said as he pulled into the driveway.

"And Tricia's been living with you all this time?"

"Yup. She's still here."

"And y'all still not together, right?" Sabrina asked with a judgmental tone.

"Nope," Marcel replied. "And believe me, Tricia is cool with it." Marcel dismissed his niece's probing. He turned the engine off and grabbed his things. Sabrina followed suit, grabbing one of her bags from the back seat.

"I gotta leave that other stuff in here for the night. I'm too tired to bring it in ," Sabrina said.

"That's cool," he replied.

Marcel got out of the car, and his niece followed him up to the front porch. He opened the door and walked inside. Sabrina followed, marveling at the size of the house.

"Damn, Uncle M," Sabrina gasped. "I see you been doing the damn thing. This place is crazy."

"Good lookin'," Marcel mumbled and dropped his keys on a small coffee table. "Business is good. You know, I can't complain."

"Hell no. This shit is off the hook." Sabrina gawked at the nice house. She looked around and felt proud of her uncle. He seemed to be doing very well for himself.

"Let me show you where your room is," Marcel said.

Sabrina followed him down a short hallway to the only bedroom on the first level. He opened the door, and immediately noticed that Tricia fixed up the room just the way he'd asked her to. The queen size bed was laced with a new comforter, and the room smelled like a spring morning. He looked over to his niece, and then pointed back into the hallway.

"There's a bathroom down the hall on your left," Marcel continued. "That one is all yours. Just make yourself comfortable, and don't even think about leaving until I figure this out."

Sabrina put her bag on the bed and looked around the room. It was a lot nicer than she'd imagined. She started feeling lucky that she had an uncle who was serious about his money. She didn't want to think about where she would be if he didn't come to the hotel and save her.

"So you still wanna see the video, Uncle M?" Sabrina quietly asked as she looked over to Marcel.

"Hell yea," he replied. "You got it?"

Sabrina reached into her bag and pulled out a clear DVD case. She handed Marcel the video and looked up to him.

"I can't watch it again," Sabrina uttered and shook her head.

"Okay. I'll check it out in a few."

"I'm gonna go to bed now." Sabrina yawned. "Will you be here in the morning?"

"Yup, I'll be right here," Marcel responded. "Get some sleep, and we'll talk tomorrow."

Marcel gave his niece a small grin and turned around. He closed the door to her room, and then headed downstairs into the basement. He was beyond curious to see what was on the video. Marcel fired up the flat screen television and put the video inside the DVD player. He grabbed the remote and took a front row seat on the soft leather couch. Marcel sat up in his seat once the video started playing. There were a couple of people on the video, but Marcel didn't recognize any of the faces. The video images were choppy for a few minutes, and then he saw Gary Banks enter the frame.

"Holy shit, that is the mayor," Marcel gasped.

He gripped the remote, rewound the video, and played it again. Marcel balled up his fist and put it in front of his lips. "What the fuck? That is him," Marcel uttered again.

He couldn't believe what he was watching. The mayor was clearly on the video, and Marcel even stood to his feet to get a closer look. There was loud screaming on the video, and Marcel turned down the television. He watched in pure shock as the video went on for nearly fifteen minutes.

"Oh my fuckin' God," Marcel uttered and shook his head. The images were horrifying, but he couldn't turn away. He was glued to the video. Marcel was standing in the middle of the floor, staring at the television, when Tricia walked in.

"What's going on, Marcel?" Tricia whispered and looked over to the flat screen.

Marcel spun around and noticed her entering the room. He quickly pointed the remote to the television, turning it off. He tried to fix his face, but Tricia could clearly see that he was shaken by something.

"What was that?" Tricia asked with a worried expression.

"It was nothing," Marcel said and walked back to the leather sofa.

"Wait a minute, Marcel, that wasn't *nothing*," Tricia pressed. "What was all that screaming?"

"It was nothing," Marcel repeated as he plopped down on the couch. "Don't worry about it. I was just checking something out."

Tricia decided not to press the issue, and walked over to her friend. She sat down on the sofa and studied Marcel's worried expression. "So is everything okay with your niece?"

"Yea, she's good," Marcel responded. "Sabrina's gonna stay here for a minute. She was staying in a hotel, and I can't have that shit."

"That's cool," Tricia whispered, not wanting to put up a fight. "I was worried when I didn't hear from you. Are you okay?"

"Yes, I'm good," Marcel lied.

His mind was still on the video, and Tricia could sense that he was stressed out. She reached over to him and started rubbing Marcel's neck.

"Are you sure you okay," Tricia asked, lowering her voice. "You know I hate to see you without a smile on your face." Marcel didn't say a word. He looked at his young friend and gave her a small grin. "No, Marcel, I need my baby to smile bigger than that. Come on, let's go to bed. Let me see if I can find a way to loosen you up."

Tricia nibbled on her lip, then gave her friend a sexy smile. Marcel knew exactly what Tricia was referring to, and he picked up on her sensual vibe. He thought about his long day, then decided that in his bedroom with Tricia is where he needed to be. The long night with his niece had gotten to him, and he needed something to take his mind away from the drama. Tricia grabbed Marcel by the hand and helped him stand to his feet. She led him out of the basement and upstairs to the top floor. Marcel got aroused as he watched Tricia slowing swaying her sexy body in front of him. She waited for him to enter the bedroom first, and knew he would be impressed at the sight. Tricia had laced the room with scented candles and soft music. She slowly closed the door to the bedroom, and got ready for a special night with her friend, Marcel.

Nine

The bright morning sunlight calmly crept through the curtains in Kimi's bedroom. The warm sunrays slowly made their way to her sleeping face, causing her to slowly open her eyes. Last night's unbelievable episodes had put her in a coma-like slumber. She calmly stretched her wings, and noticed her body was slightly aching from the waist down. She didn't mind the pain. Niko had made love to her like a champion last night. The sex with him was always incredible. She looked over to him, then smiled at his sleeping face. Images of him on top of her, pleasing every inch of her body, flashed into her mind. *Damn, you're gifted,* Kimi thought as she glanced at his peaceful expression. She looked around the room, then slowly exhaled with delight. The satisfying moment of memories was short lived when Kimi turned her attention to the digital clock on her dresser. She almost had a heart attack when she noticed the blinking numbers on the clock flashing 4:23 A.M. She knew the clock was wrong.

"Ah shit!" she blurted. Her voice instantly woke Niko.

He could barely keep his eyes open as he turned over and looked at Kimi. "What's the matter?" Niko mumbled. He kept his face buried in the pillow.

"Damn, I think we had a blackout last night," Kimi said. "My clock was reset." She reached for her cellphone on the glass table next to her bed, and her heart dropped to her stomach. "Goddammit," Kimi yelled. Niko picked up his head again from the pillow.

"What happened?" he whispered.

65

"Baby, we got to get up now," Kimi said. She pulled the covers back and jumped to her feet. "It's almost ten o'clock."

"What?" Niko blurted. His eyes were wide now. He glanced at the blinking clock and frowned.

"I'm sorry, baby. The lights must've went out last night, and my alarm clock didn't go off. Shit!" Kimi uttered. She was stressing. She rushed to her closet and pulled out a business suit.

"Damn. And you said it's almost ten o'clock?" Niko asked. He put his hand on his forehead and thought for a moment. "I'm going to miss my train."

"No you not, honey," Kimi responded. "I'll get you there. But we have to get ready. It's going to take me fifteen minutes to get dressed, and we can be out the door in twenty. I got you babe." Kimi hustled to the bathroom and turned on the shower. She walked by the bed again and looked at Niko. "You can jump in the shower first. I'm going to go check on something downstairs."

"Okay," Niko responded.

He slowly rose to his feet, then made his way to the bathroom. Kimi rushed downstairs and headed to the kitchen. All of the lights were off on the first level, and Kimi realized that her electricity wasn't fully restored.

"Geesh, all of this money I pay and they can't keep the damn lights on in this town," Kimi whispered in frustration.

She opened a wooden drawer next to her refrigerator and pulled out a flashlight. Kimi flicked on the light, then made her way down to the basement. She hated going downstairs in the dark ,but she knew she had to reset the circuit breaker. Kimi mustered up some courage and continued into the basement. After a few moments of searching the wall, Kimi spotted the breaker and clicked back on the lights. She shook her head and turned off the flashlight. She made her way back upstairs, and felt relieved when she noticed that all of the power was now working. She quickly rushed back up to the second level. Niko was still in the shower, and Kimi turned her attention to the linen closet that was in the middle of the hallway. She opened the door and looked inside. It was no ordinary linen closet. Instead of sheets, towels and hand cloths, Kimi was staring directly at a large metal cage.

Even though Kimi lived in a gated community that had a very diligent security team, she'd decided to add extra protection to her house. She had an expensive alarm system installed that included a twenty-camera hookup that surveyed her entire house. Each camera was about the size of a large marble and had been strategically placed all around the home. Kimi was so paranoid that she had a few cameras put in to videotape the outside of her house. She was serious about keeping safe. The camera system was so intricate, and it was appropriately named Big Brother.

Kimi unlocked the cage and saw that the Big Brother system was still activated and the recording featured was still disabled. Kimi never filmed the house while she was home, she only use the recording feature when she was away. She doubled checked all of the connections, then closed the cage. As she returned to her bedroom, Niko was coming out of the bathroom with nothing but a towel wrapped around his waist.

Kimi took one look at his sexy chest and slowly blinked her eyes. "Goddamn, baby," she joked. "You better be glad we're both late for appointments."

Niko smirked and started to get dressed. Kimi rushed to the bathroom, keeping her promise to make it quick. She was in and out of the shower in ten minutes and fully dressed shortly thereafter. Niko gathered his things, making sure he had his wallet, keys and jewelry. He turned his attention to Kimi, who was almost ready to go. She grabbed her briefcase and packed a bag with her essentials, including notes for today's presentation. Kimi put on her sexy fur coat and left the bedroom. Niko followed her downstairs, and they both headed toward the garage. She hated to rush him, but she knew she had to get him back to the train station in Newark. They both walked into the garage, and Kimi made sure to activate the alarm.

"Last night was wonderful, baby," Kimi whispered as she unlocked the door to her X5. Niko walked closer to Kimi and hugged her. She grabbed his face and gave him a slow kiss on the lips. "I swear I never want our time to end. You are the best," Kimi said.

"Thank you, sexy," Niko whispered. "I don't know what I would do without you."

Niko's last words were like music to her ears. She had never heard Niko talk like that to her, and it made her feel loved. Kimi and Niko were growing closer, and she was happy to have him in her life. They were becoming good friends, and the lovely sex between the two was a sweet bonus to their marvelous chemistry. They kissed again. Niko rested his lips on Kimi's forehead for a moment, and the garage fell silent.

"I'm going to miss you, baby," Niko said.

"Not more than I'm going to miss you, babe," Kimi groaned.

The two embraced again, then walked to the back of the X5. Kimi looked out her garage door window while Niko climbed into the trunk. He got comfortable in the roomy space and smiled.

She bent down and kissed him. "You are so bad," she said with a devilish smile.

"And you love it," Niko joked.

"I do." Kimi giggled and carefully closed the trunk.

She opened the garage door, and the cold wind quickly engulfed her. Kimi looked around her quiet neighborhood one last time. She hated her nosey neighbors so much that she made it a point to come in and out of her garage undetected. After living in Shady Meadows for almost two years, she knew all of the neighbors talked to each other quite frequently. She knew it would sour her friendship with Niko if people knew she was sneaking such a famous man in and out of her house. After realizing the coast was clear, Kimi rushed back to her SUV. She fired up the engine to the BMW, then smoothly backed out of the driveway. As the garage door slowly lowered, Kimi looked at the clock on the dashboard and noticed she had less than thirty minutes to take what was supposed to be a forty-five minute drive to the train station. She knew she could do it if she hurried. Kimi put the X5 into gear, set to pull off.

"Kimmmiii, wait!" a loud voice yelled from outside of the car.

Kimi looked out the window and saw the last person in the world she wanted to see jogging toward her SUV. Her neighbor, Desiree West.

Thirty-six year old Desiree was a married woman. She and her husband had lived in Shady Meadows for almost four years. She didn't have many friends, and because Kimi lived directly across the street, Desiree felt it necessary to welcome Kimi into her life. But, for Kimi, the feeling was far from mutual. She and Desiree were from two different worlds. Kimi was a girl born and raised in the rough environment of Newark, New Jersey. She always had to work hard for her position, and that energy showed everyday in her personality. But Desiree was cut from a different cloth. She was born in Scotch Plains, New Jersey, and was brought up in the safe and secure confines of the suburbs. Her parents had careers in the dentistry field, and because Desiree had no brothers and sisters, she lived a much-shielded childhood. Kimi didn't like Desiree from the first day they met, but because Desiree lived directly across the street Kimi decided to be polite every time they would speak.

"Kimi, honey, roll down your window. I'm glad I caught you," Desiree shouted, continuing to jog to the car.

Kimi took one look at Desiree's bubbly expression and resisted the urge to roll her eyes. Kimi lowered her window and greeted her neighbor. "Good morning Desi," she said with a half smile. She still couldn't believe Desiree was coming to her car.

"Howdy neighbor," Desire joked. She walked up to the car, then rested her arms on the driver side door. "Honey, I know you are in a rush, and it looks like I'm holding you up already. I just saw you pulling out, and wanted to catch you before you left. Oh my God, is that the new passion fruit air freshener I'm smelling? Oh my, that smells so divine."

Kimi looked at Desiree and was tempted to pull off down the street. Desiree's morning rambling reminded Kimi of another reason why she didn't like her neighbor. Desiree could talk the ear off of a statue. Kimi looked at the clock on the dashboard and turned back to her neighbor.

"Actually, Desi I'm in bit of a rush ," Kimi politely uttered. "I really have to go."

"You know what neighbor, I'm sorry," Desiree said. "Look at me. I know you are a busy woman, and I'm standing here running my mouth like a marathon. I'm not going to hold you too much longer. I just wanted you to know that I am throwing a dinner for my husband tonight, and I want you to come." Kimi was stunned by the invitation. Her face froze for a moment. "Listen Kimi, I know you're probably thinking like where the heck is this coming from, but his birthday is this weekend, so I figure I can throw him a nice dinner tonight before we go away. It's going to be something small, just a few friends."

"Ummm," Kimi uttered. She didn't know how to respond to the invitation. She gave Desiree a suspicious expression. "You want me to have dinner with you and your husband tonight?"

"It's only going to be about eight of us, Kimi. Like a small get-together, that's it," Desiree said. "You can even bring a friend. In fact, it would be nice if you brought a friend. Everybody's going to be coupled up."

"Oh, okay, what   time is it?" she asked. She thought about the trunk of the X5, then tried to speed up the conversation.

"About eight o'clock tonight," Desiree responded. "I would really be honored if you could make it, Kimi."

Desiree's sincerity disarmed Kimi. Desiree always invited her neighbor to dinner, but Kimi never accepted. There was something strange in today's request from Desiree, but Kimi had to make a decision so she could finally get on the road.

"Okay, Desi," Kimi mumbled. "I will call you later to get the details. But I really have to go."

"Great, Kimi. Thank you so much." Desiree smiled. "Believe me, honey, this is going to be a dinner to remember."

Kimi gave her neighbor an uneven smile. She felt uncomfortable about the invitation, but she had no time to dwell on that. She waved goodbye to Desiree, then put the car back into gear.

"Okay, Kimi, drive carefully," Desiree smiled.

"Thank you. I will call you later," Kimi said. She returned the grin to Desiree and pulled off. Kimi looked at the clock on the dashboard and noticed she'd lost five minutes. She sped through the neighborhood and quickly made her way to the main highway. She turned her head toward the back of the BMW, then yelled loud enough so Niko could hear her.

"I'm sorry, baby," she shouted. "It's going to get a little rough. Just hold on back there. But I promise you that we're going to make it."

Ten

"Baby, you up? It's almost ten o'clock," Tricia's morning voice shook Marcel out of his deep sleep. The long night of dealing with Sabrina's drama had put him out like a light. He turned his rested body over toward his friend and gave her a small grin. Tricia could tell Marcel was flashing back to their late night episodes. She gave him a seductive smile, then kissed him on his shoulder.

"Good morning," Marcel grumbled. "What the hell are you doin' up so early?"

"I wanted to talk to my special friend," Tricia whispered as she curled up next to Marcel.

"About what?" Marcel stretched.

"I need to see what he's up to," Tricia playfully uttered. "He was poking me while you was sleeping last night. I need to go down there to see if he's okay."

Marcel smoothly chuckled, then closed his eyes as Tricia reached down and rubbed on his stomach. Her soft hands felt warm on his skin, and Marcel started reacting to her caress. She continued to kiss his shoulder, and slowly moved her lips and tongue down to his chest. Marcel lifted his arms, inviting Tricia to please him. She didn't hesitate. Tricia climbed on top of Marcel's naked body, then eased her legs around his hips. Marcel became aroused. No matter how tired Marcel was, or what was going on in his mind, the sight of Tricia's tight body could grab his full attention at the drop of a hat.

MESSY SHEETS

Tricia could tell that Marcel was growing excited. She seductively arched her back and surrendered to the thought of pleasing him. She licked on his chest, and then quickly moved down to his stomach. A few seconds and a few kisses later, she found herself in the middle of Marcel's legs. His swollen dick was standing firmly upright, begging for her head game. Tricia loved the sight of it. The few moments before she started her freak show was the best for her. She loved to stare at Marcel's chocolate dick and watch it as it rocked back and forth, pulsating and gyrating with anticipation. Tricia felt herself getting hornier by the second. She made her mouth as wet as possible, and then engulfed his dick like a sweet popsicle. Marcel moaned and his head sunk into the pillows. Tricia sucked and teased him until he moaned her name. He loved it when she woke him up to play. No matter how many times Tricia went down on him, she always found a way to make it feel like the first time. She knew exactly how to please him and have him coming back for more.

"Uncle M, are you in there?" Sabrina yelled just beyond the bedroom door. Marcel quickly lifted his head. His face transformed from sheer pleasure to absolute anger. Her timing couldn't have been any worse.

He looked over to the bedroom door, yelling at his niece, "I'm busy. Come back in like twenty minutes."

Meanwhile, Tricia never missed a beat. She kept pleasing Marcel as if she was hard of hearing.

"No, Uncle M, it's an emergency please," Sabrina whined. "You gotta see this."

"What the fuck…!" Marcel snapped. He dropped his head back to the mattress, clearly annoyed. His concentration was officially broken.

Tricia noticed the change in his mood, and then rolled over. She was beyond furious with Sabrina for cock blocking.

73

"Uncle M, it will take five minute to see this," Sabrina yelled. "Please? I gotta show you this."

Marcel jumped up and out of bed. He stood to his feet, looking around the room. The sound of his niece's voice killed his sexual high and he had no choice but to see what was so important so early in the morning. He quickly got dressed, putting on his sweatpants and T-shirt. He looked back at Tricia who never took her eyes off of him.

"I'll be right back," Marcel mumbled. "Don't move."

"I won't." Tricia smiled and wiped the sides of her lips.

Marcel rushed to the door and pulled it wide open. The sudden noise startled Sabrina. "Who died?" Marcel groaned, then walked out of the bedroom.

"Come here, Uncle M, let me show you this," Sabrina replied. She walked down the stairs, and Marcel followed her. She didn't say a word until both of them reached her room. Marcel watched her as she picked her phone up from the bed.

"I got this message a few minutes ago," Sabrina nervously said.

Marcel grabbed the phone and read the text message.

UNKOWN CALLER

This is your last chance to get my shit back to me.

I know you got it.

Text me bitch and let's work this out.

"Who the fuck is this?" Marcel sharply asked. "Is this that nigga, Khalil?"

"That's who I thought it was," Sabrina responded. She took the phone from Marcel, then scrolled down to another message. "I was thinking it was Khalil, so I text him back and told him that I didn't have his money. And this is what came back to me." Sabrina handed the phone back to Marcel, and he read the message.

UNKOWN CALLER

What money? I'm talking about the video you stole from me.
You are making it super bad for yourself.
Text this number back and let's meet before it's too late.
Remember, anybody can get touched. You can't hide.

"Oh shit," Marcel gasped. He kept reading the text over and over, until the words circled in his mind. He looked up from the phone and at his niece. "So this is Gary Banks texting you about the video?"

"I think so," Sabrina uttered. She was clearly shaken by the message, and sat down on her bed. "I told you, Uncle M. I'm in serious trouble. Maybe I should just give the DVD back and leave town."

"Nah, fuck that," Marcel snapped. He was becoming increasingly angry as the text message flashed in and out of his mind. The threatening tone of the message made him feel challenged. "What the fuck does he mean *anybody can get touched*? So can he."

Sabrina looked up to her uncle, and saw that his temper was slowly getting hotter.

"So what should I do?" Sabrina quietly asked.

Her room became eerily silent, and Marcel looked away from her. He took a seat on her bed, then thought for a moment. Marcel knew his niece was scared of the mayor, but giving the video back to Gary was out of the question. Marcel was a hustler by nature, and the opportunity to make some real money from the video enticed him.

He looked over to Sabrina. "Is this the first time he text you like this?" he asked.

"I never seen this number before, but somebody sent some shit to my email account," Sabrina said. "I'm not sure if this is Gary, or somebody that he put up to this. I just want this shit to end."

Marcel didn't respond to his niece. A crazy idea came to his mind, and he put his hand on his chin. Sabrina looked at her uncle and noticed a sinister expression.

"Did you show anybody else the video?" Marcel asked.

"Hell no," Sabrina responded.

"Okay. So nobody else knows you got it, right?"

"No, I don't think so." Sabrina shook her head. "Where is the video at now, Uncle M?"

"It's downstairs in the DVD player," Marcel responded.

"Okay," Sabrina uttered.

Marcel thought for another second and looked at his niece's phone again. He started texting the number back, and Sabrina looked over his shoulder."

SABRINA
I have the video and the only way you can get it back
is by meeting me tonight. Alone.

Sabrina nervously looked at her uncle as he sent the text message. Her stomach started turning with anxiety as she tried to figure out Marcel's plan. The room fell silent again. Sabrina and Marcel both stared at the phone impatiently waiting for a response. After a few tense moments, Sabrina's phone started buzzing as another message was being received.

UNKOWN CALLER
Where do you want to meet?

Sabrina put her hand over her mouth when she read the response. Marcel started typing on the phone again.

SABRINA

I will send you the location tonight. Come by yourself and bring $100,000 if you want it back.

"What are you doing, Uncle M?" Sabrina gasped when she read the text message.

Before she could stop him, Marcel hit the send button and pushed the text message through. Although Sabrina grew more afraid, he seemed to be cool and calm. He stared at the phone as a response came in.

UNKOWN CALLER

I don't think so.

Marcel quickly started typing again.

SABRINA

You better Think So! If you don't bring the money Gary this video will be EVERYWHERE tomorrow.
And I'm starting with the news!

Marcel sent the message. He stood up, and then looked down to his niece. Her worried face almost made him chuckle. He knew they had the mayor in a tough spot, and there was nothing he could do but cooperate. The room was completely quiet for the next few minutes. Marcel never broke a sweat as he glanced at the phone, waiting for the mayor to respond. Sabrina looked up when she heard the phone buzzing. Marcel read the message, and then showed it to his niece. A devious smile emerged on his face as she read the response.

UNKOWN CALLER

I will have the money. Just bring the video and
let's put an end to this shit.

"That's what I'm talkin' about!" Marcel boasted. "We got 'em! We got this motherfucka!"

Marcel's loud voice made Sabrina jump to her feet. She was shocked by his sudden burst of energy and looked over to him.

"So what do we do now?" Sabrina nervously asked.

"Don't leave the house," Marcel ordered. "Wait here until I come back."

"Where are you going?"

"I need to see my peoples that might be able to help us. I'm serious about you staying here." Marcel looked at his niece as she shrugged her shoulders.

"Okay, I'll stay here." Sabrina groaned feeling like a stepchild.

"And if he text you back, don't say shit to him, alright?" Marcel asked with a stiff tone.

Sabrina simply nodded her head.

"Did you hear what I said? Don't say shit to him if he text you."

"Okay, Uncle M," Sabrina gasped. "I heard you."

Marcel gave his niece a serious expression, and then turned around. He left the room and headed upstairs. Marcel walked into his bedroom and looked at the time.

"I'm sorry, Tricia, I gotta go," Marcel announced.

"What? Where are you going?" Tricia whined. She sat up on the bed and looked at Marcel as he prepared to shower.

"I'm going downtown for a hot minute, but I'll be right back," Marcel continued. "Make sure Sabrina doesn't leave. Okay?"

Tricia never got a chance to answer Marcel. He rushed into the bathroom and turned on the shower. Marcel's mind raced with a thousand thoughts. He was sure that his plan to make some quick cash from the video would work. He didn't waste another minute preparing to put his dangerous plan into motion.

Ten miles away, in the bottom level of a vacant parking deck, Kimi's BMW whipped around the corner and made a screeching sound loud enough to wake the dead. Niko held on tight as his crammed body bounced around in the trunk like a pinball. She pulled up alongside Niko's car, and then put the SUV in park. She rushed to the rear and quickly popped open the hatchback.

Niko gave Kimi a crooked grin and shook his head. "I think I'm going to need a chiropractor after that ride," he groaned, and then got out. He stretched his limbs to shake off the bumpy ride.

"I am so sorry, honey," Kimi said. "But I tried to be very careful this time."

"It's okay ,baby. I'm good." Niko smiled. "I'm just glad we made it safe."

Kimi looked around the quiet parking structure and moved closer to Niko. She wrapped her arms around her friend and gave him a deep kiss.

"You know I hate to see you go," she whispered, nudging her face against his cheek.

"I know," Niko gasped. He hugged Kimi's sexy body and closed his eyes. For Niko, leaving Kimi was the worst part of his day. Despite being a married man, living a very public life, he had a deep affection for Kimi that showed with every embrace. He would grow goose bumps every time they got close. There was something perfect about the way their bodies fused together when they hugged. Niko kissed Kimi on the lips. "Baby, I have to go," he whispered, looking down into his friend's eyes.

"I know. Me too." Kimi sighed. She returned the yearning glance, and then hugged Niko tighter. "Be careful today, baby."

"Thanks," Niko whispered. "Good luck this morning on that presentation. You will do great. I'm proud of you."

"Awl." Kimi smiled. "That means a lot to me. Stay by your phone. I will call you to check in with you after I'm done."

Niko hugged her again, and they exchanged kisses. Kimi headed to her car while Niko opened his trunk and pulled out his briefcase.

"Are you going straight to the office?" she asked as she opened her door.

"No, I will be at the firm in a couple of hours. I have to see a client before my big meeting later," he responded.

"Okay, just be careful. I hear the weather is going to be rough later." Kimi smiled.

"Thanks, baby. Call me later." Niko nodded toward his friend and got into his car. He looked around the vacant area, and then fired up his engine. He had a long day ahead of him, and he was ready to get it started. He looked over to Kimi's BMW and watched as she sped out of the parking structure.

Kimi also had a hefty schedule on the horizon. The big day she had been anxiously awaiting was finally here. She went over the notes in her mind and smiled, knowing that she was well prepared to pitch her business for a very huge sale. Kimi blasted her music and sped down the city streets. She used her motivated spirit to carry her all the way to her destination.

Eleven

"No matter how intense you think your sex life is there is always room for improvement. Take a minute to think. Try to imagine what attracts you to the opposite sex. Is it the way they walk or talk? Is it the way they dress or carry themselves? How about the occupation they chose? Is there something about what a person does for a living that turns you on? Is it the small things about them that drive you crazy? A way they smile or a way they look at you in the heat of the moment? The answer to this age-old question is all of the above. Although our minds have a funny way of focusing on just a few things about a person, true attraction comes from hundreds, if not thousands, of triggers that draws us to the opposite sex. But there is one thing that needs to be present in order for us to fully take our sexual lives to the highest intensity level possible. I like to call this place orgasmic heaven."

A few loud pants and chuckles cascaded from the audience as Kimi took a moment to let her explanation sink into the minds of all in attendance. Every month for the past two years, Kimi held presentations to introduce her new products to the public. For Kimi, being a founder and CEO of a thriving company meant she had to find creative ways to grow her business and attract new clients. Her organization was doing well, and things were looking up for Kimi ,but she never let a day go by without developing new plans and strategies to stay ahead of her competition. Today, Kimi was on a bigger mission.

She was ready to pursue her dreams of putting out a lifestyle magazine, but the first step was to sell her current business.

Kimi had invited over two hundred professionals to this particular presentation. She invited the senior buyers from Macy's, Bloomingdale's, Lord & Taylor and even Wal-Mart. She also invited members of the media and small business owners throughout the Tri-State area. She'd even invited executives from the adult film industry. The conference hall in the Newark Hilton was buzzing as professionals conversed and joked with each other. Everyone had been anticipating this new idea that Kimi Moore was trying to sell to them.

Kimi's company developed a new line of silk sheets to add to the long list of products. For the past few months, she had been meticulously preparing today's presentation, and now the hour had come to pitch her new idea to the world.

"We are all professionals here, so I will try to keep the presentation as clean as possible," Kimi joked with the audience. "But there are clearly levels of sexual satisfaction. Some of us journey through our love lives having very mundane sexual experiences. This is the type of sex that goes on when one spouse, or, possibly, both of you are too busy for intimacy. We all know the story. You work all the time. Or the kids get in the way. Or your schedule is too hectic, and your spouse is too busy to make love. And, finally, once you both have time to share, the sex is very basic, and usually follows the same routine. Man on top, woman acts like she is enjoying herself, and the entire dreadful episode lasts a whopping ten minutes...if you are lucky."

The audience erupted into a loud laughter. Kimi smiled as she realized her presentation was heading in the right direction. The audience was at full attention, and Kimi decided to kick things into high gear.

"So as a couple that wants to spice things up in the bedroom, what do you do?" Kimi continued. "You buy all types of creams, lotions, gadgets, videotapes, lingerie, and even costumes to turn things up a notch. But, after a while, all of those tricks begin to wear off. Does anybody know why?"

"Because your body gets use to it," one man yelled out from the back of the room.

"Toys and lotions only work for a while, then you'll eventually have to introduce something new to the mix," one woman, in a business suit, added.

"Exactly," Kimi said to the group. "All of those toys, lotions and gadgets are meant to stimulate your body. But I'm here today to tell you that sex is not entirely a physical thing. Of course, we use our bodies for sex, and there must be a physical attraction to your partner. But the beginning of a good sexual experience starts in the mind."

Kimi paused for a moment to let her last statement linger with the audience. She reached for a glass of water, and then took a long sip. She was a great orator who understood the importance of baiting in her listeners. Letting them use their own imagination was a big part of keeping them engaged. She took another moment to reset, and then continued with the presentation.

"If I ask you guys what is the most important sexual organ in your body, most people will automatically shift their minds to imagine what's below and between your legs. Am I right?" Kimi asked. The audience murmured again with a few giggles. "But, do you know, the first sexual organ is your brain? Without your mind present and highly aroused, your body is useless. The brain is not only filled with wild sexual fantasies and creative thoughts of explorations, but the brain is also equipped to handle certain neurochemical events that make your episodes much more pleasurable. I don't want to go too deep into the inner workings of neurology, but, just imagine for a moment, the human mind is the coach and your body is the players. Without a good coach, the players can't play to full potential. This is where my company comes in. We have developed a new line of products that will be sure to change the way you look at sex and, even, your partner."

Kimi turned on a slideshow. The audience shifted in their seats, and prepared for the announcement they had been waiting for all morning. Members of the media pulled out their recorders, and photographers started to snap images of the stage. Kimi started the slideshow and continued to speak.

"I'd like to introduce to everyone our new line of silk sheets called the MS Collection." Kimi smiled as a fancy logo appeared on the screen. She clicked on a few images of different women, lying comfortably on silk sheets, with very seductive expressions on their faces. The slides drew a number of raised hands from the audience members, and Kimi decided to field the questions.

"I see a few hands now," Kimi said. "What's your question, sir?" Kimi politely called on a gentleman to her far right.

"The MS Collection?" the man asked. "What does that mean? Does the *MS* stand for anything?"

"That is an excellent question, sir." Kimi smiled. "The MS is an acronym. Because our target audience is women for this particular line, we wanted to use the MS to attract our base. And, also, MS stands for *Messy Sheets*. So, in essence, today we are introducing the Messy Sheets Collection to the world."

Women covered their mouths at the revelation. People were blushing in the audience. Kimi noticed a number of childish smiles growing on their faces as their collective imaginations started to run wild. She knew the catchy name would grab hold of people. Some would love it, and others would shy away from it. But Kimi was willing to take the gamble. By the reaction of her current audience members, she knew she made the right decision by choosing such a visual name for the silk sheets. Kimi continued to pitch the product.

MESSY SHEETS

"When couples think to spice up their lives in the bedroom, they always seem to forget to spice up the biggest asset in the room; the actual bed. Our silk sheets have been designed with the finest mulberry silk on the planet. In fact, pound for pound, our silk threads are the strongest natural fibers in the world. This makes our sheets and comforters more durable and sturdier than ever."

A few more hands began to summon Kimi for more questions. She looked to her left and called on a young professional in the audience.

"I have a question for you, Ms. Moore," the young woman said. "Why name the brand Messy Sheets? What does that mean?"

"Oh wow," Kimi responded with a curious smile. "Sweetie, if you have to ask me what the term Messy Sheets means, I do believe that you may be just a little too young for this presentation."

The audience exploded into laughter. It took a few moments for the young professional to finally grasp the concept. Her bashful expression made Kimi smile.

"It's okay, sweetie, it takes some people a little time to catch on," Kimi continued. "But this is clearly an adult line of bedding with a focus on pleasurable results."

A few more hands were raised, and Kimi called on a reporter sitting toward the center of the room.

"Yes, sir?" Kimi asked.

"I have to say that I am impressed with the name, and I think it will spread fairly quickly throughout the marketplace," the reporter said. "But there are hundreds, if not thousands, of silk bedding brands out there. What is the niche that Messy Sheets will bring to the consumer?"

"I am so glad you asked that question, sir," Kimi responded. "This will actually bring us to the most important segment of this presentation."

Kimi reached into her briefcase and pulled out a small white spray bottle. To the naked eye the container resembled perfume. Kimi placed it on the podium and changed the slide slow. The last image was of two people embracing each other with the word *desire* above them. Kimi turned her attention back to the audience and continued her presentation.

"My company conducted a survey last year with over five-hundred couples throughout the country," Kimi said. "When it came time to discuss their sex lives, we wanted to find out what was the most common complaint. After gathering all the data, we came to the conclusion that most couples have an issue with desire. Or, in other words, over time our couples seem to have lost interest in each other. And, as we discussed earlier, just like all sexual experiences begin in the brain, the same rings true for desire. Imagine for a moment that there was a way to desire your partner every time you walked into the bedroom. Imagine if there was a way to increase your sexual desire to nearly an animalistic level."

Kimi grabbed the white spray bottle and raised it in the air. The photographers in the room scrambled to get a good picture of the unlabeled container. Kimi kept the bottle elevated in the air as she continued to speak.

"This is called Rati," she explained. "Rati is a combination of fragrances and sex pheromones that increase desire. As you all know, the brain responds to these pheromones and intensifies the urge for intercourse. Each one of our bodies releases these pheromones as a form of communication to our partners that it's time to…well… for a lack of a better phrase…that it's time to get it on."

The audience chuckled again, and even Kimi tickled herself. She smiled for a moment, and continued then with the presentation.

"Without even knowing it, we send signals to each

other that shift our mood. My company has developed an amazing combination of human fragrances and pheromones that is guaranteed to increase desire. Our secret formula is non-alcoholic based and one-hundred percent totally natural."

"So the Rati perfume comes with the sheets?" one man blurted in the audience.

"Not exactly, sir," Kimi responded. "The Rati is *in* the sheets." Kimi's revelation caused a stir in the audience.

"How is the Rati in the sheets?" the man asked.

"Each one of our pieces have been specially designed and woven with the silk pheromone-dipped threads," Kimi explained. "So the sheets become a natural aphrodisiac, and increase the desire triggers in you and your partner." Kimi looked around at the faces in the room. She was excited about the reaction of smiles and nods she was receiving from her audience. "I will take one more question from the young lady right here, in the front."

"Very good stuff," the woman said. "I believe the buyers at my company will be more than interested in this product. But I do have to ask what's the formula for Rati?"

"I'm sorry guys, the formula is a secret," Kimi replied. "The contents are under patent protection, but I can tell you that the pheromones are not genetically altered. They are all natural. Besides, if I told you the formula, we wouldn't be in business for very long." Kimi smiled at the woman.

A few more laughs came from the audience, and Kimi decided to wrap up the presentation. She clicked on the last slide. The logo for Messy Sheets appeared on the screen along with the contact information for her company.

"I want to thank you guys for coming today, and I do appreciate your business. This is an exciting time for the bedding industry, and couples are begging for an opportunity to spice up things in the bedroom. If your company is interested in wholesale pricing and additional information, we have a full prospectus for you near the entrance. Also, if your company or firm is interested in buying the Messy Sheets Business, please contact our lawyers to discuss the details. Thanks again, and have a great day."

A round of applause erupted from the audience. Kimi even received a standing ovation from some women in the room who were clearly impressed with the exciting and fresh concept. A few of the women approached Kimi as she and her employees broke down the set, preparing to leave.

Kimi greeted a few people as they approached her and offered their own business cards and brochures. Kimi was making great connections, and she had a very positive feeling about today's presentation. As Kimi talked to a few women in front of her, she recognized a familiar face walking to the table. She nearly lost her cool when she looked at the young man's face. Her heart stopped for a moment, and she was instantly taken back to a place long before Messy Sheets, Shady Meadows, and the good life. The women in front of her noticed a change in Kimi's mood, then turned to see at whom she was gazing. They all watched as the tall and attractive man smoothly made his way to the table. He excused himself in front of the women, and then walked right up to Kimi.

"Marcel!" she gasped. "Oh my goodness, what are you doing here?"

Marcel smiled at Kimi, then gave her a hug. Although she was in shock, her smile grew from ear to ear. She hadn't seen or heard from Marcel in over six years. She gave him a tight hug and became slightly emotional. She quickly brought herself back to reality.

"Wow, Marcel, what a surprise this is," Kimi said.

"I know. It's been a long time," he responded. "I wanted to surprise you. But I know you're busy, Kimi. I would love to meet you for lunch if you have some time after this."

"Sure," Kimi quickly accepted. She looked at Marcel's face, and still couldn't believe he was here. It was getting harder for her to maintain her composure around him. She looked at the small group at her table and smiled. "I will wrap this up, and should be free within the hour."

"Sounds great, Kimi," Marcel said. "Let's meet at Kings on Clinton Avenue."

"My favorite spot," Kimi uttered.

"I remember." Marcel smiled. "I'll meet you there, let's say, at two?"

"Perfect. I will be there," Kimi responded.

They both hugged again, and Marcel turned around and left. Kimi took a moment to gather herself, then turned her attention back to the small crowd at her table. She continued to network with the women, but her mind was fixed on Marcel. He was looking more handsome than she had ever seen him, and Marcel was clearly doing well for himself. Kimi's mind wandered off to the past, and she unconsciously looked at her watch. She couldn't wait to meet up with him to reminisce about old times.

Twelve

One hour later, Marcel pulled up to King's Restaurant and parked his SUV directly in front of the building. The cold afternoon made the usually busy Clinton Avenue seem like a ghost town. The normal flow of traffic had been reduced to only a couple of cars and a few pedestrians trekking though the cold weather. But no matter how cold it was, and no matter how much snow fell to the ground in Newark, Marcel could always count on his favorite restaurant to be open for business.

Marcel walked up the shoveled staircase and through the double glass doors of King's restaurant. The gorgeous hostess near the front entrance greeted him.

"Okay now, I knew I smelled big money walking through the door." The young woman winked at Marcel.

"Hey, beautiful." Marcel smiled as he returned a pleasant compliment.

The good food was not the only reason he loved the restaurant. The female employees were always so warm to him, and never passed up an opportunity to flirt. Marcel soaked up the attention. He continued to make his way into the dining area of the restaurant, and personally greeted all of the waitresses. Marcel was definitely a hood celebrity in Newark. His name was always circulating in and out of the gossiping mouths when the topic of money came up. Everybody knew Marcel for being a young baller on the rise. For the waitresses in King's, seeing Marcel coming through the door was like a holiday for them. He always took care of his servers, and there was always a scramble to be the first to seat him.

"Hey, Money Marcel," a sweet voice said.

Marcel looked over and smiled at his favorite waitress. She returned the polite look and motioned for him to follow her.

"I'll be your server today."

Marcel didn't put up a fight. He followed the waitress to the middle of the dining area, and then took a seat in the booth facing the window.

"Thank you, babe," Marcel said. "I'm waiting for one more person, and I'll be all set to go."

"Okay, darling." The waitress smiled. "I'm finishing up with my last table, and then I'm all yours."

The waitress gave Marcel two menus, and then headed to the other side of the room. He watched her as she strolled to a table occupied by three men. Marcel looked them over. He recognized the bunch from the Belmont Apartments. The shortest guy at the table was Erick Ruiz, a Spanish hustler from 18th Avenue. Marcel had known Erick back when they were teenagers, but hadn't seen him lately. Erick had locked up most of his adult life. Erick took one look at Marcel, then got up and walked across the restaurant.

"Look at this baller right here!" Erick yelled as he bopped over to Marcel.

"Damn homie, look at you." Marcel cracked a grin and stood up. "Nigga, I ain't seen you in a hundred years. What's poppin'?"

"The same old shit," Erick said as he shook hands with Marcel, then gave him a hug. "What you doin' out here, back in the hood?"

"Back?" Marcel laughed. "Shit, a nigga never left." The two men chuckled for a moment. "What you been up to?

I heard you came home last year," Marcel said.

"No doubt. Been home for eleven months," Erick continued. "But, you know, a nigga like me had to hit the ground running."

"Word," Marcel uttered. "I'm not mad at that. You back in the hustle?"

"Hell yea." A grin came to Erick's face as he looked around. "I got hooked up with Marquez and his team. They got me out here movin' that Charlie Sheen, my nigga."

"You crazy as hell, my dude." Marcel shook his head and started laughing. "Do what you do, fam. Don't be like these other lames out here. Get that money, E!"

"Always. So what's up with the old crew? What's up with your cousin, Boogie?" Erick asked.

"He's good," Marcel responded. "I haven't seen him in a few months, but I dropped some money on him last week. So he's good. No news is good news, right?"

"I heard that."

"Now that you mention my cousin, let me ask you this," Marcel said, looking around the restaurant. "You ever heard of some dude named Khalil, out here?"

"Damn Marcel, I know a million Khalil's," Erick confessed. "Every nigga in the hood is a Muslim now."

"Nah, this dude said he knows my cousin Boogie," Marcel continued. "He said he put in some serious work up there with him."

"You talkin' about big Khalil from the Belmont Houses?" Erick asked. "Brown skinned dude. He got a big scar on his left cheek?"

"I don't know if he's from down the hill, but this nigga did have a cut on his face," Marcel said.

"You got beef with him?" Erick asked with a suspicious look.

"Nah, not at all," Marcel lied. "Just need to know my surroundings, you know."

"Damn, I was about to get worried for you, my nigga," Erick said. "He's definitely a killer."

"What?" Marcel blurted.

"Yea man." Erick looked around for a moment, then turned back to Marcel. "He's definitely a monster out here. The last notes on him was that he was clippin' niggas for the Marquez boys."

"Say word," Marcel mumbled.

"I put that on everything, homie. He's like a ghost though. I haven't seen him around in a while," Erick continued. "But if you do got beef with him, just watch ya moves, homie. Khalil is definitely not that nigga you wanna fuck with."

Marcel's mind flashed back to the altercation with Khalil in the hotel room. A shot of anger ran through his body as he thought about how he missed his chance to finish off Khalil. He shook the thought, and then turned back to Erick.

"Okay, thanks for the info, fam," Marcel said. "I will definitely watch my back." Marcel looked over Erick's head and noticed Kimi walking through the glass doors of the restaurant. He locked eyes with her and smiled.

"Right on time," Marcel mumbled. He turned to Erick and shook his hand. "Okay, boss. I gotta cut this convo short. I gotta tend to more important things."

Erick turned around and watched as the sexy woman walked toward the table. He picked up on Marcel's hint, then shook his hand.

"Okay bro," Erick nodded. "I'll catch you later."

Erick headed back to his table as Kimi walked up to Marcel. She was clearly excited to see her old friend, and gave him a long hug.

"Damn boy, it's so good to see you," Kimi moaned her

words as she squeezed him like a teddy bear.

"It's been a long time, for real," Marcel responded. He quickly changed up his tone, and lightened his mood when he looked at Kimi's smiling face.

Kimi kissed him on the cheek, and then sat down across from him. "Well, look at you all grown up," she joked. "You look like things are going really well for you."

"I'm managing," Marcel humbly responded.

"Shit, boy, stop being like that." Kimi waved at him. "You're shining."

"Thanks, Kimi," Marcel said. "Just trying to make a dollar outta fifteen cents."

"Whatever man," Kimi laughed. "More like a million dollars out of fifteen cents."

"You still funny," Marcel said with a wide smile. He looked into Kimi's eyes, and then smoothly shook his head.

Kimi reached into her bag, and then handed Marcel her cellphone. "Before you say another word, put your phone number in my BlackBerry, so I'll have it." Kimi smiled. "I wanted to hit you up a few times, but I didn't know how to reach you."

"Oh okay. Damn, so how long has it been?" Marcel questioned as he did as she asked. He handed her the BlackBerry and smiled.

"Since when?" Kimi continued. "Since you decided you was too cute for me, and left me standing in the cold?"

"Is that how you remember it?" Marcel asked and started laughing.

"Yup," Kimi responded. "I remember us doing just fine for two years. And then you stepped up and started playing God again, then shut me right down." Kimi laughed with Marcel.

"Damn, I don't remember all of that."

"You wouldn't remember. You're a guy," Kimi giggled.

"But it's okay. I think we're better people now that we're not together. It took a while for me, but I'm over it."

Kimi gave Marcel a crooked smile and looked at him. She knew he was digesting her last statement, and decided to wait for his response.

"Sounds like there's still something left brewing, if you ask me," Marcel joked.

"Something like what?" Kimi replied with another smile.

"I don't know. Maybe some built up tension between us. Maybe there's something still on your chest that needs to be worked out," Marcel added and slowly licked his lips. "Maybe it's been building up since the last time we saw each other. I don't know. But it definitely sounds like something's there. I'm not a professional, but if you need me to, I can help you work that out. I can try to make it all better."

Marcel gave Kimi a deep glance and smiled. Kimi's face started to grow warm with embarrassment, and the mood started to slowly change at the table. She hadn't seen Marcel in over six years, but the two still had a deep connection. Marcel picked up on her body language and smiled.

She dropped her head and started chuckling like a high school freshman. "I'm not messing with you," Kimi said. "I haven't seen you in six years, nigga. There is no way you're going to help me work out anything today," Kimi joked. "Baby boy, you're going to have to work a lot harder than that."

Before Marcel could respond to Kimi's statement, the waitress returned to the table and politely interrupted the conversation. "Would you guys like to start off with some drinks?" the waitress asked.

"Yes, I'm going to take a medium uptown," Kimi requested.

"Make that two," Marcel added.

"Un-originalllll," Kimi playfully sang.   Marcel laughed and looked at the waitress.

"That's all for now." He nodded. The waitress walked away from the table, and Marcel turned his attention back to Kimi.

"So where were we?" he asked.

"You was about to tell me how the hell you found me," Kimi responded.

"You're not that hard to find," he said. "Your face is everywhere, Kimi. Everybody is talking about your company. I was on my phone the other day, and I saw a post that you was gonna be downtown at the Hilton."

"Damn, for real?" Kimi said.

"True story," Marcel responded. "So Messy Sheets.... wow, what an idea."

"Thanks babe." Kimi smiled.

"So keep it real with me. Does it really work?" Marcel asked.

"Does what really work?" Kimi quickly responded.

"The messy sheets? Can those sheets really make you horny?" Marcel blurted.

"Damn." Kimi laughed at his statement. She almost gagged as she tried to answer his question. "I really don't like to put it like that, but, yes. The sheets are serious. If you put those sheets on your bed they will turn you into an animal."

"Really?"

"Hell yes. My sheets are off the hook," Kimi continued. "The next time I see you, I will give you a set. And you can let me know if they work for you."

Kimi smiled at Marcel, who nodded his head toward her. He was clearly impressed.

"So why are you trying to sell the company?" Marcel

asked.

"I've been running this business for a few years now, and I think it's time to move on," Kimi continued. "I'm ready to start my magazine and live my real dream."

"Damn, Kimi, you are really doing it. I'm so proud of you." Marcel gave her a genuine smile. "I'm glad that I came down there today. This might be the last chance I get to see you."

"Last chance? Before what?" Kimi asked. "Before you go."

"Go where?"

"Before you go all Hollywood on us," Marcel joked.

"Wow." Kimi laughed. She playfully waved her hand at Marcel and shook her head. "I'm not going anywhere yet. I'm a Jersey girl. I might not be in the Bricks no more, but I'm still in Dirty Jersey."

"That's good," Marcel said. "But, seriously, I'm proud of you, Kimi. You really followed your dream and made it happen for yourself."

Kimi smiled at Marcel. The waitress came back with the drinks and placed them on the table.

"Are you guys ready to order?" she asked.

"Give us five more minutes, please," Marcel requested. The waitress nodded her head, then walked to the other side of the room. Marcel raised his glass to Kimi. "Let's make a toast to winning," he said.

Kimi agreed and raised her glass. "Okay...to winning." Kimi smiled. She took a sip of the lemonade and iced tea mix, then nodded her head. "Damn, now that is how you make an Uptown. This is some good shit, right here."

"Yea, this place is still the bomb." Marcel picked up his menu. "So what do you want to eat? It's all on me."

"Is that right?" Kimi asked. "So you're going to buy me lunch today?"

"Yup. And don't even try to reach in your purse for a thing," Marcel joked. "I'm buying everything."

"Okay big spender. I don't have a problem with that."

"Good." Marcel smiled. "Because today is Kimi Appreciation Day."

Kimi dropped her menu and looked at Marcel for a moment. He noticed she was watching him and smiled at her.

"Uh oh," Kimi grunted.

"What?" Marcel asked.

"Kimi Appreciation Day?" Kimi questioned.

"Yup," Marcel responded.

"What the hell do you want?" Kimi smiled.

"Huh?" Marcel uttered. "Why you asked me that?"

"Because when you start to say corny shit like that, it means you're looking for something." Kimi laughed.

"Damn girl," Marcel said with a busted smile. "I'm not looking for anything. It's just good to see you."

"Whatever, Marcel," Kimi laughed. "I didn't get dumber in those last six years. And I still remember how you *are*. When you're overly nice to me that means you're trying to soften me up for something. What is it?"

"Damn, I guess you saw that coming, huh?" Marcel laughed.

"Just ask me, boy," Kimi said. "You never know. I might just say yes."

"Wow, I must be losing my touch for real." Marcel shook his head. "Okay, I was gonna wait until we finished lunch to bring this up, but I do need a favor."

"That's fine," Kimi uttered. She took another sip of the drink and looked at Marcel. "Shoot. I'm all ears."

"You remember my niece, Sabrina?" Marcel asked.

"Of course, the pretty one, right? Yup, I remember her."

"You remember what she used to do when you met her?"

"When she was working for you?" Kimi responded. "Is she still doing the call-girl thing?"

"Yea, something like that," Marcel continued. "But she's not working for me no more. She's out there on her own. Anyway, last night she showed me this video she got from Gary Banks' house. He used to be a client of hers."

"The Mayor of Newark?" Kimi quickly whispered. "Oh shit."

"Yup. Gary Banks," Marcel continued. "This video is serious, Kimi. I mean... it is...fuckin' serious."

"What kind of video?"

"It's a video of Gary."

"What is he doing?"

"He is ummm....damn. Gary is...ummm," Marcel mumbled for a moment and shook his head. "I can't even say it out loud. You just gotta see the video, Kimi. It's fucking sick!"

"Whoa," Kimi uttered. "Now I'm curious as hell."

"Yea, that dude is definitely a fucking sicko." Marcel looked around the restaurant and looked back to Kimi. "Anyway, my niece was telling me that she's been gettin' all these death threats and shit from Gary. She said she got some in her emails too."

"Are you sure the threats are coming from the mayor?" Kimi asked.

"I'm a hundred and ten percent sure of it," Marcel continued. "All I know is that it's clearly the mayor on the video, and, if I was him, I would do anything to get that video back. Feel me?"

"Hell yea," Kimi agreed. "So what's the favor?"

"Are you still friends with that girl from the news station?" Marcel asked.

"Yes, we're still friends," Kimi responded. "She is going to help me put out this magazine. I haven't spoken to her in a few days or so, but I can reach out to her."

"Good shit," Marcel said. "I wanna make sure I can get the video to the news if I have to send it there."

"What do you mean *if you have to*?" Kimi asked.

Marcel looked around and turned back to Kimi again. "I think the mayor will pay big money to get this video back from me." Marcel gave Kimi a curious look. "If he thinks I can get the video to the news, I bet he would pay some serious cash for it."

"Marcel, are you crazy?" Kimi asked, wrinkling her face. She couldn't believe what was coming from his mouth. She looked around and leaned over the table. "Marcel, that is blackmail."

"Exactly," he fired back. "I know what it is. That's the whole point."

"Wow." A nervous expression came to Kimi's face. "I don't know where your mind is, but they send people to jail for that kind of shit."

"Nah, nobody is going to jail, trust me." Marcel rubbed his chin. "That's the first thing I thought about when I came up with this idea. On some real shit, Gary don't want nobody to see this video, so I think he'll do just about anything to get this shit back from me. And if he tries to get me locked up, we can just put him on blast and his ass would be the one going to jail. Believe me, this video is fuckin' crazy."

Kimi thought for a moment. She was shocked by what she was hearing. Marcel's disclosure about the video was the last thing she expected to hear today. She leaned back in her seat and closed her mouth. Kimi was speechless.

"I'm tellin' you this is gonna work," Marcel uttered. "I'm meeting with him tonight."

"Marcel, you have officially gone crazy," Kimi cut him off. "What makes you think he's going to give you any money for a video? I'm sorry. Let's change the subject. I can't hear any more of this."

"Wait, Kimi listen to me." Marcel gave his old friend a hard glance. He was surprised to see her so panicky about the idea. "Hold up for a second. Don't tell me that Brick City Kimi is scared of a little drama?" Kimi shook her head and looked away from Marcel. "Damn, Kimi, back in the day you woulda' been all over this shit. You been gone too long."

"Shit right," Kimi gasped and nervously chuckled at Marcel's last statement. "You might be right. I've been in those hills for too long. I don't have the stomach for this type of shit no more."

Marcel nodded his head and took a sip of his drink. He smiled at his friend and continued speaking. "Listen, don't worry about a thing," he whispered. "I'm going to take care of everything. All I need you to do is call your friend at the news station and let her know that I may have a crazy video for her. So if Gary doesn't act right tonight, I'll call you and we can put his crazy ass out there."

"Just that simple, huh? Kimi skeptically asked.

"Hell yes. Just that simple," Marcel responded.

"Wow," Kimi mumbled. She gathered her thoughts and gave Marcel a smirk. "I swear you will never change, Marcel. You'll be a hustler 'til the day you die."

"And even when I die, I'll still be trying to hustle my way into heaven," Marcel laughed at his own joke, and Kimi joined in with a slight chuckle.

The tension at the table lifted and Kimi started to feel more relaxed. She took a drink of her iced tea mix and calmly looked over to Marcel. "Okay, so all you need me to do is call up my friend at the station, and then I'm out of the middle of this?" Kimi asked.

"That's it," Marcel replied.

"Okay. I can do that." She nodded her head.

"Thanks, Kimi, for real. I knew I could count on my road dog."

"Not a problem. Just do what you got to do," Kimi continued. "And be safe. I don't want to read about you in the paper tomorrow."

A crooked grin came to Kimi's face as the both of them laughed at her joke. Although Kimi was kidding about the newspaper comment, she was praying that Marcel knew what he was getting himself into. Everyone in Newark knew that Gary Banks was a dangerous man with ties to all types of gangsters in the Newark area. Kimi didn't want to dwell on Marcel's plan, so she changed the subject.

"Enough about this Gary Banks stuff." Kimi turned her attention to the menu on the table. "I'm starving. Let's get something to eat, Marcel."

"Sounds good to me." He smiled.

Kimi and Marcel flipped though the menus, and then spent the rest of the lunch date catching up on old memories, reminiscing about the good and bad times they both shared.

Thirteen

*A*nd in local news, authorities are searching for three suspects in yet another violent carjacking in Newark. This makes the tenth carjacking incident this month, bringing the total for the year to a nationwide high of thirty-eight. Police are knocking on doors, and asking the public for their help after a thirty-five year old Maplewood woman was forced from her Mercedes Benz at gunpoint on the 800 Block of South Orange Avenue in Newark. Police said the three suspects managed to force the woman to stop her car in the middle of the street. The suspects proceeded to assault her, and tried to force her from the car. When the woman refused, she was shot one time in the chest. Some witnesses on the scene stated that the men were heavily armed and working as a team. The woman was taken to an area hospital and treated for the gunshot wound. She's currently listed in critical condition. Newark police have posted more information on the suspects and the victim's vehicle on their website.

Niko listened to the news report on his car radio and shook his head. The horrible story agitated him and forced him to shut off the radio. All he wanted to hear was the growling of the Audi A8 engine as he pushed the luxury car well beyond the speed limit. He was late for his appointment, and tried to make up the time by racing through the main streets of Newark. Niko's phone was ringing off the hook, but he refused to answer the calls. His office, his clients, and even members of the media had been blowing up his phone all morning. After

103

nine years of being a lawyer, Niko learned the valuable lesson of never taking a call before he reached his office. Being unprepared to answer an important question about any of his cases was worse than not answering the question at all. And just like every other morning on his commute to work, Niko sent all calls to his voicemail.

Twenty minutes later, Niko pulled up in front of 723 Broad Street. The front of his office building was buzzing with news vans and reporters. He looked around in search of a familiar face. After a few moments, he saw Raymond Bowser, a lawyer who'd been working at his firm for nearly six years. Raymond was a great defense attorney, and his hard work helped build Niko's firm. Today Raymond was getting hassled by the cluster of story-hungry journalists, urging him to make a statement. When he recognized Niko's car pulling up to the building, he rushed over to greet his boss.

"I'm sorry. It's a madhouse out here today, Niko," Raymond grunted in frustration. Niko got out of the Audi and looked at Raymond, who continued shouting. "We tried to get them to back away from the building, but they are not cooperating."

"What the hell is going on?" Niko raised his voice.

"The mayor is considering calling in the National Guard to curb some of the violence in the city," Raymond responded. "After that crazy carjacking last night, everyone is in an uproar."

"Shit," Niko mumbled.

"Tell me about it," Raymond added. "I'll park your car for you, and will be right up. It's a feeding frenzy right now."

"Okay." Niko handed over the keys to his car. Raymond grabbed the keys and waited for Niko to grab his briefcase and mobile phone. Niko looked at the reporters and put on his game face. Without a second to lose, he walked away from Raymond, and right into the center of the cameras and reporters, and then tried his best to back them down.

"Counselor Stanton, what are your thoughts about the latest string of carjackings in Essex County?" one reporter yelled, shoving a small tape recorder in Niko's face.

"Guys, as of right now, you know I don't have any comments...unless it is about a case surrounding one of my clients," Niko responded.

"Sir, you do know that many authorities are pointing the blame to your client, Leon Marquez," another reporter yelled.

"Mr. Marquez has maintained his innocence of any involvement in illegal activities in and out of Essex County," Niko responded. "Any details about his currently legal battle with the city of Newark cannot be discussed at this juncture ,but I can assure you that my client will be cleared of all charges so he can carry on with his life as a successful businessman. Furthermore, in regards to the latest outbreak of violence in Newark, I would suggest you guys camp out in front of the mayor's office for those answers because my client is innocent and time will prove this to be the case. Thank you guys, and, please, no more questions. I'm late for an important meeting."

The group of reporters exploded into a loud uproar of questions and interview requests. Niko refused to speak again and pushed his way into the building. When security noticed Niko, they rushed over to the reporters and forced them back outside.

"Thanks guys," Niko stuttered as he let out a gasp of air.

He hurried through the building lobby and jumped into the elevator. He hastily pushed the button and looked at his watch. *I can't believe I'm an hour late for this shit,* Niko thought . He gathered his thoughts, and then waited for the elevator to take him to the top floor, to his firm.

*

Back at King's Restaurant, Marcel and Kimi were finishing up their lunch date. Marcel paid the check as promised, and the two were heading out the door when Kimi turned to Marcel and gave him a warm smile.

"I'm happy that we had a chance to talk today," Kimi said. "Thanks for inviting me out."

"No problem, Kimi." Marcel smiled. "I'm glad that you didn't bite my head off for asking you for that favor."

"Never that," Kimi said. "Why would I bite your head off, sweetie?"

"I don't know," Marcel continued. "I know things between us didn't end on the best of terms. And I didn't know if you would blast me right there at the table." Marcel let out an uncomfortable laugh, then looked at Kimi.

"Can I be honest with you for a second?" she asked.

"Of course."

"When I saw you walking up to my table after the presentation, I almost screamed like a mad woman." Kimi laughed. "I know we haven't seen each other in a thousand years, but I do think about you from time to time."

"Same here," Marcel smiled. "So let's not make it another thousand years okay?"

"That's cool with me. Let me make sure I got your number locked into my phone." Kimi scrolled through her numbers. Marcel did the same. "I got it."

Marcel and Kimi headed out the restaurant, and Marcel walked his old friend to her BMW.

"Don't forget to call your peoples at the news station," Marcel uttered.

"I won't," Kimi responded. "I will call you later with her information once she gives me the okay."

"Cool." Marcel nodded his head.

Kimi opened her arms and hugged Marcel. An emotional feeling came over her when they embraced. Marcel hugged her much tighter than he did inside the restaurant. Kimi's mind flashed back to the good old days when she and Marcel were together and going strong. Her emotions were jolted back to a time when Marcel could do no wrong and the very mention of his name would send chills up her spine. Kimi rested her forehead on his chest, and thought for a moment. She didn't want to let him go.

"Don't forget to be careful tonight," Kimi whispered.

"Thanks. I won't," Marcel responded.

Kimi returned the pleasant smile to Marcel, and then kissed him on the cheek. She got inside of her BMW and watched as Marcel walked to his truck. Seeing Marcel today was clearly getting to her emotions. Before she could dwell on her thoughts any longer, the ringing of her cellphone snapped her out of her trance. Kimi scrambled for her purse, grabbing the phone. She looked at the name on the display and cursed out loud. Kimi went against her better judgment and answered the call. It was her neighbor, Desiree.

"Hello," Kimi answered with a dry tone.

"Kimi, darling, how is your day going?" Desiree greeted.

"It's going good," Kimi responded. She tried her best to be polite ,but she was clearly disgusted by Desiree's bubbly tone.

"I was calling to see if you had a chance to think about my invitation," Desiree said.

"The invitation you gave me this morning?" Kimi sarcastically asked.

"Yes, darling," Desiree whined. "I need to count you in, Kimi. Did you decide to bring a date?"

"Ummm," Kimi uttered and looked out the window

of her SUV. Her eyes were still fixed on Marcel as he got into his truck and started the engine. "I don't think I'm going to bring a date, Desiree. That's if I'm able to come at all."

"Oh no, Kimi, you have to come," Desiree groaned.

Kimi rolled her eyes. She hated that Desiree didn't have a lot of friends. She started to grow impatient with her neighbor, and decided to rush her off the phone.

"Desiree, I tell you what," Kimi continued. "Let me make a few calls, and I will see if I can get a date for tonight. But, as of right now, I'll be coming alone."

"Okay, Kimi, darling," Desiree said. "See what you can do, and I'll save a place for your date. Just let them know they don't have to go too far. I'm right across the street." Desiree laughed at her own joke.

Kimi gave her a fake laugh and decided it was time to end the call. "Desiree, I will call you a little later and let you know what I decide," Kimi said.

"Okay neighbor," Desiree replied. "Have a good one."

Kimi hung up the phone and shook her head. She was still sitting behind the wheel when Marcel made a U-turn and sped down Clinton Avenue. She thought about calling him and inviting him to her neighbor's dinner, but she didn't want to send him the wrong message. She decided to call Niko to check to see if he made it to his office safely and on time.

Back at 753 Broad Street, Niko was exiting the elevator on the 16th floor when his cellphone started buzzing in his jacket pocket. He quickly looked at the phone and decided to answer the call before he reached his office. He looked at the display and smiled. It was Kimi.

"Hi," Niko answered.

"Hey superman," Kimi joked. "Did you make it to your meeting on time?"

"I didn't. I'm just walking into my office now," he responded.

"Damn. I'm sorry," Kimi apologized.

"Don't be sorry. It's not your fault. How did your presentation go?"

"It was marvelous and very effective," Kimi reported. "My inbox is already filled with a order requests."

"That is great news," Niko said. "I'm so proud of you."

"Thank you," Kimi whispered. "I know you're busy, so I'm not going to hold you. Call me when you can. I wanted to ask you something."

"Okay," Niko responded. "Today is going to be a crazy day. I think the mayor is going to make a major announcement any hour now. So if I can't call you right back, I will try to call you later."

"That sounds good ,baby," Kimi said. "Just make sure it's before seven o'clock."

"Sure thing."

"Okay, baby. Have a good day," Kimi sweetly said.

"You too."

Niko hung up the phone and headed toward the entrance to his office. He looked at the gold letters on his glass doors and took a deep breath. Any other day those three words on his door-STANTON LAW FIRM-would electrify his drive. The firm had been his lifelong dream, and Niko fought long and hard to turn it into a reality. Because of his hard work, his law office quickly became one of the most powerful firms in the state. But his latest case was threatening everything he'd worked for.

Leon Marquez was a powerful businessman in Newark. His ventures included lucrative real estate deals, restaurant franchises and a bookstore chain in Newark. But despite Marquez's public record of rising companies, there was a dark side to his business ventures. Marquez was known throughout the streets as a true gangster. Because of his power and wealth, Marquez employed an army of thugs who roamed the streets of Newark and carried out any order that came down from his crew. Everything from simple robberies to carjackings to murders came from Marquez. Few people ever knew the true dark side to Leon Marquez, but Niko knew the corrupt side of his client all too well.

Niko was fighting hard to get his client released from jail after his latest arrest. Marquez was facing a number of serious charges, including money laundering, theft by deception and conspiracy to murder. In the past, Niko had no problem getting his client acquitted of any charge that Essex County tossed his way. This time things were different. The district attorney gathered a mountain of evidence and boasted a star witness that was set to testify against his client. As a result, the judge denied him bail to make sure Marquez would be available for trial. Niko was feeling a lot of pressure, not only from Marquez, who was looking for a bail hearing, but from the DA and mayor, who were both looking for Niko to take a plea deal. The mayor wanted to send a message to every thug in Newark that he meant business, and taking down Marquez would send a major one. Every day, Niko found himself in the middle of a firestorm, and, as he walked into the lobby of his firm, he sensed that things were only about to get hotter.

"Good morning, Mr. Stanton," a professional voice sang.

"Good morning," Niko said, greeting his secretary. "Is my twelve o'clock appointment still here?"

"Yes, and he's been here since ten this morning," the secretary nervously responded. Niko recognized the worried expression on her face, and knew that something was wrong.

"Is he by himself?" Niko asked. The secretary didn't say a word. She simply nodded her head. Niko looked around the office for a moment. "Alright, hold all of my calls and, put

the phone on speaker...just in case things get out of control."
The secretary's face turned serious. "It's going to be okay,"
Niko tried to calm her. "I'm sure this is going to be a quick
in-and-out for him."

Niko put a tighter grip on his briefcase and walked
inside of his office. He was clearly nervous ,but he tried his
best to stay cool. A young man wearing an angry expression
on his face greeted Niko.

The fuming scowl belonged to twenty-six year old
Ronald "Rojo" Marquez, the eldest son of Leon Marquez.
Rojo was in charge of the family business while his father
was awaiting trial. Rojo got his nickname from the Spanish
word for red. People called him Rojo, not only because of his
skin tone, but, also, because of his hot temper. Rojo was well
known for his tendency to flip out over the smallest issues.
He was the perfect captain to run Marquez's crew because
everyone feared him who crossed his path. For the past few
weeks, Rojo and Niko were meeting to figure out the best way
to handle his father's case. But Rojo was growing impatient
with Niko. He'd threatened him on a number of occasions,
and Niko walked into his office today expecting the same.

"Where the fuck you been?" Rojo snapped as Niko
walked behind his desk. Niko didn't respond to Rojo's
aggressive tone. He calmly sat down in his leather seat, and
then gave Rojo a firm glance.

"I told you before, Ronald," Niko calmly continued.
"There is no need to get hostile with me. I'm not the enemy
here. I'm the one here to help your father. He's been my client
for almost seven years now. And, like I said last week, these
things take time. There is nothing you or I can do to speed this
up. He's facing some serious charges."

"Fuck those charges," Rojo shouted.

"I agree," Niko uttered. "But you can't *fuck those
charges* until the court date. Until then, those charges are here,

and we have to deal with it."

"Don't talk that lawyer shit with me, Niko," Rojo shouted. "My father paid you a lot of money to get this shit done and handled. It's been almost two months, and my father is still behind bars. We need him on the streets. You been reading the papers? It's a goddamn war out there. Every man for himself. Niggas is robbing and shooting motherfuckers like its Iraq out there. We need to get shit back in order."

"Listen Ronald, what goes on out there in the streets is not my concern," Niko said. "My only concern is your father's case. Have you got a chance to talk to him about the plea?"

"What the fuck is up with you and this fuckin' plea deal shit, Niko?" Rojo shouted. He was growing angrier by the minute. "How many times do I have to tell you that we are not pleading out of this shit!"

"Have you even looked at the terms?" Niko snapped.

"What the fuck? You deaf, nigga?" Rojo shot to his feet and stood over Niko's desk. "Maybe I got to say it slower for you. No…fucking…plea…deal!"

"Okay." Niko leaned back in his chair. "So what do you want to do?"

"Who's this witness that everybody is talking about?" Rojo asked. "Niggas is saying that somebody from the streets is gonna testify against my father."

"I haven't been given any details about the witness," Niko responded. "But, whoever it is, the district attorney is banking his case on them."

"Okay, so we gotta find out who it is," Rojo barked.

"It's a lot more complicated than it sounds, Ronald," Niko protested.

"I don't give a fuck how it sounds," Rojo yelled. "You need to find out who it is, so we can hunt 'em down and give 'em a serious reason not to testify."

"Whoa, Ronald what the hell are you doing?" Niko shouted and stood to his feet. "You can't talk like that in my office."

"I don't give a fuck who's listening," Rojo fired back. "My father paid you a lot of money to handle his case, and you need to handle it."

"I'm a lawyer," Niko shouted. "There are rules in place-"

"Fuck the rules!" Rojo yelled, cutting off Niko. "We are changing the fucking rules. We losin' damn near fifty thousand dollars every day my father is locked up. So do the math. If we don't get this shit handled soon, it's gonna be bad for everybody. Even you!" Niko didn't say a word. He gave Rojo a long hard stare, and stood completely still. "So fuckin' find the witness!" Rojo yelled, then turned around and reached down into his jacket pocket. He pulled out a thick white envelope, and then slammed it the desk. He let out a weird groan and pulled out his gun.

Niko was startled by the move, and backed away from his desk. He nervously watched Rojo as he pulled out a metal clip from under the pistol, and then flicked a single bullet into his palm.

Rojo smoothly placed the gold bullet on Niko's desk, right next to the envelope. "You got two choices here, Niko," Rojo stated with a sinister tone. "There's twenty-five thousand in that envelope. You need to pay off whoever you gotta pay off to get that name for me. I don't care how you do it. Just do it."

"This is crazy," Niko nervously whispered.

"And if you don't make this happen, Niko," Rojo continued with a threatening tone. "They gonna be digging one of those out of you." Rojo pointed to the bullet on Niko's desk and gave him a hard stare. "And I don't mean from your leg. I promise you." After a few tense moments, Rojo turned around and left the office.

Niko dropped his head, then fell to his seat. His heart was racing out of control as he glared at the money and the bullet. He had been dealing with the Marquez bunch long enough to know that the ultimatum was serious. He had no choice but to figure out a way to find the star witness in the case against his client, Leon Marquez.

As Rojo left the office, he scowled at the frightened secretary. The buzzing of the elevator grabbed his attention, and he turned around just in time to see Raymond. The two exchanged peculiar stares as they passed each other in the lobby of the law firm. Raymond took one look at Rojo's war tested face, and felt a shot of fear rush to his stomach. Raymond quickly looked away, and continued to make his way to Niko's office as Rojo left the firm.

"Is everything alright?" Raymond asked as he poked his head into Niko's office. He put Niko's car keys on the desk, then noticed the bullet and envelope. "What the hell is that?" he asked.

Niko snapped out of his deep trance. He was thinking long and hard about Rojo's threat, and Raymond could read it all over his face. Niko snatched the bullet from the top of his desk and put it in his pocket.

"Fuckin' guys from the street always think they can come in somebody's office and intimidate them," he blurted.

"What happened, boss?" Raymond asked. "Did Rojo leave that?"

"What do you want to know for?" Niko fired back.

"Damn, Niko, I'm sorry. I was just asking a question," Raymond uttered.

"Well, don't worry about it," Niko shouted. "I'll handle it."

Raymond closed his mouth and watched as Niko

gathered his things. He snatched the envelope and placed it inside his briefcase, then he got up and headed for the door. He planned to walk right by Raymond without saying a word.

"Where are you going?" Raymond quietly asked.

"I need to go see somebody about this Marquez case," Niko quickly responded.

"Oh okay." Raymond dropped his eyes and peered at Niko. Raymond was taken aback by Niko's secretive tone, but decided not to push the issue. "I'm going to stay in the office for a few more hours. But I also wanted to ask you about tonight?"

"Don't worry, I'll be there," Niko grumbled.

He walked away from Raymond, and furiously continued to the elevator. Niko was clearly stressed out, and Rojo's threat was still floating around in his mind. Niko thought for a moment as he entered the elevator. He had no clue how to handle his new Marquez situation, and decided to call up an old friend to see him through this. He grabbed his phone and made a quick call. After a few seconds, a female voice politely answered from the other line.

"Hi, this is Niko."

"Good afternoon, Mr. Stanton," the woman responded.

"I'm heading over to your office now. Can you meet me outside in about fifteen minutes? This will only take a second," Niko said with a sense of urgency.

"Okay. I was about to leave the office, but I can wait for you," the woman continued. "I'll wrap up this paperwork, then meet you downstairs."

"Thanks. See you in a minute."

Niko hung up the phone, thinking about his next move. He knew he didn't have long before Rojo and his father turned up the heat on him. Niko had to come up with something fast to avoid the inevitable.

*F*ourteen

*B*ack at Marcel's house, Sabrina was calmly flicking through the channels on the flat screen television in her room. Although her eyes were searching for something good to watch, her mind was fixed on trying to figure out what Marcel was planning for later tonight. She was growing more nervous with each passing minute she didn't hear from her uncle. Sabrina kept checking her phone ,but there were no calls from Marcel. Sabrina looked at her watch and realized it had been a couple of hours since he'd last called. She was too nervous to sit still. She reached for her phone, deciding to call her uncle to make sure everything was going along as planned. She quickly dialed his number, then waited for him to pick up.

The phone rang for what seemed to be a year before his voicemail was activated. "Where the hell are you at?" Sabrina whispered in frustration. She let out a chest full of hot air and disconnected the call. She found herself on her feet, pacing back and forth. Her mind began to race with cynical thoughts. She looked at her watch, and then started to dial Marcel's number again. Before she could send the call, she heard a gentle knock on her door.

"Sabrina, are you sleeping," a female voice quietly asked from the hallway. It was Tricia.

"No, I'm not sleeping," Sabrina yelled out. "Give me one second."

Sabrina looked around the room. She slowly walked

over and opened the door.

"Hi, Sabrina," Tricia said with a soft smile. "I'm about to make a sandwich, and wanted to see if you were hungry."

"Oh, okay," Sabrina uttered. She thought for a moment and nodded her head to Tricia. "That's fine. I can use something to eat."

Tricia turned around and headed to the kitchen. Sabrina followed close behind. "I didn't think you was still here. I thought you left already," Sabrina said.

"Yea, I was about to go shopping, but I decided to stay inside," Tricia continued speaking as the women entered the kitchen. "It's too cold out there to be going to the mall."

"Girl, you never lied," Sabrina uttered.

Tricia went to the refrigerator and pulled out a loaf of bread. Sabrina sat at the kitchen table and placed her phone next to her.

"So how you been, Sabrina?" Tricia asked, trying to make small talk.

"I been as good as I can, girl," Sabrina said with a low tone. "What about you? I see you still puttin' up with my uncle."

"Oh yea," Tricia said as both of the women laughed. "Marcel is a good dude. I know he can be an asshole sometimes, but he means well."

"You right," Sabrina uttered. "So y'all are still *just* friends?"

"Yup," Tricia quietly answered. "You know how your uncle is. He doesn't like to get too attached."

"Tell me about it. Did he call you at all today?"

"I tried to call him about an hour ago, but he didn't pick up," Tricia responded. "I don't know where he is."

Sabrina turned her attention back to her phone. She called Marcel again, but there was no answer. She left him another quick voicemail, then set the phone back down.

"He's still not picking up?" Tricia asked.

"Nope," Sabrina responded. She was growing more concerned.

"Maybe he is out of range somewhere," Tricia uttered. "I swear, Marcel is always on the move."

Sabrina didn't respond to the statement. She sat quietly at the table, and looked at her phone again. She started reading through the text messages that Marcel had sent Gary Banks earlier that morning. Sabrina started zoning out and becoming nervous as she read the hostile texts. Sabrina went against her uncle's wishes, and decided to reach out to Gary Banks. It was clear that the fear was getting to her.

SABRINA
Are you still there?

Sabrina looked down at the phone, eagerly awaiting a response. Tricia continued to talk while she made the sandwiches, but Sabrina paid her no attention. Her phone started buzzing, and Sabrina's heart skipped a beat as the response came through.

UNKOWN CALLER
Yes

Sabrina thought for a moment, trying to figure out how to proceed. The entire ordeal worried her, and she was more than ready to put the unnecessary drama behind her. She started typing again.

SABRINA
That wasn't me texting you earlier.

MESSY SHEETS

UNKOWN CALLER
Is that right?

SABRINA
Yes and I don't want any money from you.
I just want to give you this DVD and move on with my life.

There was no response to Sabrina's message for a few minutes. Tricia sat down across from her, noticing that Sabrina's mind was in a totally different world.

"Earth to Sabrina," Tricia joked.

"Give me a second. I'm reading this message," Sabrina groaned.

"Must be from a dude," Tricia uttered.

Sabrina waved off Tricia, and then continued to glance down. The buzzing of the phone shook her again. She quickly clicked on the message and read it.

UNKOWN CALLER
Where are you ?

SABRINA
In Newark

UNKOWN CALLER
Let's meet

SABRINA
Meet where?

UNKOWN CALLER

Meet me in one hour in the parking lot of Tops Diner
across the bridge.
Come alone and no fucking games this time.

SABRINA

I will be there

The harsh tone of the text message made Sabrina stand up. Tricia looked at Sabrina's eyes and sensed that something was wrong. Sabrina dialed Marcel again, but the phone continued to voicemail.

"Godammit, Uncle M!" Sabrina shouted, disconnecting the call.

"Sabrina, what happened?" Tricia quickly asked.

"I gotta leave," Sabrina stammered. She rushed into her room, then put her shoes on. Tricia jumped up from the kitchen table, the followed Sabrina.

"Is everything okay?" Tricia yelled.

"I gotta meet somebody really quick," Sabrina stuttered as she put on the rest of her clothes. She looked over to Tricia as she stood in the doorway. "Is that your car out front?"

"Yes," Tricia responded and dropped her eyebrows. "Why?"

"I need to use it real fast," Sabrina pleaded. "Please Tricia. This is serious."

The emotion in Sabrina's voice changed the entire mood in the room. There was no way she could refuse Marcel's niece. She walked away from the doorway as Sabrina continued to gather her things. Sabrina put her cellphone in her pocket and walked out of the room. She rushed downstairs into the basement, remembering that Marcel told her the video was in the DVD player. Sabrina didn't waste a minute grabbing the DVD and rushing back upstairs to the first floor.

"Tricia!" Sabrina yelled as she went back to her room. She shoved the DVD inside her purse, then put on her coat.

Tricia walked back into the bedroom.

"Sabrina, listen, she's all I got so take care of her," Tricia said as she handed Sabrina the keys to her car.

"This is not going to take long at all. I just need to drop off this DVD, and I will be right back. I promise." Sabrina nodded toward Tricia.

"Okay, that's cool. There's no gas in the car, so I hope you got gas money," Tricia added.

"Oh damn, okay. I'll stop by the gas station on my way over there." Sabrina took the keys from Tricia, and headed to the front door. "If you speak to Marcel, please tell him to call me."

"I will," Tricia whispered.

Sabrina quickly opened the door and rushed out into the cold weather. She stomped though the thick snow, then jumped inside of Tricia's car. As she fired up the engine, Sabrina realized that she had more than enough time to make it to the gas station before heading over the bridge. She slammed the car into gear and quickly sped off the block.

A few miles away, Marcel felt a strange feeling in the pit of his stomach as he drove though the snowy streets trying to make it back to his house in North Newark. He was still excited about the meeting with Kimi, and he was hoping she could keep her promise and get in contact with her friend at the news station. Even though Marcel was doing well with his business, he was still hungry for more money. He lived by the hustler's code. For people like him, the only thing better than getting money was getting even more money. If Gary Banks made good on the deal to bring the cash for the video, Marcel knew he would be set.

As he continued to drive through the streets, he decided to call home and make sure Tricia and Sabrina were okay. He reached into his pocket and pulled out his cellphone.

"Oh shit," Marcel mumbled, realizing his battery had died. Marcel quickly plugged up his phone to the car charger, then waited for it to turn back on. He kept pushing through the snow when his phone lit up in his lap. He looked down and saw he had several missed calls from Tricia and Sabrina. Marcel decided to call Tricia and see what she wanted. He quickly dialed her number, then waited for her to pick up the phone.

"Where have you been?" Tricia shouted when the call connected.

"What?" he barked. He was shocked by Tricia's tone.

"We been trying to call you for the past couple of hours," Tricia said. Her voice cracked with panic.

"What happened?" Marcel yelled.

"Your niece just left," Tricia reported.

"What!?"

"She told me to tell you to call her," Tricia said.

"Why the hell did she leave?" Marcel quickly asked.

"I don't know why. She was texting somebody, and then she just up and left. I let her use my car."

"Fuck!" Marcel shouted. "I'm goin' to call you back."

Before Tricia could respond, Marcel quickly disconnected the call and scrolled up to Sabrina's name. He dialed her number, praying that she would answer the call. After a few rings, Sabrina picked up on the other line.

"Damn, Uncle M, I've been trying to reach you," Sabrina shouted through the phone.

"Where are you?" Marcel fired back.

"I have to get rid of this DVD, Uncle M," Sabrina groaned. "I'm sorry. I'm on my way to meet Gary."

"What Sabrina?" Marcel shouted. He was clearly upset. "I told you we gonna meet with him tonight."

"I don't want no money for this, Uncle M. I just want this to be over."

"Shit!" Marcel grumbled. He put his hand on his head as the car started to speed up. "I just set everything up, Sabrina. We got this motherfucker. Trust me, we can do this."

"I can't, Uncle M," Sabrina whispered. "I can't wait. I need to take care of this and just move on."

"Where are you?" Marcel asked.

"I need to stop off and get some gas," Sabrina responded.

"Which gas station?" Marcel quickly asked.

"I'm going to stop off at the Gulf Station on Bloomfield Ave," Sabrina responded.

"Okay, you talking about the one with the store right?' Marcel asked.

"Right," Sabrina uttered.

"Okay listen, I'm on my way to you . Stay there and don't make a move," Marcel ordered.

"How far are you, Uncle M? I gotta meet Gary real soon."

"I will be right there in less than ten minutes. Just wait there," Marcel shouted.

His strained voice shook Sabrina. She grew quiet, and didn't know what to say.

"Are you still there?" Marcel shouted.

"Yes, Uncle M," Sabrina mumbled.

"So meet me at the gas station, and don't leave. I will

be right there."

"Okay, I will," Sabrina whispered.

Marcel hung up the phone, then dropped it in his lap. He was beyond angry with his niece for disobeying him. Sabrina didn't realize how much he was counting on the meeting with Gary tonight. He checked his watch, and then sped up the car as he made his way to the gas station. He was hoping his niece would change her mind and not destroy his big plans.

MESSY SHEETS

Fifteen

Despite the cold weather and snowy streets, downtown Newark was buzzing with traffic and pedestrians as everyone prepared for their afternoon commute. Niko looked at his watch as he pulled up to the Essex County Courthouse. He parked his Audi A8 directly in front of the building and looked around. After a few minutes, he spotted his friend as she headed to his car.

Forty-six year old Laura Sanchez was a hard-nosed prosecutor for Essex County. She was well known for being one of the sharpest legal minds in the state. After battling tough cases against Niko for the past few years, Laura developed a professional respect for him and his firm. Although they worked diligently from opposite sides of the courtroom, Niko and Laura became good friends, and often sought each other out for advice. Today Niko was coming to her with a sensitive issue. Laura was the lead prosecutor on the Marquez case, and Niko knew he was crossing the line by discussing his client's business with her. But Rojo's threat shook Niko beyond the point of rational thinking. He was ready to find an exit, and he was hoping Laura could help him come up with a plan.

"Good afternoon, Mr. Stanton," Laura greeted Niko as he got of the car.

"Good afternoon." Niko smiled.

Laura walked right up to Niko and gave him a firm handshake. Although they had been associates for years,

125

Niko and Laura never hugged in public. They both feared the media and knew if an inappropriate photo showed up in the local newspaper, it could damage their reputations.

"Let's take a short walk," Niko uttered and grabbed his briefcase from the car.

"Excuse me?" Laura said. "I don't know if you can feel that, but it's only thirty degrees out here."

"I know it's cold out, but I need to ask you a few things without the spotlight on us." Niko gave Laura a soft expression.

Laura sensed something different in Niko and nodded her head. She turned around and they started to walk up the street.

"What's on your mind?" Laura asked as she cut to the chase. It was too cold outside for small talk.

"Listen, Laura, I have a serious dilemma," Niko said. "I got a visit today from Leon's son."

"Is this about the Marquez case, Niko?" Laura sharply asked.

"Yes."

"You know we can't discuss that right?" Laura uttered.

"I know, but we have to discuss it today," Niko responded. "This problem is not going to go away by itself."

"What problem?"

"This problem," Niko blurted as he reached into his pocket. He showed Laura the gold bullet, and then stared at her. "This came to me courtesy of Ronald Marquez today."

"What...seriously?" Laura scowled.

"Yes," Niko quickly responded. "And you can only imagine the threat that came along with it."

Laura thought for a moment as they continued to walk. She looked over to Niko as he put the bullet back in his pocket.

"What exactly is going on over there at that firm, Niko?" Laura asked with a stern tone.

She gave Niko a suspicious look, and he picked up on the reason for the questioning. He looked around the busy street again, and then started talking.

"Look, Laura. You and I both know that Leon is no angel," Niko whispered. "You probably know more than I do when it comes to his background. So I'm not here to discuss whether or not Leon Marquez is guilty."

"So what are you here to discuss?" Laura questioned.

"My life was threatened today, and I don't know how to handle it," Niko confessed. "I'm not speaking to you now as an attorney. I'm speaking to you as a friend."

"Of course, Niko." Laura gave him a supportive expression. She relaxed her guard for a moment and tried to be sympathetic. "So what are you going to do about this issue?"

"I think I'm going to write the judge and request to be removed from the case," Niko whispered.

Laura stopped in her tracks and looked at Niko. She gave him a piercing stare, trying to read his body language.

"Is this a joke?" she snapped. "Now, you wouldn't be trying to trick me would you, Niko?"

"Laura, I am serious," Niko uttered. His voice was even and very direct. "I have been defending Leon Marquez for many years now, and he has never threatened my life. And his son..." Niko paused for a moment, then grabbed Laura by the arm. He motioned for her to keep walking. "His son is very dangerous, and I'm not sure why they are threatening me like this, but I don't think I will survive either way."

Laura grew quiet as she listened to Niko. They continued to walk up the street until they reached the corner. Laura turned to Niko and stopped him for a moment.

"How serious are you about this?" Laura asked.

127

"Honestly, this just happened, so the first thing I thought about was having myself removed." Niko glanced at Laura.

"Are you being totally honest with me, Niko?" Laura asked with a harsher tone.

"Absolutely," Niko quickly defended himself. Laura looked away from him as her mind started working. Niko gave her a peculiar glance and waved his hand in front of her face. "You know something, don't you?" Niko asked.

"What do you mean?" Laura responded.

"I know that look, Laura," Niko said. "I've been studying that look for years now. Every time I see that look, you drop a bombshell on me."

Laura's expression never changed. She gave Niko a serious look and just stared at him.

"Look, Laura, we are not in the courtroom," Niko pleaded. "If there's something on your mind, just tell me. I'm asking for your help ."

Laura let out a gasped and shook her head. Niko's voice sounded desperate, and she hated to see him suffering like this.

"Niko, what I'm about to tell you is strictly between you and me." Laura nodded to Niko.

"Yes, of course," he responded.

"Your firm is being investigated."

"What?" Niko blurted. "For what?"

"Damn, I can get burned bad for telling you this," Laura groaned and looked around. "Niko, we got an audio tape two weeks ago with Ronald Marquez speaking with his father."

"Okay!" Niko mumbled as he tried to prepare himself for the worse.

"On the tape Ronald and Leon are discussing how to quote un-quote remove a key witness from this case." Laura folder her arms and continued to speak. "They were discussing how to permanently remove the witness when your name was brought up."

"Son of a bitch!" Niko cried out, then put his hand on his head. "I swear Laura-"

"Wait, let me finish," Laura snapped as she cut Niko short. "The only reason why I'm telling you this is because I respect you, Niko. As a result of the tape, we started our own investigation into Ronald Marquez." Laura gave Niko another hard glance. "We know that you are not involved in this plot, but somebody at your firm is."

Niko closed his mouth. Laura's last statement raced through his mind.

"Our investigation uncovered that Attorney Raymond Bowser is working with Ronald Marquez to find the witness," Laura said.

"What? Are you sure?" Niko's expression dropped as he thought about Raymond's face.

"We are absolutely sure of it," Laura continued. "Raymond Bowser made contact with Ronald Marques last month to discuss this case. During that conversation, they devised a plan to find our key witness and make an attempt to dispose of them. "

"Jesus Christ, this can't be happening," Niko uttered and continued to rub his forehead.

"Later on in that conversation, Attorney Raymond Bowser suggested that Ronald give you twenty-five thousand dollars to find the witness."

Niko looked up to Laura. "So Raymond suggested getting me involved in all of this?" He was growing more irate by the second.

"Yes," Laura responded. "According to the audio, it seems that they are trying to set you up, Niko. Once you got caught trying to buy off a witness, there'd be a mistrial, and you would go to jail-"

"And Raymond would take over my firm," Niko whispered. "That son of a bitch!"

"Listen, they are going to come down pretty hard on you and your team," Laura said. "You need to get in front of this thing, and get your house in order."

"Jesus, this can't be real," Niko gasped.

"Oh, it's real, Niko. And you don't have much time."

"Indictments?" Niko quietly asked.

"Yes. And they are coming really soon," Laura said.

"I can't believe Raymond would do this shit to me." Niko's face stiffened.

"Believe me. If there's one thing I learned down at this courthouse, people will do anything for money."

Niko turned away from Laura and shook his head. Her words seemed to cut deep into his conscious. He thought about all the years that Raymond worked for his firm, and tried to figure out the reason why he would try to destroy his life. Niko composed himself and turned back to Laura.

"I know you didn't have to pull my coat to this, so, thank you, Laura. Seriously." Niko nodded toward her. "I need to take a long hard look at everything, and I will call you on Monday to let you know what I'm going to do."

"Sounds good," Laura said. "You know the mayor is up for re-election, so he can easily use this case as a stepping stone. I know you two are on the outs now."

"Shit, don't remind me," Niko gasped. "I know Gary Banks doesn't like me, and he would do anything to burn my ass right about now."

"Exactly, Niko," Laura continued. "Just know that the case is building fast now, and you don't want to get caught with your pants down."

Niko thought about the white envelope full of money in his briefcase and closed his mouth. It was bad enough to know that Raymond and the Marquez bunch were out to set him up, but now he had to worry about the mayor using his influence to shut him down. As Niko weighed his options, Laura turned around and started heading back to the front of the courthouse. Niko followed suit, and then started walking next to her. The cold wind forced them to move fast.

"Don't forget to call me on Monday," Laura said as she turned and shook Niko's hand.

He gave her a reassuring nod, and then watched as she headed back to her office. Niko turned around and went to his car. His first thought was to double back to his firm and confront Raymond about the news, but he decided to suppress his anger and devise a bigger plan to handle the situation.

Niko grabbed his phone and checked the time. He noticed he had a missed call from Kimi, and he quickly dialed her number.

"Hey, baby," Kimi answered. "How is it going?"

"Not good at all," Niko uttered.

"Oh no. What happened?" Kimi quickly asked.

"I can't talk about it, but I will call you back a little later," Niko continued. "I have to make one more stop, and then I will try to reach you back."

"Okay babe, but I really wanted to ask you something about tonight," Kimi softly said.

"I know, but this is really not a good time. I ran into a serious problem at the firm today." Niko's voice sounded strained and Kimi picked up on his stress. She decided to drop the issue.

"Fine. Just call me when you can. I will be home until eight or so," Kimi said.

"That's good. I will speak to you later?"

"Yes. Goodbye," Kimi mumbled.

He heard the phone disconnect from the other line. He knew Kimi was upset that he had no time to talk, but Niko was in the middle of a serious issue. He turned his focus back to Raymond Bowser, and tried to figure out how to deal with his new enemy.

Sixteen

A few miles away, Sabrina couldn't stop her hands from shaking as she reached for the volume button on the car stereo. She turned up the music to a deafening level as she tried to drown out the fear that was still running through her body. She couldn't shake the jitters as she carefully drove down Bloomfield Avenue in search of the huge orange Gulf gas station sign. For the past few minutes her mind was racing out of control, trying to figure out why Marcel was so focused on extorting Gary Banks. All of his talk of getting money from the mayor only scared Sabrina. While her uncle was focused on a big payday, Sabrina couldn't ignore the scary possibility of things going terribly wrong with Marcel's plans. Sabrina was beyond ready to get rid of the DVD and move on with her life. For the past year, she had regretted ever taking the video from Gary's house. Today, she promised herself that it was time to bury this issue and focus on her future.

Sabrina carefully pulled into the drive of the gas station. There was a long line in front of her as nearly seven cars crammed into the small station to take advantage of the cheap gas prices. Sabrina turned down the music and sat back in her seat. She tried to calm her nerves again, but the rumbling in her stomach would not go away.

"Damn, I need to eat something," she whispered.

She impatiently waited until it was her turn to pull up to the pump. She got out of the car and was greeted by a short gas station attendant.

"Can you fill up the tank, sir?" Sabrina requested. "I'll be right back."

"No problem," the man said.

Sabrina turned around and headed to the convenience store near the rear of the gas station. It seemed like the entire world was getting gas today, and Sabrina found herself in the middle of the rush. People were coming in and out of the store like it was a train station. She squeezed by a few people, and then walked inside. She headed straight for the grill and snatched a turkey sandwich from the oven. She was tempted to order something more, but knew she was pressed for time. She grabbed a cold soda from the cooler, and made her way up to the cashier. The long line was moving slow, and Sabrina let out a gasp in frustration. People started complaining about the slow service, and Sabrina decided not to join in with the bickering. As the line continued to move one person at a time, Sabrina reached into her pocket and pulled out her money. Another group of customers came through the door. A few minutes later, Sabrina found herself next in line. She was waiting for an older woman in front of her to pay for her items when a few angry customers started yelling in the back of the line.

"Why is there only one person working?" one woman shouted.

"I just want ten dollars worth of gas, geez," another woman squawked.

A few groans came from the line as the people started to grow impatient. Sabrina heard the front door swing open as a few more patrons walked in and out of the store. One man saw the long line and yelled toward the cashier behind the register.

"Habib, what the fuck is up with this line? Let's move it up there!" the man yelled.

Everyone in the store chuckled at the racist slur, except Sabrina. She was frozen stiff. The man's burly voice was like an alarm to her ears. She thought she recognized the voice, but she was too afraid to turn around, fearing the worse. The older woman paid for her stuff, and then made room for Sabrina, who nervously approached the counter. Sabrina slowly handed the cashier the money, and then took her change. A bizarre emotion came over her, making her freeze for a second. She was having an out-of-body experience, and could see herself standing at the counter. A cold chill rushed through her soul, unlike anything she ever felt before. Before she could dwell on the emotion any longer, the husky voice brought her back to reality.

"What the fuck lady, let's go!" the angry man yelled.

Sabrina almost dropped her bag to the floor. Her face twisted with fear, and she stood motionless. The customers in the line screamed at her, but Sabrina refused to move.

"Yo lady, we don't got all fuckin' day to wait for you. Hurry the fuck up!" the man continued to yell.
Sabrina slowly closed her eyes and almost started to cry. She was certain she knew the man's voice. The cashier glanced at Sabrina's face and gave her a confused look.

"Are you okay?" the cashier asked.

Sabrina opened her eyes and looked at the clerk behind the register. Her mouth fell open, but no words came out. She didn't know what to say. She tried to speak to the cashier with pleading eyes, but it wasn't working. The customers in the store started to grow angrier. The frustrated man in the back of the line rushed to the front and grabbed Sabrina's arm.

"Okay lady, you got your stuff, now keep it moving--" the man stopped himself as he spun Sabrina around by her shoulder. Her face turned to pure terror as their eyes met. Sabrina's worse fears were confirmed. It was Khalil.

Sabrina took one look at his bruised face and panicked. She tried to pull away from Khalil, but he instantly went into attack mode. He slapped Sabrina across the face, and then brutally slammed her against the counter. Everyone in the line gasped in horror as Khalil mercilessly beat Sabrina to the floor of the convenience store.

"What the hell are you doing, man?" the cashier yelled at Khalil, who totally ignored him.

Khalil continued to punch Sabrina in the face with cold-blooded intentions. Everyone stood around in shock. The cashier knew he had to act fast. He grabbed a bat near his feet, and then ran around the counter. Without a moment to lose, he grabbed Khalil by the shoulders, trying to pull him off Sabrina. The clerk underestimated Khalil's fury when he turned his aggression on him.

Khalil stood up and swung on the cashier, who never expected the move. "Get the fuck off of me!" Khalil yelled.

He punched the cashier square in the face, then slammed him into the magazine rack. People started to run out of the store as the scene turned extremely violent. Khalil grabbed the bat out of the clerk's hand. Before he could hit him again, the cashier bolted out of the door. Khalil's rage intensified. He looked back over to Sabrina, who was barely conscious on the floor. Khalil was still angry over the beat down he'd gotten from Marcel last night, and he was dying to get some payback. Sabrina was in the wrong place at the wrong time today, and Khalil refused to let the opportunity slip.

"Please," Sabrina uttered in pain from the floor.

Khalil ignored her plea. His eyes were emotionless, and the evil look on his face froze Sabrina. As he raised the bat over Sabrina's head, her world just stopped. She was too petrified to scream, too weak to defend herself. The last thing

Sabrina saw was Khalil swinging the heavy bat toward her face, and he continued to beat her without mercy.

*

Fifteen minutes later, Marcel approached the Gulf station and twisted his face. There was a large clump of people standing on the sidewalk, and nearly a dozen cars were doubled parked out the front. There was something clearly happening, and Marcel started to get a bad feeling. He sped up the truck, and then parked as close as he could. He grabbed his phone and jumped out of the SUV. A few people were murmuring about the incident inside the store. As Marcel ran up to the gas station, he noticed Tricia's car that Sabrina had driven, but it was empty.

"What the fuck?" Marcel uttered, looking around the lot.

There was no sign of Sabrina. He noticed that a few people were looking through the window of the convenience store, and he rushed over there.

"What the hell is going on?" Marcel yelled.

"Some nigga beat her ass pretty bad," a woman coldly said, never looking away from the window.

Marcel heard the words, then rushed to the front entrance to the store. People were clogging up the front area, trying to get a look at the carnage. Marcel found himself pulling people away.

"Let me in!" Marcel shouted.

"You don't want to go in there. It's a fuckin' mess," one man yelled as he tried to hold Marcel back.

"Who is it?" Marcel shouted again, then pushed the man to the side.

He squeezed through another group of people, and managed a small glimpse of the horrid sight in the store.

137

Blood was everywhere near the front counter, and a few people were tending to an injured woman. Marcel took one look at the woman's shoes and knew it was Sabrina. His heavy heart buckled, and he nearly collapsed to the floor. He held his breath as he rushed to get a look at her face.

"Oh God, Sabrina," Marcel shouted.

His eyes were instantly flushed with tears as he fell to her side. Sabrina had been beaten unconscious, and she was barely hanging on to life. One woman was covering a large gash in Sabrina's head with a towel, while another man was yelling on his mobile phone, telling the police to hurry to the scene.

Marcel grabbed his niece's hand and looked at her battered face. The tears rushed from his eyes like an endless river. He couldn't believe that it was his niece who was bruised and fighting for her life.

"Come on, Sabrina, stay with me," Marcel uttered though the heavy lump in his throat.

Sabrina's eyes twitched when she heard her uncle's voice calling for her. Marcel saw her reacting and squeezed her hand tighter.

"You're going to be okay, Sabrina." Marcel started weeping. "Please…just hang in there."

Sabrina forced her eyes to open slightly. She slowly looked around until she found Marcel's face. Her eyes were weak, and Marcel could tell that she didn't have much longer. Sabrina had lost a lot of blood and was fading fast.

"I'm….sorry," Sabrina whispered.

"Shhhhhh….don't talk, Sabrina. It's okay," Marcel mumbled.

"I'm so…sorry," Sabrina whispered again.

A few tears started to trickle from the sides of her eyes, and Marcel felt her hand shaking. Sabrina was sensing the end was near, and she was so scared. Marcel tried to give her a reassuring smile, but Sabrina could see the pain on his face. She started mumbling, but Marcel couldn't make out the words. He moved closer to her face, and realized that Sabrina was saying a prayer. She squeezed her uncle's hand, and Marcel's face cracked with more tears. Before Sabrina passed she was able to say a few words to her uncle.

"Khalil did it," Sabrina uttered. She never breathed again.

*S*eventeen

Later that evening in Shady Meadows, Kimi stepped out of the steamy shower feeling like a brand new woman. The hot water felt like heaven after a long day of phone meetings and long discussions with potential buyers. Kimi was tempted to stay in the shower for another twenty minutes and let the hot water relax her tense body, but she knew she was running late for Desiree's dinner. As Kimi dried off she shook her head at the thought of playing the good neighbor tonight with Desiree and her husband. She didn't want to cause a rift with Desiree, so she decided to make good on her promise and show up to the dinner. As the seconds clicked away on her clock, Kimi grew more apprehensive about her visit. Before she could sink into her thoughts any deeper, her cell phone started ringing in the bedroom. Kimi rushed out of the bathroom and grabbed the phone.

"What the hell?" Kimi whispered as she looked down at the name on her phone. It was her neighbor calling. "Hello," Kimi coldly answered.

"Hey Kimi, is everything alright?" Desiree asked from the other line.

"Everything is fine," Kimi responded.

"Oh okay," Desiree groaned. "I was getting a little worried. It's almost a quarter after eight, and you're not here. I thought something happened."

"No, nothing happened," Kimi uttered and shook her head. "I'm leaving out the door in two minutes. I'm already dressed," Kimi lied.

"That's wonderful," Desiree cheered. "I'll look out for you. Our other guests have already arrived."

"Okay," Kimi uttered. "Let me finish up here, and I will be across the street in a few minutes."

"Fine, Kimi. I will see you when you get here."

Kimi disconnected the call, and then tossed the phone back on the bed. Her uneasy feeling about Desiree started to grow. She couldn't figure out why Desiree was so hard pressed to get her to the dinner tonight. Kimi couldn't connect the dots. She knew Desiree didn't have a lot of friends so maybe there was something else going on in Desiree's mind. *Who were the other guests at the dinner?* Kimi thought for a moment and continued to get dressed. Whoever it was had to be somebody important if Desiree invited them over.

Kimi wanted to look good tonight, so she went with her sexy brown dress that made her body look like royalty. She checked herself in the mirror and smiled. Kimi headed to the closet and stepped into her coffee-brown Paris Hilton shoes that matched her dress flawlessly. She didn't know what to expect tonight, so Kimi made certain to look her best. Before Kimi left her bedroom, she decided to top her outfit off with one last piece. She put on a platinum necklace with a diamond star pendant. The necklace made her shine even brighter.

Fifteen minutes later, Kimi left the house and headed across the street. The brisk air made her put some extra pep in her step as she trekked through the light snowfall. A strange feeling of nervousness came over Kimi again as she got closer to the house. Desiree's driveway was packed with cars. Kimi quickly realized that she was undoubtedly the last to arrive to the dinner. Kimi knew that tonight was not going to be an ordinary night inside of Desiree's home. In order to survive she would have to put on the performance of a lifetime. She calmed down her suspicions and proceeded to the front door. Kimi rang the doorbell twice, then slowly exhaled a lung full of air. There was no turning back now.

Desiree came to the door and smiled when she saw Kimi. She swung the door open and greeted her neighbor with a casual hug. Kimi was thrown off by the move, but hesitantly returned the gesture.

"I am so glad you made it, Kimi," Desiree sang. Kimi gave her neighbor a pleasing grin. "So I see you decided to come by yourself?" Desiree questioned as she looked behind Kimi.

"Yes, I wanted to come alone. You know how men are," Kimi said, putting on a fake smile.

"Oh okay," Desiree mumbled. "Come inside, honey. We got to get you out of this cold."

"It smells like somebody was slaving over this dinner all day," Kimi said as she slowly walked inside of her neighbor's nice home.

"Oh no, darling. I didn't cook," Desiree continued. "I hired three chefs out of New York to come and prepare dinner for us. Believe me, tonight's dinner is going to be divine," Desiree bragged.

Kimi nodded her head at her neighbor. She was impressed that Desiree was sparing no expenses for her husband this evening. She handed Desiree her winter coat and watched as she placed it in the closet near the front door.

Desiree was dressed to the tee this evening. Her jet-black dress was very flattering, and Kimi couldn't help but notice that it fit perfectly on every curve. She was sure Desiree had the dress designed. Kimi's neighbor had extravagant taste, and it showed in the type of clothes she wore. Although she was shorter and less attractive than Kimi, Desiree still had a sexy way about herself. Her busty chest and curvy ass was just enough to make any man break his neck to look her way. Tonight Desiree wore four-inch heels to give herself a more commanding air. And it worked. She wanted everyone to know that she was the lady of the house, and Kimi picked up on her swagger.

"Follow me darling," Desiree said. "I want to introduce you to everyone."

Kimi followed close behind Desiree as they walked down a small hallway and into her social room near the den. Kimi raised her eyebrows when she noticed two men in tuxedos playing violins in the far corner of the room. The soft music gave the home a serene feeling as if they were gathering in a prominent museum. There were four couples in the room conversing with each other and drinking wine. Desiree grabbed Kimi by the hand, then walked her over to each one of them.

"I would like you to meet, Mr. and Mrs. Douglas," Desiree announced the first couple.

"Hello. I'm Kimi Moore. Nice to meet you," she said, shaking the hands of a middle-aged man and his wife.

"Here we have Mr. and Mrs. Brookheim." Desiree smiled.

"Hi. I'm Kimi Moore," she repeated as she greeted another middle-aged couple.

"Now, this interesting character here is Mr. Charles Holmes, and this is his wife, Eleanor," Desiree joked with a lighthearted smile.

"Hello Mr. and Mrs. Holmes. I'm Kimi Moore," she politely greeted them, then continued to follow Desiree to the last couple.

An older man in his late forties stood to his feet. He reached out and smoothly grabbed Kimi by the palm.

"Don't worry, Desiree, I will introduce myself," the man said with a slightly flirtatious tone. "You make me feel old when you call me by my last name."

Kimi recognized the gentleman. She remembered seeing him in a number of newspaper articles and local new stories for the past few years.

"Good evening, my name is Raymond Bowser," he said. "Attorney at law."

"Good evening ,sir," Kimi humbly greeted him.

"This is my wife, Charlene Bowser," Raymond said.

Kimi shook her hand. Charlene gave her a crooked grin and nodded her head. Kimi could tell that Charlene didn't appreciate Raymond making an extra effort to meet her. Kimi kept her cool and blew off the woman's slight attitude. Raymond was not her type. He was an older gentleman who reminded Kimi of a computer geek more than a lawyer. His grey suit hung from his frail body awkwardly and looked like he snatched it from a clearance rack at Wal-Mart. Mrs. Bowsers' appearance was just as tacky. Her flower dress was outdated, and her makeup looked like a blind woman helped her with it. The couple was clearly well beyond their glory days, and both of them were searching for just about anything to spice up their insipid lives. Kimi turned away from the couple and looked at Desiree, who was smiling at Raymond. There was something mysterious in the way she looked at Raymond, and Kimi picked up on the energy.

"Raymond works for my husband down at the law firm," Desiree reported to Kimi. "He is a major reason why the firm is doing so well. I even heard rumblings that he will be a partner soon."

"Stop it, Desi," Raymond smiled and gave Desiree another peculiar expression. "I just met the young lady, and here you are telling her lies about me already." The small group laughed at Raymond's joke.

"Now, don't be modest, Mr. Bowser. Believe me he's

MESSY SHEETS

a great lawyer." Desiree winked at Kimi. "Raymond set a firm record last year. What was it, fourteen acquittals in one year?"

"Sixteen." Raymond smiled. "But who's counting?" The group laughed again.

"See, there's the Raymond Bowser I know and love," Desiree joked. "Very confident, very smart-"

"And a total fucking show off!" a male voice shouted from the hallway.

Everyone turned around just in time to see the man of the hour walking into the room. Kimi's heart dropped to her stomach when she saw her neighbor's husband approaching them. Desiree smiled, and then grabbed Kimi by the hand again.

"There he is." Desiree shook her head and walked up to her husband. "Here is the man who will probably be late to his own funeral." Desiree chuckled at her own joke and hugged her husband. She kissed him on the lips. "Baby, you remember our neighbor from across the street right?"

Desiree's husband looked at Kimi. Her heart was racing like a motorbike, and she felt a rush of emotions. Keeping her cool was going to be a lot harder than she thought. Kimi almost looked away, but she had to play her position. Kimi smiled at Desiree's husband, and then reached out her hand to greet him. Unbeknownst to Desiree, Kimi was all too familiar with her husband already. It was her good friend, Niko.

"Of course, I remember our neighbor," Niko said as he shook hands with Kimi. He gave her a comfortable glance, and politely nodded his head. Kimi was surprised to see Niko so relaxed. But after years of defending thieves and murderers in high profile trials, Niko had a knack for keeping very still under serious pressure. Niko's tone helped Kimi calm her nerves. Seeing his handsome face gave her a few flashbacks, and she tried her best to hold back excitement. Kimi simply

145

smiled at Niko, continuing to play her role.

"How are you tonight?" Kimi calmly asked. "Happy birthday."

"Why, thank you, neighbor," he responded. Niko was cool as a fan in the middle of January. He gave Kimi a pleasant expression, then continued speaking. "Actually, today is not my birthday. It's this Saturday, but my wife felt tonight would be the perfect night to celebrate with everyone. I really don't know why my wife insists on doing these shindigs every year for my birthday."

"Because this is your special time of year," Desiree explained.

"I know honey, and I appreciate it. You only turn twenty-five once, right?" Niko joked.

The small room erupted into a loud laughter. Kimi smiled and looked around at the other guests. The light-hearted moment opened up an opportunity to take off some of the edge.

"You know, if it was up to me, I would just have a barbecue in the back yard with a couple of my good friends," Niko smirked.

"Oh stop it, honey," Desiree said, cutting her husband short. "Don't be so ghetto."

The guests chuckled at her joke. Niko gave Kimi an awkward look, and then slightly shook his head. He was clearly agitated by his wife's statement. But before he could respond, Desiree grabbed him by the arm and playfully spun him around.

"Okay, everybody, let's move this party to the dining room," Desiree announced. "It's time for dinner."

Desiree cuffed her husband by the arm and led him out of the social room. Kimi watched the married couple, and started to feel a pit of jealousy in her stomach. Seeing

146

Niko with his wife made her feel uneasy, yet triumphant. Knowing that he was a totally different person when he was around Kimi made the sight much more ironic. Kimi forced herself to shake the ugly emotions, and knew she had to keep her cool if she was going to make it through the dinner.

Kimi and the other guests followed the couple to their dining room just beyond the kitchen. Kimi's mouth fell open when they entered the room. She was impressed with the immaculate space. Desiree walked her husband over to a large cherry wood table that sat in the middle of the room. Twelve hand-carved chairs surrounded the round table, and a huge crystal chandelier illuminated the space. The scene reminded Kimi of something out of the nineteenth century. As she walked over to the table, she noticed that Desiree had placed name markers on each plate. Everyone circled the table looking for their assigned seats.

"Kimi, I had two seats for you, so you can choose either chair," Desiree said as she took her seat.

"Okay thanks," Kimi mumbled.

She walked to the other side of the round table and sat in her chair. She noticed that Raymond Bowser tried to sit next to her ,but his wife switched chairs with him. Now that Kimi was seated next to Stay-Away-From-My-Man-Charlene, Kimi knew her night was only going to get longer. She looked across the table and noticed Niko and his wife sitting directly across from her. She felt like a sitting duck in the middle of the pond for all to survey. Her heart started racing again, and she took a drink of water. The night was still young, and Kimi could only imagine what she was in for this evening.

Desiree's four-course dinner lasted nearly an hour, and was filled with light-hearted discussions and anecdotes. As the women sparked up conversations about jewelry and the latest episodes of Real Housewives, the men conversed about sports and world politics. Kimi tried her best to be cordial with the guests, and involved herself in the meaningless dialogue. As everyone finished up their dinner, Desiree stood to her feet and made an announcement that the amazing dessert would be served in a few minutes.

"Now, I know there are a lot of different personalities in the room, so I decided to go with two desserts this evening," Desiree addressed everyone. "I had our chefs make a delicious hot apple-crumb pie and a death-by-chocolate cake." Desiree smiled as a few guest chuckled.

"So we have two choices?" Niko asked with a curious expression.

"We sure do, honey," Desiree responded with a girlish smile.

"Let's flip for it," Niko blurted.

Kimi almost choked on her own air. She discretely reached for her drink, then buried her face in the glass. Desiree gave her husband a strange look.

"Flip for it?" she asked.

"Yup." Niko smiled. He reached inside his pocket and pulled out a shiny quarter. He looked around the room and smiled at all the guests "Hey, life is too short. Let's have some fun tonight, right?"

A few of the guests giggled and nodded at Niko. Raymond gave his boss the thumbs up, and they laughed like two schoolyard boys.

"Honey, I don't think that is really appropriate," Desiree whispered. She was slightly embarrassed.

"Oh come on now, Desiree," Niko joked. "It's my birthday, right? It's a simple coin flip."

Desiree shrugged her shoulders and sat back in her seat. Niko stood up and looked around the table for a moment.

"Kimi," Niko said, raising his voice.

"Huh?" Kimi smiled. She was thrown off by Niko's

commanding voice. She tried her best to keep her cool, and hated the fact that Niko was putting the spotlight on her.

"You can call it," Niko said. "Heads or tails?"

Kimi dropped her head and laughed. What seemed to be a very innocent game to everyone else in the room, had a very intimate effect on Kimi's body. Her mind started flashing back to their sex-capades back at her house. Niko was toying with her tonight, and Kimi picked up on the game. She lifted her head up and gave him a controlled glance.

"Tails," Kimi whispered.

"Tails is a good choice," Raymond blurted, causing his wife, Charlene, to roll her eyes.

"Okay, tails it is," Niko said. "Let's say heads for apple pie and tails for chocolate cake." Niko spun the quarter on the table, and the room erupted into a few cheers. The guests were rooting for heads or tails like they were at a football game. Niko laughed at the excitement, then looked over to Desiree, who was not amused. As the quarter landed on its side, everyone looked at Niko for his reaction.

"Chocolate cake it is," Niko announced. Cheers and groans came from the table.

"I told you tails was a good choice." Raymond laughed.

Desiree pulled Niko down into his seat and gave him a stern expression. Niko waved her off, and then ordered the chefs to bring in the chocolate cake. Kimi laughed with everyone at the table, and kept her eyes away from Niko. She knew his wife was upset with him, and she didn't want to draw any unnecessary attention. As the dessert plates came out more conversations started to brew in the dining room.

"So what in the world is going on down there in your city, Niko?" one of the female guests asked.

"What do you mean?" Niko responded.

"Newark is becoming a seriously dangerous city," the

woman said.

"Newark was always dangerous," Niko continued. "It's just in the newspapers more, now that the big basketball stadium is in town."

"That is exactly right. Newark was always a cesspool," Charlene Bowser added, taking a sip of her drink. "Let's hope things get better in that city."

"Let's hope they don't," Raymond joked and chuckled at his own words. "That would be bad for business."

"That's a terrible thing to say," Charlene gasped. She tapped her husband and dropped her eyebrows.

"Let's see if you say that when I become a partner down at the firm," Raymond boasted.

A few people chuckled around the table. Kimi looked over to Niko and noticed that he was giving Raymond an uneasy glance. The mention of Raymond becoming a partner seemed to touch on a sensitive nerve.

"Whoa Kimosabe," Niko mumbled. He gave Raymond a stiff expression. "You and I both know we are a long way from that day," Niko said and turned his attention to his dessert.

"Oh, okay you're right," Raymond uttered. He raised his glass of wine and took a few sips. His perturbed expression let everyone know that he was clearly aggravated with Niko's response. "I've been working for you for what? Only, umm...six years now, right?" Raymond sarcastically asked. "But you're right; we are a long way from that day."

Niko raised his head from his plate and glanced at Raymond. If looks could kill, Raymond Bowser would have died a quick death right there at the table. Desiree looked over to Raymond and shot him a stiff glance. Charlene noticed the mood in the room darkening and tapped her husband again.

"Let it go, honey," Charlene whispered.

"I will not let it go," Raymond uttered just loud enough

for Niko to hear him.

"Listen to your wife, Ray and relax," Niko said in a low tone. "Now this is a nice dinner. Let's not ruin it by talking about business. We can discuss work at work."

Niko's voice was very serious. Everyone in the room could tell that something deeper was brewing between Niko and Raymond. The room fell silent as most of the guests pretended to be enjoying their cake. Raymond dropped his head and decided to let go of the topic. He was clearly embarrassed. Charlene looked over to her husband and closed her mouth. It felt like the entire room was focusing on them. Charlene didn't like the heat. She continued to drink her wine, trying to shake off the awkwardness. Niko was still staring at Raymond with a disappointed expression, when Charlene decided it was time to take the focus away from her husband. She looked over to Kimi, who sat quietly enjoying her dessert.

"So what about you, Ms. Moore?" Charlene mumbled like a mother questioning her child.

"What about me?" Kimi uttered and looked over to Mrs. Bowser.

"You never told us what you do for a living," Charlene responded.

"I own my own business," Kimi replied.

"Don't we all." Charlene chuckled and looked around the table. A few of the dinner guests smiled and glanced over to Kimi, who was not amused.

"Don't mind, Charlene." Desiree waved to Kimi. "She is always poking fun."

"It's okay," Kimi said, forcing a fake smile to come to her face. "My company is actually doing quite well. I just signed a major contract with Macy's, and looking to add on Bloomingdale's soon." Kimi made sure she sounded confident when she announced the news.

"Very impressive," Niko said from the other side of the table. He was clearly trying to lighten the atmosphere in the dining room.

"So it sounds like you work very hard to keep up with it all, Kimi," Charlene continued to grill her.

"Eight days a week," Kimi responded.

"So is that why you don't have a man of your own, because you work so hard?" Charlene blurted.

"Alrighty then!" Niko playfully yelled from the other side of the table. "Time to change the subject."

Kimi looked over to Charlene and shot a laser at her. She couldn't believe Charlene's nerve. Kimi felt a rush of adrenaline run through her body. She wanted to smack the evil expression off of Charlene's face for trying to embarrass her. Kimi stared at Mrs. Bowser.

"Charlene, that is really not right," Desiree gasped. "You don't have to answer that, Kimi."

"Oh come now, Desi. She's a big girl," Charlene continued to dance on Kimi's nerves. Despite her polite tone, Kimi could sense the tension in her words.

"You're right, Mrs. Bowser, I am a big girl." Kimi's temper was flaring, but she refused to give Charlene the satisfaction of knowing she was getting to her. She dropped her fork down to her plate, and then looked over to Mrs. Bowser. "Well, if you must know. The reason I don't have a man is because I choose to be single. I refused to be in a relationship just to say I have a man, or marry somebody just so I can stay home all day and spend his money. I don't want to end up being forty-five years old, dejected, and picking on younger women just to justify my miserable life."

A few groans came from the room as everyone reacted to the verbal jab from Kimi. Charlene tried to keep her face still ,but she was clearly affected by Kimi's gut punch.

"So my assumptions about you were correct then?" Charlene snickered.

"What assumptions?" Kimi quickly snapped.

"You strike me as a go-getter," Charlene continued. "You're young and pretty and very driven. I can clearly see that you are the type of person that sees something you want and you go get it. There's nothing wrong with that."

"Okay," Kimi mumbled and readjusted her chin.

"But when you see something that belongs to somebody else you better be careful trying to go after it," Charlene warned. "You might just get those pretty wings of yours clipped." Charlene gave Kimi a menacing look, but Kimi didn't back down.

"Okay ladies," Desiree interrupted. "Put a lid on that fire over there."

"Trust me, nothing and nobody is getting clipped over here," Kimi snarled, ignoring Desiree. "Don't worry, Charlene, I would never go after something that's yours. I'm already seeing somebody, and he fucks me like a champion." Kimi's words electrified the dining room. Niko dropped his head and almost laughed out loud. Kimi's emotions had clearly gotten the best of her, and she was beyond ready to give Mrs. Bowser a piece of her mind. She continued to badger Charlene. "I'm almost tempted to give you his number because, it's clear to me, somebody is not getting fucked right at home."

"You classless bitch!" Charlene shouted and stood up.

"Here we go," Niko blurted, jumping to his feet. He rushed over to Kimi's side of the table.

"You're fucking miserable," Kimi yelled and quickly jumped up. Raymond held his wife back as the two women shouted at each other.

"And you're a fucking whore," Charlene roared. "What kind of woman would flirt with somebody's husband right in front of his wife?"

"I wasn't flirting with nobody," Kimi defended herself. "You have no idea what flirting is. If you did, your husband wouldn't be looking at every other woman's titties at this dinner table."

"Ladies, please relax," Niko yelled, getting between the women. "This is ridiculous."

"No, this bitch is the one who's ridiculous," Charlene growled. "Who invited this trash to your dinner anyway?"

Charlene's words seemed to slam dance on Kimi's last nerve. She quickly raised her arms, and then tried to smack Charlene with her open hand. Niko blocked the hit, and then grabbed Kimi in a bear hug.

"Ladies, what the hell is going on?" Desiree yelled. She almost passed out at the sight of her dinner becoming a disaster. The other guests at the table looked at the argument with sheer amazement. Raymond grabbed Charlene, and then dragged her out of the dining room. She cursed Kimi out with every breath.

"Ladies, please stop!" Desiree shouted again. Kimi fired back at Charlene with a barrage of insults of her own. Niko shook his head at Kimi, and then tried to calm her down. When he noticed her temper was clearly out of control, he turned to his wife.

"You know what," Niko mumbled. "This dinner is over. It's time for everybody to leave. Especially you, Kimi."

Niko's words were like a light switch that turned off her anger. She looked at Niko and dropped her head.

"I'm sorry, guys," Kimi said, trying her best to calm down. She looked over to Desiree. Her angry expression told the whole story.

"I'm out of here. I got to go," Kimi gasped with frustration. She forced herself out of Niko's grip, then stormed out of the dining room. Niko followed close behind to make sure Charlene wasn't waiting for her in the hallway. Kimi never turned around as she grabbed her winter jacket from the closet and opened the front door. She turned back to Niko and shook her head.

"I wasn't flirting with him," Kimi uttered.

Niko didn't respond. His silence was loud enough to let Kimi know he was upset with her. Kimi turned around and walked out into the cold. As she headed back to her house across the street, she couldn't help but think that tonight was not going to be the last time she heard from Charlene Bowser.

€ighteen

Three hours later, Kimi's eyes were wide open as she quietly stared at her eggshell-colored ceiling. She had been lying in bed thinking about Desiree's dinner for a while. The fight with Charlene made her beyond upset, and Kimi was still shocked by her accusation. Charlene's venom had caught her by surprise, and, usually, the mild mannered professional woman in Kimi would have prevailed. But tonight, Kimi let her temper get the best of her. She felt embarrassed as she thought about the faces in the room and how they judge her during the altercation. But one face haunted her the most. She had never seen Niko so disappointed since she known him. The look on his face bothered her enough to keep her up well past midnight, thinking of how their relationship was going to be affected. She thought about calling him, but decided against making such a risky move. The suspense was killing her.

After a while, Kimi found herself looking out of her bedroom window and staring at Niko's home across the street. All of the lights were off, and she could only try to imagine what was going on in his mind. Even though Kimi and Niko never had a disagreement, Kimi realized that tonight would test their relationship. Kimi knew it was going to be tough ,but she had to make it through the night and reach out to her good friend in the morning to apologize for ruining his dinner.

Kimi walked away from her bedroom window and stretched out across her soft mattress. She turned over on her side and closed her eyes. Before she could get some much-needed rest, her cell started buzzing from across the room. Kimi jumped up and rushed to the phone. She almost dropped it when she noticed that Niko was texting her. Kimi's heart skipped a beat as she focused in on the message.

NIKO (Cell)
Kimi please meet me at your back door in 10 minutes
I need to talk to you.

Kimi looked up from her phone and covered her mouth. She couldn't believe her eyes. She rushed back to the window and looked across the street. She noticed that Niko's car was gone and a few lights were on in his house. A million thoughts rushed through her mind, and her hands started shaking from nervousness. She stumbled to her closet and put on her nightgown. Kimi checked the time on her clock and walked into her hallway. She disabled her Big Brother system. Kimi wanted to make sure the video cameras in her house were not recording when Niko showed up. Kimi waited for the cameras to disable, and then rushed down the stairs. She didn't want to bring any attention to her house, so she decided to keep all of the lights off. Kimi held her phone tight in her hand and headed to the kitchen. She sat anxiously at her kitchen table and waited for Niko to come knocking.

Fifteen minutes later, a loud banging shook Kimi. She jumped to her feet and rushed to the back door where a freezing Niko was waiting for her. She opened the door, and Niko bolted into the house. Kimi stepped back as her friend stumbled into the kitchen. Niko was wearing thin slacks and a sports jacket. Kimi could tell that he was not prepared to be outside. She looked at him closely as he gathered himself.

"Baby, what the hell is going on?" Kimi nervously

questioned and looked at Niko.

He didn't say a word. He looked at Kimi for a moment and took off his jacket. She didn't recognize the look on his face. His eyes were fixed on her, but Kimi sensed that his mind was somewhere else. She stood motionless in the middle of the kitchen, continuing to read Niko as he walked over to her. Kimi felt a rush of fear boil in her stomach. She assumed that her friend was still upset with her. Niko moved closer, and Kimi instinctively took a few steps back from him. Without warning, he lunged at Kimi and grabbed her by the neck.

"Oh my God, Niko!" Kimi yelled.

He forcefully pushed her against the refrigerator. The weight of both of their bodies shook the kitchen. Niko's eyes grew more intense, and Kimi's heart started pounding out of her chest. She grabbed his cold hand and tried to pull it away from her throat ,but Niko's grip was tight and wouldn't budge.

"Niko, what are you doing?" Kimi whined. She was almost driven to tears.

Niko stared deep into his friend's eyes. His emotionless face intimidated Kimi, and she reached for his arm again with both hands. He was so strong tonight. Kimi's mind started to race as she tried to figure out how to escape his grasp. She panicked and wildly pulled on Niko's arms again. He refused to let her go.

"What the fuck is wrong with you, Niko?" Kimi shouted.

Her loud voice set Niko off, and he reached around her back with his free hand. He pulled her close and gave her a passionate kiss. His stiff tongue entered her mouth with a surprising force. Kimi was completely thrown off by Niko's move. He loosened his grip on her neck just enough to stop hurting her, but kept it tight enough to control her. Her heart fluttered again. A huge chill ran up her spine. Niko pushed his body up against hers and pinned her against the refrigerator.

He started kissing her like it was his last day on earth.

"Niko...!" Kimi cried out.

She realized that her friend was not there to hurt her tonight. The mood in the kitchen instantly shifted when Niko ran his hand down the side of Kimi's body and lifted her leg. She wrapped her arms around Niko's shoulders and started to flow with him. The mix of fear and adrenaline made Kimi feel like she was on a powerful drug. Niko grabbed her by the face and kissed her deeply again. He lifted up her nightgown and put a firm grip on her soft ass. His cold hands made her shiver and woke up her body. Kimi moaned his name. Her voice echoed off the walls in the dark kitchen, and Niko became more aggressive. He pulled his lips away from hers and ran his tongue down the side of her neck. He forcefully licked her jugular until Kimi started shaking. She never felt so vulnerable. Niko had her trembling from the moment he rushed through the door.

Before Kimi could kiss him again, Niko suddenly dropped to his knees. He grabbed her by the hips and put his face between her legs. Kimi dropped her head back against the refrigerator when she felt Niko rubbing his lips against her panties. His warm breath tickled her like a feather, and Kimi shuttered at the sensation. She didn't know what to think. The instant outburst of affection from Niko had her body trembling like crazy. She grabbed the back of Niko's head as he clutched her underwear with both hands. Niko quickly slid her underwear down to her ankles. He became aroused at the sight of Kimi's exposed pussy. Niko's tongue fell out of his mouth, and he felt compelled to taste her. Kimi shook her panties off her bare feet as Niko grabbed her ankle. He threw her leg over his shoulder, moving closer to her.

"Ooooh ,baby," Kimi moaned.

There was always something about Niko's first touch that drove her crazy. Tonight was no different. Her pussy started dripping wet the second she felt the tip of Niko's tongue. He teased Kimi for a moment, licking softly between her thighs. Kimi rocked to his slow rhythm until her body couldn't take it anymore. Her hands started begging him to go harder. Niko gently pulled her lips apart and pushed his tongue deeper into her wetness. Kimi screamed and cuffed the back of his head. Niko knew exactly what she wanted. He made his tongue as hard as possible, and then started tongue-fucking Kimi.

"Niko, please don't stop!" she moaned.

Niko jerked his head back and forth for her. Kimi's heavy breathing turned into heavy moaning, and the sound excited Niko. Her sensual body language invited him to taste every drip of her. She put a tighter grip on him and pushed Niko's tongue deeper inside of her.

Kimi looked down at Niko. The sight of his handsome face pleasing her was all she needed to see to take her over the top. Kimi yelled his name as a rush of pleasure trickled down her spine. Niko felt her body climaxing and tightly grabbed her legs. Kimi bounced her pussy against his tongue as the orgasm got closer.

"Oh my God, Niko....I'm--" Kimi cut herself short and tightened her jaw. She tried to back away from Niko ,but there was nowhere to go. Niko pulled her closer as the orgasm caught her off guard. Kimi exploded in a massive rush. Niko moaned realizing that her pussy was getting wetter with every jolt and every quiver. He didn't let her go until she was completely finished and her leg collapsed to the kitchen floor.

Niko stood to his feet and kissed Kimi. The smell of his tongue drove her insane. Kimi was extremely horny now. Niko's warm hands pulled her tighter and Kimi was ready for more. She unbuttoned Niko's shirt and started kissing on his bare chest. Niko took the shirt off and tossed it to the floor. He smiled as Kimi squeezed his broad shoulders. Niko reached up to her neck again and thought about kissing her. Kimi grabbed his hand and slammed it to his side. She gave him a serious look and bit her bottom lip. It was now her turn to be the aggressor. Kimi pushed Niko back and away from her. She slowly stalked him and nudged her hot body up against his. She playfully forced him against the counter on the other side of the kitchen. Niko didn't resist, and kicked off his shoes. Kimi's excited expression turned him on. She waited until Niko was comfortably rested against the wooden countertop, and then leaned over in front of him. She quickly unbuckled his belt and dropped his slacks to the floor. Niko rested his hands on the top of his head as Kimi tugged on his boxers. She wanted him so badly, but she didn't want to rush the moment. She kissed Niko on the stomach and licked around his navel. She knew he was enjoying her tongue as his body shook a little. Kimi dropped his boxers and purred as the sight of Niko's stiff dick.

"There he is," Kimi mumbled with a devilish grin.

Niko looked down just in time to see Kimi licking on her palm. She placed her wet grip tightly around his soldier and started stroking him. Niko moaned. Kimi squeezed his dick a few times and looked up to him. She had never felt Niko so hard before. Niko was beyond excited tonight, and all Kimi could do was shake her head as the anticipation warmed her body. Kimi kept Niko in her hand and stood up in front of him. She stroked him harder and kissed him on the lips.

"You mad at me, baby?" Kimi whispered and gave her friend a deep glance.

"You ruined my dinner," Niko quietly responded and returned the kiss.

"I'm so sorry about that ,baby," Kimi whined. "I don't know what got into me."

"Me neither," Niko whispered. "But I think you need to be punished for that."

A subtle grin came to Kimi's face. Niko's choice of

words only excited Kimi more. She moved closer to Niko as if she was accepting a challenge from him.

"You wanna punish me, baby?" Kimi asked as she dropped her voice to a seductive whisper.

Niko never responded to her. Without warning he grabbed her by her neck again. This time Kimi yelled out his name and closed her eyes. Niko leaned over and kissed her. He tried to force his tongue into her mouth ,but Kimi playfully resisted. The more she tried to resist Niko, the more aggressive he became. The mischievous tussle excited both of them. As Niko forced himself against Kimi, the couple stumbled back and landed against the kitchen sink.

"Baby...!" Kimi moaned when she felt Niko's hands gripping her shoulders. He spun her around and forced her to bend over near the sink. Kimi didn't put up a fight and lifted her nightgown for Niko. She exposed her bare ass to him and moaned when he rubbed her. Kimi reached around and grabbed Niko by the arm. Before Kimi could say another word, she felt Niko's throbbing dick entering her yearning pussy in a rush.

"My God...!" Kimi yelled with pleasure.

She grabbed onto the edge of the sink as Niko pushed himself deep inside. Kimi found herself moaning uncontrollably as Niko stroke her with passion. He fucked her so hard, and Kimi loved every second of it. It had been a while since they played the punisher game, and Kimi missed the adrenaline rush of feeling Niko being so aggressive.

"Spank me, baby...!" Kimi yelled as she felt Niko's hips pounding against her. Niko smacked Kimi on the ass and rode her like a stallion. Kimi bounced wildly on him and yelled again.

"Hit me harder, baby....!" Kimi moaned.

Niko cocked back and smacked her stiffly on her wanting ass. Kimi moaned in pleasure, and her body started shaking. Niko knew she was close to another orgasm and started moving faster.

"Do it again, baby…please," Kimi yelled.

Niko raised his hand high in the air and smacked her again. The high-pitched sound echoed throughout the kitchen, and Kimi screamed like she was dying. Niko grunted loudly as he pleased her.

"Is that what you want?" Niko uttered.

"Yes, please, baby. Do it harder," Kimi screamed. "Spank me harder!"

Her begging seemed to set Niko off again. He curiously looked around the kitchen and continued to hump Kimi's backside. An idea came to Niko's mind, and he smiled at the devious thought. Before Niko could stop himself, he'd reached over toward Kimi's dish rack. Kimi looked up and her mouth fell open. She dropped her eyebrows when she noticed Niko grabbing a stainless steel spatula from the counter. She looked back just in time to see Niko's arm swinging from the air. Niko spanked Kimi's ass with the steel, just hard enough to send a shot of pain though her body. Kimi's head fell back and she yelled to the heavens.

"Yes, baby!" Kimi screamed. She loved it.

The mix of pain and pleasure sent Kimi's body to euphoria. Niko continued to tap on her ass with the cooking utensil, and the graphic scene made him even more aroused. He pushed himself deeper and deeper until Kimi cried out with joy. Her body started trembling again as another orgasm flushed through her. Niko couldn't control himself. He pounded her faster and started climaxing. Kimi felt his body shuttering. His knees were becoming weaker. She started grinding her ass up against his hips, forcing him to succumb to her will. Niko dropped the spatula to the kitchen floor and gripped her waist.

"Oh shit, Kimi…!" Niko grunted.

Hearing Niko shouting her name was more pleasing to Kimi's ears than the best song ever recorded. She pushed her ass up against him again, and Niko erupted like a geyser. He reached over to the counter and held on tight as the orgasm took over his body. Kimi moaned with pleasure. She felt his manhood gyrating inside of her and cooed at the sensation. Kimi contracted her muscles and squeezed every bit of pleasure out of Niko as he collapsed on her back.

"Wow Niko," Kimi gasped. "That was fucking amazing."

Niko let out a chuckle and tried to catch his breath. Kimi's face was filled with bliss. She moaned and groaned for the next few minutes as Niko's body heat soothed her. Neither one of them made a move as they leaned up against the counter in silence and tried to recover from the incredible sex.

Nineteen

Back in the cold city of Newark, Marcel slowed down his SUV to a creeping pace. He had been driving around the city for nearly five hours searching for the man responsible for killing his niece. Images of Sabrina's battered face haunted Marcel, and he was clearly motivated by anger and vengeance. The snowy streets were empty tonight. But that didn't stop Marcel from questioning every street hustler and trick-bitch he'd seen hugging the snowy block. Marcel continued to come up empty each time he decided to stop. No one on the street seemed to know Khalil or know where to find him. A few hustlers heard about his niece's killing earlier that day ,but no one could help Marcel find her murderer.

After a few hours, Marcel lost track of time and found himself growing tired and frustrated. He continued to drive around the city until he made his way to 18th Avenue. He circled the neighborhood a few times, hoping he would see anyone from his old crew on the block. Marcel was just about to give up when he spotted the familiar face of Erick Ruiz walking out of his building. Marcel's mind instantly flashed back to their conversation in King's Restaurant. He was sure that Erick had more information on Khalil. Marcel made a U-turn and pulled in front of him. The SUV startled Erick for a moment and he jumped back. Marcel rolled down the window and shouted at Erick.

"Aye homie, I need to holla at you," Marcel yelled in

an aggressive tone.

"Yo, what the fuck man?" Erick stuttered. He peered into the truck and noticed it was Marcel. "My nigga, you was about to get it for real. Rolling up on me like that. Shit man, that ain't cool."

"That's my bad, fam," Marcel shouted. "I need to holla at you, for real though. Jump in, my nigga."

Erick thought for a moment and looked around. He noticed that Marcel was dead serious, and he decided to find out what was on his mind.

"What's the deal, bro?" Erick asked as he sat down in the passenger seat and closed the door. Marcel pulled off the street and looked at Erick.

"You heard about that shit today in North Newark?" Marcel coldly asked.

"What shit?"

"This nigga killed my fuckin' niece today," Marcel uttered. His voice cracked a little ,but Marcel refused to look weak in front of Erick.

"Damn fam," Erick gasped and put his fist in front of his lips. "You talkin' about that shit that happened at the gas station?"

"Yea man, that was my niece, Sabrina," Marcel said.

"Aww fuck, my nigga. The whole hood is talking about that shit," Erick continued. "They said her boyfriend killed her over some domestic shit."

Marcel looked over to the passenger side of the truck and twisted his face. Erick noticed his mood growing darker.

"It wasn't no fucking domestic shit," Marcel scowled. "It was Khalil that did that shit to her. And on some real shit, I need to find this nigga."

The news hit Erick like a ton of bricks. Marcel turned his focus to the road, and Erick took a closer look at him. He looked at Marcel's hands and his clothes. Marcel had dried up blood on his fingers and sleeves.

"So you think Khalil did it?" Erick quietly asked.

"I know he did that shit, my nigga," Marcel snapped.

"How do you know?" Erick pressed.

"My niece told me. Right before she died," Marcel's emotionless voice scared Erick. Marcel gave him a death stare, and then pulled his truck over to the side of the road. "Now listen my, nigga," Marcel uttered, looking around the dark street. "I know you hustle for them Marquez boys. And I know you want to stay loyal to them niggas. And that's cool. But I need to find this motherfucka." Erick didn't say a word. He gave Marcel a blank stare and tried to keep his cool. "There is no way you can sit here and tell me you don't know where this nigga is," Marcel snapped.

"Come on man, why you wanna come at me like this tonight, my dude?" Erick looked away from Marcel. "I don't know where this nigga be at."

"E....!" Marcel raised his voice. "Look at me."

Erick turned around and looked at Marcel. Between the hard glare in his eyes and the blood on his hands, Marcel was looking like a man with nothing to lose.

"This ain't got shit to do with business," Marcel snapped. "Sabrina was a civilian, and Khalil fucked her off. All I'm asking you to do is point me in the right direction, and I'm gone."

"Come on, Marcel, don't make me do this," Erick uttered in frustration.

"You know the rules, my nigga," Marcel groaned. "Sabrina was my family. She was my blood. That motherfucka gotta go!"

The truck fell silent as Erick looked out the window again. He tried to gather his thoughts before he spoke.

Erick was caught between his loyalties, but he knew Marcel was right. Khalil had violated the rules by killing Marcel's family, and things needed to be rectified. Erick turned to Marcel who continued to coldly stare in his direction.

"So what's in this for me?" Erick asked.

"What do you mean?" Marcel responded.

"For you, it's personal. For me, it's business. So I need to know what's in it for me."

"What you need?" Marcel twisted his expression.

"If I tell you this shit, man, I gotta lay low for about a month," Erick continued. "And I won't make no bread while I'm skating, so I need enough to hold me down until I come back."

"Okay, so what's that lookin' like?"

"Twenty," Erick said with a straight face.

"Twenty stacks?" Marcel blurted.

"Hell yes. I should ask you for more than that." Erick readjusted in his seat and turned to Marcel. "My nigga, you are asking me to push Khalil in front of traffic for you. That type of information is gonna cost you."

Marcel closed his mouth and looked at his hands. His bloody knuckles made his adrenaline rush throughout his body. He thought about Sabrina's face and nodded his head.

"Okay, E. That's a deal," Marcel whispered.

"Cool, but you can't do this shit tonight," Erick warned him. "These niggas will figure that shit out blindfolded. So you gotta wait for this. Give it at least a week."

Marcel didn't say a word. He simply nodded his head and thought for moment. Although his heart telling him to seek revenge tonight, his common sense agreed with Erick. He calmed down his emotions and reached to put the truck back into gear. Erick stopped him.

"Nah, my nigga. I will get out right here," Erick

said. "I don't want nobody around there to see me with you."

"What? Why not?" Marcel sharply asked.

"My nigga, you are hot right now," Erick responded. "I didn't know that was your family that got killed today. So there's definitely a spotlight on you right now. Just lay low, my nigga. Trust me. In a week or two, holla at me and we will handle that shit. I got you."

Marcel nodded his head again. Erick gathered himself, reached over, and gave Marcel a pound. He jumped out of the SUV and stomped through the snow, heading back to 18th Avenue. Marcel put his truck in gear and pulled off the quiet street. He decided to take Erick's advice and lay low until everything blew over. Marcel pushed his truck through the snow and made his way back to his house. He knew he had more than enough time to plan the right attack to eliminate Khalil.

*J*wenty

Back in Shady Meadows, there was a hovering silence in Kimi's bedroom. After another sexual episode, Kimi was out like a light. But Niko had been lying awake for about an hour contemplating the new stress in his life. The problems with the Stanton firm were reaching a boiling point, and Niko had been racking his brain trying to figure out how to solve the issue. For most of the day, Niko had been mulling over a plan of simply shutting down his law firm and starting a whole new life. After his discussion with Laura, Niko realized that his firm would not survive such a big investigation of corruption. Even though Niko was confident that he could beat any charges tossed his way, the embarrassment of the arrests at his firm would scare off potential clients and would call his prior cases into question. Niko was disgusted at the fact that Raymond had put him in such a tight squeeze. He realized that his life as a high profile attorney was over. Niko had to concentrate on how to make a new life for himself. But there was still one piece to his puzzle that remained in question. Tonight, Niko decided it was time to take a leap of faith and start a whole new chapter in his life.

"Baby, are you sleeping?" Niko whispered, breaking up the silence in Kimi's bedroom. He turned over and gently shook Kimi to get her attention. Kimi jumped up out of her sleep and turned to Niko. Her wide eyes were clearly tired, but she looked around the room as if something dangerous was lurking.

"I'm sorry, baby," Niko uttered. "I just wanted to

let you know that I have to go. Sorry for waking you up."

Kimi glanced over to Niko again, and then let out a sigh of relief. She leaned up against the headboard and grabbed her face.

"I was having a nightmare," Kimi gasped.

"Damn," Niko whispered.

"I was getting chased by all these people," Kimi groaned. "It was crazy. What time is it?"

"Almost 4:30," Niko responded. He sat up on the edge of the bed, and then stretched his tired bones. "I have to get back across the street before she sends out a search party for me."

"Okay," Kimi said, nodding her head. She hated when Niko had to leave her. She looked at him and gave him a soft expression. "I'll walk you downstairs."

"No, not yet," Niko said and turned away from Kimi. He put his feet on the floor and tried to brace himself to give Kimi the sad news. "I have to tell you something ,baby."

Kimi pulled down the covers and looked over to Niko. Although he had his back turned to her, Kimi could sense that something heavy was on his mind. She turned on the lamp, got up, and put on her nightgown. Niko turned around and looked at her as she walked over to him. The slight fear in his eyes confirmed that something was clearly wrong.

"Hey, what's the matter?" Kimi softly asked.

She sat next to Niko on the side of the bed and put her arm around him. Niko looked down to the floor, taking a moment to gather his thoughts.

"I'm leaving my wife," he whispered.

Saying the words felt like a weight was being lifted from his body. Niko had been having marital problems for a few years, but he never mentioned them to his friend. Niko decided it was time to make a big change.

"Are you serious?" Kimi asked.

She was clearly stunned by Niko's news. She didn't know how to feel about his revelation. Kimi had always fantasized about having Niko to herself ,but now the reality made her nervous.

"Kimi, I've been thinking about this for a while now," Niko mumbled. "There are some things going on at my firm that will come out soon, and I will have to shut my business down."

"Seriously?" Kimi gasped. She dropped her forehead toward Niko and gave him a deep glance.

"I'm very serious. "I...ummm." Niko paused for a moment and nervously rubbed his forehead. "I fucked up," he stuttered. He looked over to Kimi with remorse in his eyes.

"Niko, what happened?" Kimi whispered. "You're scaring me. Talk to me. What happened?"

"Okay, Kimi," Niko took a deep breath and looked up to his friend. "You remember how I got my start-up money for the law firm?" Niko asked.

"Huh?" Kimi mumbled. "Niko, you told me your wife gave you the money to start your business. Twenty-thousand dollars right?"

"Yeah, that's not the total truth," Niko confessed and slowly shook his head. "Desiree gave me the money to start the company ,but I blew it." Kimi didn't respond. She was clearly taken aback by the news. She continued to listen to Niko vent. "Yup. I fucked up." Niko dropped his head and buried his face in his hands. "I was so stupid back then. I thought I could flip the money with some people I knew. One thing led to another, and the next thing I knew, I was down almost thirty-two thousand dollars."

"Holy shit, Niko." Kimi covered her mouth. "But how did you-"

"I got the money from Marquez," Niko said cutting off Kimi. He let out a lung full of air as he thought about a darker time in his life. "I couldn't go back to my wife for more money, so I got it from Marquez." Niko rubbed his forehead in frustration. "I known Leon Marquez for over ten years. We were never friends like that ,but I knew him from Newark. I represented him back when he first started out. He knew I was in the middle of some financial issues and offered to step in. He ended up giving me fifty thousand to start my law firm. That's why the company took off so fast. I had enough cash to buy the world at that time."

"Damn, Niko." Kimi couldn't believe her ears. She stood up and walked to the other side of the room.

"Nobody knows about this, Kimi," Niko said. "Nobody, but me and Marquez, and, now, you."

"So what else is going on?" Kimi asked with a dubious tone. "This is why you want to leave your wife?"

Niko closed his mouth and thought for a moment. The air in the room seemed to get thicker as Niko thought about his troubles. He glanced over to Kimi. "Marquez is threatening my life if I don't get him acquitted," Niko revealed.

"What?" Kimi gasped.

"Yea, he's out of his fucking mind, and now he's turning against me." Niko became frustrated with every word. "This son-of-a-bitch even had his son come to my office today and threaten me. And I found out that they are even trying to set me up. So basically, they are trying to blow the lid off of my firm. I have no clue how this is going to go down ,but, either way, it won't be good for me. So that's why I need to make a move. And make a move soon."

"Shit, Niko." Kimi shook her head and walked over to the bed. She sat down next to her friend and consoled him. "So what are you going to do?"

"I set up a meeting with the judge and the lead prosecutor for next week," Niko said. "I'm going to cooperate with them ,but it will clearly mean the end of the Stanton Firm."

"My God, Niko this isn't good at all." Kimi sighed.

"You telling me." Niko rubbed his forehead. "Plus, I'm not exactly Mr. Popularity down there. The prosecutor and the district attorney and the mayor are itching for a reason to put my nuts in the grinder. They would love a chance to bury me with this Marquez bullshit. But I refuse to give them the satisfaction. I will just shut my own shit down and start over."

The room fell silent as a cemetery. Niko's voice was full of conviction and disappointment. Hearing himself talk about his situation out loud added more stress to his mind. After a few quiet minutes in the bedroom, Niko looked over to his friend and gave her a strange expression.

"Kimi, I don't know how to ask you this, so I'm just going to say it," Niko uttered and took another deep breath.

"Ask me what?" Kimi whispered.

"I don't love my wife," Niko blurted. "Seriously. I mean I use to love her. But now I don't. It took me a while to come to grips with that ,but now I know it for sure. There is really not a lot left between us. I've been feeling like this for a couple of years now. The only reason I'm even here is because of my firm. And without my firm, I really have nothing to keep me here." Kimi didn't know what to say. She started feeling anxious as Niko continued speaking. "Things got really ugly tonight. Me and my wife had a huge fight after you left."

"Niko, I'm so sorry about the dinner." Kimi shook her head. "I don't know why I snapped on that lady-"

"It's okay, Kimi," Niko cut her short. "It's not your fault. Charlene is a bitch just like most of my wife's friends. You don't have to apologize for that. But truth of the matter is, I'm leaving my wife. Seriously. She would never divorce me without a fight, so I decided to walk away from everything and start over somewhere else."

"Niko are you serious?" Kimi dropped her eyebrows.

"I'm very serious," Niko responded. "If I don't leave here soon, things are going to turn out bad between me and Marquez. Even if I get removed from the case, my enemies down at city hall will eventually find out the truth and try to put me in jail."

"Jail? Niko? For what?" Kimi was confused.

"Kimi, I started my company with money I got from a known criminal," Niko continued. "I could face money laundering, tax evasion, falsifying federal documents. You name it, and the district attorney will be up my ass for it. This is serious."

"Jesus Christ."

"Yes, this shit is going to explode soon, and I just need to get in front of this thing." Niko's mind was racing as he looked down to the floor again. "I've been putting money away for the past few months, and I almost got enough to make my move."

"So you're really going to leave?" Kimi asked with an uneven expression. She was clearly uncomfortable with the news.

"I already got one foot out the door, Kimi," Niko whispered. "But I don't want to go at this alone."

Niko turned to Kimi and looked into her eyes. The sincere look on his face made Kimi's heart skip a beat. She opened her mouth to ask the next question, but she was too afraid to let the words out.

"I want you to come with me, Kimi," Niko softly said.

"Niko, what are you asking me?" Kimi shook her head. "I can't go with you."

"Why not, Kimi?" Niko quickly questioned. "This is a chance for us to be together...and away from here."

"But Niko, we're not together," Kimi uttered.

"I know. But seeing you tonight at the table with my wife made me realize that just how miserable I am over there," Niko said. "You got that fire in you that I'm missing. I saw it again in you tonight. I know we would be happy together."

"Niko, wait. Back up for a minute," Kimi said as she stood up. "Just because you're miserable over there doesn't mean you're going to be happy with me."

"I know that's true, but I'm willing to try," Niko said, standing up with Kimi.

"Okay, that's fair. But try where? A thousand miles from here?" Kimi asked.

"Why not?" Niko snapped. "We can start over. Start fresh. Just me and you."

"Niko, do you hear yourself?" Kimi asked with frustration in her voice. "I'm not a teenager. I just can't drop everything I've worked for and run away with you. This is not a movie. That's not how real life works."

"Kimi, baby. I know this sounds crazy." Niko moved closer to his friend. "Just think about it. You said it yourself that you are ready for a change. You can sell your company while I'm shutting down mine, and we can move on. Believe me, baby, we can do this."

Kimi looked at Niko. The intensity in his eyes was something she had never seen before in her friend. He was clearly desperate to leave, and the fact that he was considering taking her along was flattering. Every since she'd met him, the fantasy of him belonging to her always hovered in her mind. Tonight the opportunity was there, and Kimi decided to take it.

"Baby, are you serious about this?" Kimi softly asked. Her voice trembled with emotion.

"Extremely serious," Niko responded. "I want to make this move, and I want you right there next to me."

Kimi lowered her head, and she almost dropped a few tears. Niko's words were very powerful, and they seem to speak to something deeper inside. She looked back up to her friend and gave him a soft smile.

"Niko, you know I would do anything for you, right?" Kimi quietly asked.

"Yes," Niko responded.

"Baby, I'm serious," Kimi continued. "I would do... anything for you." Kimi's voice was serious. Niko closed his mouth as he found himself wrapped up in her eyes. "Baby, don't play with me. If we are going to do this, it needs to be just me and you, okay?" Niko nodded his head. "I'm serious ,baby. I will go with you, but it has to be just me and you now."

"Okay, baby. It's just me and you," Niko whispered.

He gave Kimi a deep kiss on her lips. He knew exactly what Kimi was asking. Niko was at the point in his life where he needed a change, and he was willing to sacrifice for it. Kimi and Niko embraced for a long moment. He realized that things would never be the same.

Niko kissed Kimi again and headed for the bedroom door. He walked out of the room and Kimi followed him downstairs to the back door. Kimi couldn't help but think back to what a crazy night this was. From Desiree's dinner party, to the fight with Charlene, to the episode with Niko in her kitchen, and, now, this. Her mind was spinning out of control. Niko brought her back to reality when he opened the back door. The cold wind shook her, and she turned to Niko's handsome face.

"Be careful," Kimi whispered and gave him a tight hug. Niko kissed her on the lips and gave her a pleasant smile.

"Let's talk in a couple of days. Okay ,baby?" Niko whispered.

"Yes," Kimi softly responded.

She watched as Niko turned around and started jogging through her backyard. She kept her eyes fixed on him until he disappeared deep into the darkness.

Twenty-One

One Week Later...

And in other local news, city officials are bracing for a huge rally near city hall today. Community leaders say they are expecting over ten thousand people to descend on the capital to call for the end of the violence in Newark and surrounding cities. The recent outcry from concerned residents comes after the latest murder of Sabrina Harris at a local Gulf station last week. Community organizers are calling on the mayor to intensify the police presence around the city and increase spending on various programs previously implemented to curb the violence. A spokesperson for the mayor's office offered no comment when asked if the mayor plans to attend the demonstration.

Marcel sat quietly in his basement, watching the morning news on television. His face turned hard as stone when the broadcaster mentioned his niece's name. It had been nearly a week since her despicable murder, and Marcel found himself becoming thirstier for revenge with each passing day. The news clip hit him directly in the heart, and Marcel felt his temper boiling. He grabbed his remote and turned off the television. He reached for his phone and made the call he had been dying to make all week. He stood to his feet and waited for the call to connect.

"Yo, who is this?" a rough voice asked from the other line.

"Erick, it's me, man," Marcel barked.

"Me who?" the voice demanded.

"It's Marcel motherfucka, where you been at?" he continued to yell into the phone. "I been tryin' to get at you for the past few days. Don't tell me you dippin' me."

"Nah, fam. That's my bad, my nigga," Erick continued to apologize. "I been hustlin' like crazy, homie. These niggas is goin' through some major paper . I don't know what's goin' on ,but they got me pickin' up and droppin' off packages like fuckin' UPS out here."

"Yea, I heard it's hot in the hood," Marcel said.

"Hotter than lava out here, homie!" Erick added.

"So what's up with that thing we talked about?" Marcel questioned. "I'm ready to put in some serious work out this bitch."

"Man, I was hoping you didn't ask me about that shit," Erick mumbled.

"Why not?" Marcel snapped.

"Because, my dude... I know exactly where this nigga is stayin' now."

"On some real shit...that's what's up," Marcel raised his voice again. "So what's the problem?"

"The problem is...nobody is supposed to know he's there, "Erick said.

"Man, you know I don't give a fuck about that. Where is he?" Marcel blurted. He felt himself becoming furious.

"Okay, my nigga, listen," Erick lowered his voice. "This nigga Khalil got into some more shit this week. I heard he's staying at one of the stash houses downtown. From what I'm hearing, he's been down there for a couple of days."

"Say word?" Marcel quickly asked.

"Yea," Erick responded. "But check it, Marcel. He's definitely not by himself. It's a lot of powder down there, so it gotta be like three or four guns down there with him."

"At the house?" Marcel asked.

"Yea man," Erick replied. "You know them Marquez boys don't trust nobody. So they always got a crew down there watching the dope."

Marcel didn't respond. He digested Erick's words and continued to think about a plan. His mind was dead set on getting at Khalil despite the fact that the odds were stacking against him.

"So where's this fuckin' house?" Marcel questioned Erick.

"Wait a minute, homie," Erick snapped. "Let's talk about this money first."

"It's whatever…!" Marcel quickly responded. "How you want to do this?"

"I tell you what. Meet me at Weequahic Park, and I will give you the address to the stash house," Erick said.

"What time?" Marcel was anxious to get the information.

"Let's do it around eleven o'clock, my nigga."

"I'll be there with the money," Marcel snapped. "Don't even sweat it."

"That's what it is, Marcel. I will check you later."

Marcel disconnected the call and clinched his fist. His blood started boiling at the thought of finally having a chance to find Sabrina's killer. All week he'd been haunted by the images of his niece's bloody face. He woke up depressed and furious every single day. He'd begged for an opportunity to confront Khalil again, and now he could sense the time was drawing near.

Marcel slowly walked upstairs to the first level. He was heading to his bedroom when he felt the urge to walk into Sabrina's room. An eerie feeling came over Marcel as he walked inside the bedroom and looked around. He noticed that Tricia had put all of his niece's clothes and belongings on the bed in a neat pile. Marcel had no clue what to do with her things. He looked down and noticed Sabrina's purse on the mattress. A rush of adrenaline hit him when he saw the white DVD just barely peeking through the opening to her bag. Marcel quickly snatched the video and stared at it. In the midst of all the drama, the video totally slipped his mind.

"Damn," Marcel whispered .

The DVD was a sad reminder of why Sabrina had got caught up in all the drama in the first place. Getting the money for the video was not important to Marcel now. He didn't care about the money at all. Marcel thought for a second and slowly nodded his head. He had a better plan for the DVD. He reached for his phone and scrolled down to Kimi's name. He dialed her number and waited for Kimi to pick up.

"Oh my God, Marcel are you okay?" Kimi groaned as she answered the phone.

"I'm getting better," Marcel uttered. His voice was slightly emotional.

"I tried to call you all week," Kimi gasped. "I heard about Sabrina. I'm so sorry. Did they find the guy?"

"No," Marcel coldly answered. "They still calling it a domestic case. They don't know what's going on."

"Oh God, that is so sad. Do you need anything?" Kimi asked.

"I'm good," Marcel lied. "This shit is going to get handled real soon."

There was something sinister in Marcel's tone. Kimi didn't know how to respond, so she decided to stay quiet as Marcel continued speaking.

"I was calling to see if you can come to Newark today," Marcel asked.

"I'm sure I can. Why? What's going on?"

"I wanted to give you this video?" Marcel responded.

"What video?"

"Of Gary Banks. You remember the one I told you about?"

"Oh….okay," Kimi stuttered. She was puzzled by Marcel's request.

"I'm about to get caught up into some other shit, and I'm not gonna need the video anymore," Marcel said. His voice was cold as ice.

"What do you mean?" Kimi uttered. She grew concerned for her old friend. "What's going on?"

"I'll tell you about it later," Marcel quickly replied. "Can you please meet me back at King's restaurant around twelve?"

"Okay Marcel," Kimi agreed. She keened in on Marcel's voice and realized that there was much more going on than he was trying to reveal to her. "Marcel, are you sure you don't need anything?"

"I'm sure," he responded. "I just need to give you this video."

"Okay. I will see you at twelve o'clock."

"Thanks, Kimi. I'll talk to you later."

Marcel abruptly hung up the phone and headed upstairs. Tricia was just getting out of the shower when he walked into his bedroom. She took one look at Marcel's eyes and knew something was eating him up inside. She quietly got dressed as Marcel walked to the closet. He pulled out an outfit to wear and grabbed a huge shoebox from the top shelf.

"Come here, Tricia. I need to talk to you, baby," Marcel said as he walked to the bed and sat.

Tricia turned to her friend and walked over to him. He grabbed her by the hand and motioned for her to sit next to him. Tricia watched him closely as he pulled the top off of the shoebox. Her eyes grew wide as Marcel exposed all of the money he had saved over the past few years. Marcel pulled out three large stacks of money wrapped in brown rubber bands, and then tossed them to the side. He closed the lid and handed the box to Tricia. She instantly became nervous by the move.

"Marcel-" she uttered.

"Wait, Tricia, just listen," Marcel said, cutting her short. "I need to handle somethin' today, and I might not make it back." Marcel dropped his head and took a deep breath. He tried to gather his words ,but he was clearly emotional. Tricia was already in tears by the time Marcel turned and looked over to her. Tricia had been dreading this conversation since Sabrina died. She knew Marcel loved her, and he would eventually try to find the man who killed her. She knew exactly where the conversation was going, so she tried to brace herself.

"I gotta do this today, Tricia," Marcel said as his face stiffened. "I might not get another shot at this. So today is the day."

Tricia wiped a few tears from her eyes and nodded her head. Part of her wanted Marcel not to go through with this ,but the other part was also seeking justice. No matter how crazy Sabrina was, Tricia felt she didn't deserve to be beaten to death like an animal. She reached over and gave Marcel a kiss on his lips. She tried to be strong for him.

"What do you want me to do, baby?" Tricia whispered.

"It's more than enough money in that box to hold you down, Tricia." Marcel looked deeper into her eyes. "I just need you to stay by the phone in case things go wrong. And if I don't call you by tonight, you know what to do."

Tricia nodded her head again. A few more tears trickled down her cheek and she hugged Marcel. He reached out and embraced his friend like it was the last time he would see her. He realized that going after Khalil was going to be a dangerous

184

deed he might not survive. Marcel pushed the morbid thoughts from his mind and concentrated on the moment. He hugged Tricia tighter and realized that the only thing that mattered was the last few moments he had left to spend with his friend.

Twenty-Two

Just a few miles away, down at the Stanton Law Firm, Niko calmly stared out of the huge window in his office. The Newark skyline was hazy, yet peaceful this morning and Niko found himself reminiscing on all the clients he had served throughout the years. His eyes slowly scanned over the vast sea of tall buildings and historic structures of downtown Newark. Although his body was relaxed and his face was serene, his mind was in the middle of a chaotic episode. For the past week, Niko had been quietly preparing his firm for a total shut down. He'd called up most of his clients and given them the bad news. He also prepared some of his employees that the possibility of a shutdown was looming. But there were still two issues plaguing Niko's mind. Raymond Bowser and Leon Marquez. Niko was still unclear how to handle his closest enemies. Before he could think about a new plan his office phone blared from his desk.

"Stanton Law Firm," Niko quickly answered the line.

"Good morning, Niko, this is Laura Sanchez. I was calling to see if you got my fax this morning."

"Good morning, Laura," Niko replied to the prosecutor. He looked around his desk and grabbed a few sheets of paper. "I did receive the fax, Ms. Sanchez."

"And what do you think about the terms?" Laura asked.

"Honestly, I'm not totally comfortable with

everything," Niko responded. "But if this guarantees no charges will be brought against me, I will agree to them."

"Niko, I reassure you that we have already discussed this case with the judge and you will not face any type of prosecution for your cooperation," Laura said. "But I can't say the same for some of the other members of your firm."

"I completely understand," Niko uttered. "I will sign these documents, and then shoot them right over to you."

"Great," Laura continued. "The motion to have you removed from the Marquez case is still under review, but I don't see a problem with it going through. It should be completed within a couple of days."

"Okay. That sounds great," Niko uttered. His voice became lower with conviction.

"Believe me Niko, you are doing the right thing," Laura assured.

The line fell silent as Niko thought about the prosecutor's words.

"I guess only time will tell if this is right for me," Niko whispered.

"Absolutely," Laura responded. "Just stay out of trouble, and we will be in touch in a couple of days."

"Okay. Thanks again." Niko hung up the phone and signed the documents. He walked over to his fax machine and sent the paperwork to Laura. It wouldn't be long now before the firestorm of reporters turned their attention to his firm. Niko was clearly heading toward unchartered territory, and he could only imagine what he was in store for.

Niko looked at his calendar and noticed that he was scheduled to visit one more client today. He packed up his things and was getting ready to leave when Raymond Bowser entered his office.

"Boss, you got a minute?" Raymond asked as he

slowly walked toward Niko's desk.

"Not really," Niko quickly responded. "I need to head out to see a client."

"Okay, but I have to ask you a question," he uttered. Niko turned to Raymond and raised his eyebrows. The sound of Raymond's tone let Niko know that this was a conversation that couldn't wait.

"Okay, what's the question?" Niko asked and continued to gather his things.

"Do you need anything else for the Marquez case?" Raymond sharply questioned.

"What?" Niko snapped. "Anything else like what?"

"I don't know," Raymond blurted. "Anything that can help with the case?"

"No!" Niko stiffly replied, trying to shut down the conversation.

"The only reason I'm asking is because I got a call this morning from Ronald Marquez," Raymond revealed.

"You got a call?" Niko asked and stared at Raymond.

"Yes, Ronald called me this morning."

"And why is my client calling you?" Niko gave Raymond a suspicious glance.

"I don't know. He called me and asked me about the case," Raymond continued.

"Why the hell is he asking *you* about the case?" Niko let out a frustrated gasp of air and shook his head. "You're a piece of work, Raymond."

"What is that suppose to mean?" Raymond barked.

"Never mind," Niko uttered. He was clearly still fuming over Laura's revelation that Raymond had been trying to set him up. Niko didn't want to let him know that he was aware of his scheming, so he decided to let go of the conversation until later. "So is that all you needed?" Niko asked.

"No," Raymond fired back. "Ronald wanted to know if you could meet him to discuss the case."

"Sure, tell him to meet me here in my office tomorrow."

"Actually, he was hoping you could meet him at a neutral location," Raymond said.

"Neutral?" Niko uttered. He didn't like the choice of Raymond's words. "Why can't he come here?"

"I'm not comfortable with him being up here after that incident with you last week," Raymond said. "I told him that if he wanted to meet and talk, it would have to be somewhere else." Niko didn't say a word. He coldly stared at Raymond while he continued speaking. "I was thinking you could meet him at Albert's Soul Food Restaurant."

"You mean the same restaurant that Marquez owns?" Niko quickly asked.

"Yes, the one on South Orange Avenue," Raymond responded.

Niko lowered his eyes to his desk and grabbed the rest of his things. He was tempted to lunge across the table and choke Raymond for his disloyalty. Niko knew the meeting was just a way to get him in deeper trouble and add more evidence to bury him with. Niko played it cool and tried not to show his hand. He simply put on his coat and walked around the desk. He couldn't believe how deep Raymond's treachery was. Niko looked at Raymond and gave him a long hard stare. Raymond grew nervous, and Niko could tell that he was hiding something. The look in Raymond's eyes was beyond devious, and his expression was nearly soulless. Raymond was hiding a much deeper secret, and Niko could sense it. He knew that if met with Rojo at the restaurant he would not come out of the meeting the same way he went into it. Either he would leave in handcuffs, or, even worse, Niko would leave in a body bag.

Niko didn't want to make Raymond suspicious, so he decided to agree to the meeting. He knew he would have to come up with another plan to make sure he left the meeting alive.

"Okay, Raymond, set the meeting up, and I will be there," Niko said. He gave Raymond a cold glance and continued to the hallway.

"I'll set it up for Friday," Raymond replied.

Niko nodded his head and walked out of his office. He passed by his secretary and smiled at her.

"Can you call my eleven o'clock appointment and let him know that I'm on my way," Niko said.

"Sure thing, Mr. Stanton," the secretary politely responded.

Niko smiled at her and continued to the elevator. Niko's mind was fixed on Raymond and his corrupt ways. He knew he only had a few days left to tie up all of his loose ends before his professional world came tumbling down. As the elevator door closed, he couldn't help but think of how to turn the tables on Raymond and Rojo.

Back in Shady Meadows, Kimi paced back and forth in her living room while she spoke on the phone. Half-packed boxes and large moving containers filled the area. For the past week, she had been preparing to move all of her belongings out of the huge house. The idea of moving away with Niko had started to grow on her. Despite the fact that New Jersey was home for her entire life, Kimi was thirsting for change. After weighing her options, she decided to put her immaculate home on the market. She was sure she would find a buyer, and, now the only thing left was to finalize a deal to sell the business. As Kimi continued to walk though her house, she yelled into the phone, continuing to battle with her broker.

"So exactly how long will it take for the paperwork to

be processed?" Kimi shouted through the phone.

"Ms. Moore, what you are asking us to do has never been done before," a male voice strained from the other line. "Vanguard Enterprises is very interested in buying the Messy Sheets company, but there is no way we can process this sell before the end of the month. I'm sorry--"

"Sir, if I can interrupt you for one moment," Kimi blurted. "Let me remind you that when I first came to your company to broker this deal, I was assured that the process would be in its second phase at this juncture of the negotiations." Kimi tried to stay professional, but she was clearly upset. "Now you are telling me you are still negotiating the terms? I have to say ,sir, that this is unacceptable. I really don't have another month to wait for you guys to play catch up."

"Again, I personally do apologize, Ms. Moore, for the hold up," the man on the other line groaned. "Please give me another week to make this right, ma'am. I am more than confident that we will finalize the paperwork and get this ball rolling as soon as possible. But I do ask you to allow at least another week for this sell to be completed."

Kimi thought about the broker's words and decided to calm herself down. She was upset that the negotiations to sell her business were moving slow.

"Okay, sir, please keep in mind that this is a time sensitive matter." Kimi lowered her tone and sat down on her sofa. "I need you guys to keep me posted on the progress, and if you need any additional documentation please reach out."

"I will, Ms. Moore," the man said. "You have a great day, and thank you so much for your patience."

"No problem," Kimi mumbled and abruptly hung up the phone.

Kimi sunk into her sofa and thought for a moment. For the past two weeks she had been putting most of her energy into selling Messy Sheets. Although the firm she contracted to broker the deal was moving at a slow pace, Kimi realized that once the money made it into an escrow account things would be smooth sailing. She was becoming more excited every day about the adventurous move. Kimi smiled as she thought about how fast time was moving. It wouldn't be long before she and Niko would finally leave all the drama behind and start things over again.

A few minutes later, Kimi was shaken out of her daydream by the doorbell. She looked toward her front door and twisted her face. Kimi checked the time on her watch, trying to imagine who could be coming by her house so early in the afternoon.

"One second," Kimi shouted as she headed to the door.

Without a thought, Kimi twisted the knob and swung open the front door. Her heart dropped to the floor when she took a look at her visitor. It was Charlene Bowser. Kimi froze for a moment, and then tried her best to read Charlene's demeanor. She could tell that Charlene was troubled by something by the distant look in her eyes.

"I'm sorry to come by here un-announced, but I didn't know where else to go," Charlene mumbled.

Kimi slowly stepped away from the door. Charlene was looking disheveled and confused, and just the sight of her standing at the doorway made Kimi feel anxious. She looked down and noticed that Charlene was holding an oversized yellow envelope in her hand.

"Can I come in?" Charlene quietly asked. "I didn't come here to start no trouble with you. I just want to talk."

Charlene's humble disposition disarmed Kimi. Today, Charlene was acting very different from what Kimi experienced the first time she'd met her at Desiree's dinner. Kimi hesitated for a moment, and eventually decided to invite the woman into her home. She motioned for Charlene to come inside, and then stepped to the side. Kimi watched her closely.

"Like I said, Kimi, I'm sorry for coming by like this," Charlene uttered. "I hope I am not catching you at a bad time."

"It's no problem," Kimi replied and motioned to the living room. "Have a seat. Can I get you something to drink?"

"Just a glass of water would do," Charlene calmly responded.

Charlene slowly walked into the living room and took a seat on the sofa. Kimi headed to the kitchen and returned with a tall glass. She handed the cold water to Charlene and watched her as she took a long gulp like she'd been stranded in the dessert for weeks. Kimi almost felt sorry for her as the woman struggled to keep her calm.

Kimi sat down directly across from the sofa. "So what's on your mind, Mrs. Bowser," she calmly asked.

"Please don't call me that," Charlene grumbled. She finished up the water and glanced at Kimi. "I won't be Mrs. Anyone soon enough. You can call me Charlene."

Kimi twisted her face at the statement. She had no clue what Charlene was talking about, and dropped her eyes to the yellow envelope again.

"You know how I met my husband?" Charlene whispered.

"No I don't," Kimi quickly responded and gave Charlene a strange glare.

"Of course, you don't," Charlene uttered with an embarrassed smile. "How would you know, right?"

"Right," Kimi blurted.

"I was on my way back home from a business trip for my company." Charlene took another drink of water and continued speaking. "This was almost fifteen years ago. I was so tired when I was on that flight. But I was sitting next to this man that would not shut his mouth. He kept talking to me, trying to make small conversation ,but I would not give him the time of day. For almost the whole flight, he kept waking me up and flirting with me. Don't get me wrong, he was a handsome man. But for some reason, he was not making a breakthrough."

Kimi looked around her house for a moment. She had no clue why Charlene was telling her the story, or why she was even at her house today. Kimi decided not to say a word to find out where Charlene was going with her story.

"So about two hours into the flight, he finally let me get some sleep," Charlene continued. "And I was out like a newborn baby. Then all of a sudden, we started hitting turbulence. The plane started bouncing up and down in the air like a goddamn yo-yo. We were falling like five feet at a time, and it scared the devil out of me. Everybody on the plane was yelling and panicking. I looked over to the man who wouldn't shut up, and he was calm as a cucumber. He looked over to me and gave me a sure expression, like he knew we were going to make it out of the storm. We dropped another five feet, and everybody screamed again-everyone except for the handsome man next to me. He grabbed my hand, and I swear it was like a light bulb exploded in my mind. I really don't know how to describe it. It was almost like we had a connection from a thousand years ago. My heart calmed down, and I wasn't scared no more. The man held my hand for the entire flight home, and 'til this day I have never let him go."

Kimi looked over to Charlene and noticed that she was very emotional. The story touched both of the women, and the living room fell silent. Kimi didn't know what to say.

"I have stuck by Raymond through everything, and I always get upset when somebody is too close to him," Charlene said. She gave Kimi a serious look. "And lately I have learned something scary about myself. I've come to

194

the conclusion that I will kill for my man." Kimi closed her mouth and gave Charlene a serious expression. She noticed Charlene's demeanor was becoming cold and very stiff. Charlene's tone dropped as she continued to speak. "Raymond has been coming up here to Shady Meadows about five times a month, and I couldn't figure out why, Kimi. His boss lives up here, and I just figured he was coming up here to see Niko. Until I found out that you lived up here too."

Kimi readjusted in her chair and returned the hard stare back to Charlene.

"So what are you saying?" Kimi asked.

"Look at you, Kimi. You're young, attractive, and single," Charlene responded. "I figured Raymond was coming up here to see you, and when I saw how the both of you were carrying on at Desiree's dinner, I figured something crazy was going on."

"Charlene, there is nothing between me and your husband," Kimi said, defending herself.

"I know that, Kimi," Charlene said with a cold tone. "Please let me finish."

"Okay," Kimi whispered.

"I was so tired of my husband lying to me every week, so I hired a private investigator to follow him and see what the hell was going on," Charlene said. "And I was right. Raymond is definitely cheating on me."

Charlene handed Kimi the large envelope and sat back on the sofa. Her eyes were filling with water and Kimi didn't know what to think.

"Open it up," Charlene said.

Kimi turned the envelope around and peeled it open. She pulled out ten black and white photos and stared at them. Kimi's mouth fell open as she thumbed through the images.

"Jesus Christ, Charlene," Kimi gasped.

The shocking images made Kimi twist her face. Kimi couldn't believe she was looking at pictures of Raymond and her next-door neighbor, Desiree, together. The private investigator had caught them both in action, not only at Desiree's house ,but there were pictures of them leaving hotels and restaurants throughout the area. Kimi continued to stare at the photos for a few more minutes. She couldn't believe her eyes.

"So, Desiree is cheating with your husband?" Kimi gasped.

"Can you believe that fucking bastard?" Charlene groaned. Kimi could sense the venom in her words.

"I'm so sorry about this, Charlene," Kimi whispered.

"No you're not," Charlene fired back.

Kimi quickly looked up from the pictures and peered at Charlene. Her face had changed, and Kimi couldn't recognize the expression.

"What?" Kimi uttered.

"When I hired the private investigator, I hired him to follow you and my husband," Charlene said. She wiped her mouth in frustration before she spoke again.

"I told you Charlene," Kimi blurted. "There is-"

"Nothing going on with you and my husband," Charlene snapped and finished up Kimi's sentence. "I know you're not cheating with Raymond. But I do know that you are cheating with Niko."

A cold chill rushed though Kimi when the words fell out of Charlene's mouth. For a moment, Kimi felt the room spinning around, and she almost rushed to the kitchen to get herself a tall glass of cold water. She looked over to Charlene, whose eyes seemed to be staring right through her.

"I don't know what you are talking about," Kimi said.

"Sure you do," Charlene quickly responded. "Believe me, this private investigator is good. And he got a lot of pictures of you. I have to be honest, Kimi. Sneaking Niko into your house in the back of your car was very clever," Charlene said.

Kimi closed her mouth and stared at Charlene. Kimi was busted. There was nothing more she could say to defend herself. The living room fell silent again, and Kimi sat back in her chair. She didn't know what to say.

"Don't worry, Kimi. I really don't give a shit what you do with Niko," Charlene said. "My problem is not with you. My problem is with that dirty whore, Desiree. I can't believe she is always smiling in my face, and that bitch was fucking Raymond the whole time." Charlene was beyond upset. The temperature in the living room seemed to raise a few degrees with Charlene's last statement.

"So why are you telling me all of this?" Kimi asked.

"I'm going to get this bitch back," Charlene threatened as she pointed across the street. "I don't know how yet, but as God is my witness, I'm going to make this bitch pay for destroying my marriage."

Kimi looked at Charlene and kept her eyes fixed on her. Charlene's threats were serious, and Kimi sensed that she meant business. The house fell silent again. Kimi didn't want to speak.

"You know I brought a gun up here to confront this bitch today?" Charlene callously revealed as her face turned to stone. She glared at Kimi for a moment. Her eyes became eerily dull. "I was about to go to her house, knock on her door, and blow her fucking brains against the wall."

Kimi's heart started beating out of her chest as she listened to Charlene and her threats. The fire in her words was real, and Kimi froze as she continued to listen to Charlene vent.

"I'm telling you, Kimi, this bitch really don't know how close she came to getting it." Charlene dropped her head. "Something told me that today was not the day to do it, so I didn't. Instead, I came over here to talk to you."

Without warning, Charlene stood to her feet. Kimi quickly responded by standing up with her. She didn't know what to expect from Charlene, so she stared at her.

"Relax, Kimi," Charlene uttered with an uneven smile. "I'm getting ready to leave. I just wanted you to know that I know what's going on up here. I do have the pictures at my house, and, as long as you help me, I won't say a word."

"Help you do what?" Kimi quickly asked.

"I don't know yet," Charlene responded with a hard expression. "But I'm going to get this bitch back real soon, and I might need your help. Don't refuse me when I come calling."

Charlene grabbed the photos from Kimi's hands. She pulled out a pen and wrote her number on the back of one of the photos, and then handed it to Kimi. Charlene put the rest of the images back in the yellow envelope, and then slowly headed to the door. Kimi followed closely behind her. She opened the front door for Charlene and watched as she walked outside.

"I don't have to tell you to keep this conversation between me and you, right?" Charlene asked.

Kimi nodded her head.

"Good girl. Just remember what I told you. This is going to happen real soon, so look out for my call."

Kimi didn't say a word. She just gave Charlene another quick nod and closed the door. She heard Charlene fire up the engine to her car and speed away. Kimi had to take a seat on her sofa and think for a moment. She looked at the photo of Raymond and Desiree, and started to feel dizzy. She couldn't believe what was happening. Now that Charlene knew about her and Niko, it wouldn't take long for Desiree to find out. Her heart raced as she thought about the consequences and what it could mean for Niko's career. Kimi stood up and grabbed her coat. She wanted to call Niko and give him the devastating news ,but she knew this was something that needed to be handled in person. She looked at her watch, and then rushed to her BMW. Kimi put the photo under her seat and quickly headed downtown to Newark.

*J*wenty-*J*hree

The inside of Marcel's truck was dead silent as he drove through the Newark streets. His mind was speeding faster than the SUV as he made his way to Weequahic Park to meet with Erick. Marcel tried his best to keep his mind clear ,but his ruthless thoughts were focused on how to bring the pain to Khalil. Marcel made sure to pack enough guns and bullets, anticipating a mini-war with whoever stood in his way. His heart pumped with everything except fear. He was driven by vengeance, and there was no turning back now. As Marcel's vehicle turned into the entrance to the park, he felt relieved when he saw Erick standing next to his car, awaiting his arrival.

"My nigga, you're right on time," Erick shouted as Marcel parked directly behind him. He walked to Marcel's truck and opened the passenger side door.

"What's good, homie?" Marcel asked as Erick got inside the truck.

"I can't call it, my dude. Just ready to make this move," Erick responded.

"So, is this nigga still downtown?"

"He's still there," Erick quickly said. "But, my nigga, you must be rollin' with an angel on ya shoulders."

"What?" Marcel snapped as he turned to Erick. "Why you say that?"

"Man, some ill shit went down last night, and a lot of niggas got moved around. So right now, it's only Khalil down there with two other dudes."

"So it's just the three of them?" Marcel blurted. "Are you sure?"

"Last time I checked," Erick continued. "And these other dudes they got down there are some pussy niggas. You won't have a big problem with them. But they all got heat, so I don't know how you gonna handle this."

"Don't worry about that shit. I got this. What's the address?" Marcel asked.

"One oh seven Orchard Street," Erick uttered. Marcel looked away and started to think. "You not gonna write it down, my nigga?" Erick quickly asked.

"Nah, trust me, I won't forget it," Marcel answered. He reached down under his seat and pulled out a brown paper bag. He tossed the bag to Erick, and then fired up the engine to the truck.

Erick looked in the bag and discovered three large stacks of money. He quickly closed the package and looked around the park. "So when you gonna handle that?" Erick mumbled.

"I'm on my way over there ," Marcel uttered. "I got one more stop to make and it's on."

"In broad daylight?" Erick gasped.

"Motherfuckin' right," Marcel barked. "He did my niece dirty while the sun was still shinin', so I figured I can return the fuckin' favor."

Erick's face froze as he looked into Marcel's eyes. Marcel's piercing glare confirmed that Marcel meant business. He was ready for war, and Erick read it all over his face.

"Okay, my nigga, be careful and don't forget what I said," Erick continued. "They all got heat in that spot, so don't run up in there tryin' to be Rambo."

Marcel simply nodded his head and gave Erick a

pound. Erick got out of the truck and headed back to his car. Marcel slammed his SUV into gear. He didn't hesitate for another moment. His truck sped out of Weequahic Park in a rush. Marcel turned his focus to the DVD in his pocket. He grabbed his phone and quickly called Kimi.

*

A few miles away, Kimi's heart was racing out of control as she sped down the New Jersey Turnpike. She had been trying to call her friend Niko for the past hour ,but he was not picking up his phone. Kimi's mind raced with flashbacks of the incriminating photos Charlene had shown her of Raymond and Desiree. After a dozen failed attempts, Kimi grew tired of waiting for Niko to answer the phone. She decided to head down to the Stanton Firm to find him. Kimi needed to see him right away. She looked over to the passenger seat, and then grimaced at the photo. She couldn't believe Raymond was sleeping with Desiree. She just knew Niko was going to flip when he found out. Kimi picked up her phone again and tried to call him. Before she could dial the number, her cell buzzed with an incoming call. It was Marcel.

"Hey," Kimi quickly answered.

"Where are you?" Marcel asked. He sounded like he was out of breath.

"Damn Marcel, I totally forgot about meeting up with you." Kimi grabbed her forehead. "Where are you?"

"I'll be in front of King's Restaurant in about five minutes," Marcel responded.

"Okay. I will be there in ten." Kimi looked at her watch. She increased the speed of the BMW as she approached her exit. "I don't have long, but I will come straight to you ."

"Please do," Marcel uttered. "I need to make something happen like yesterday."

"Okay, I'll meet you in the front," Kimi assured.

"Okay, see you then."

Kimi disconnected the call, then quickly scrolled down to Niko's number. She looked at her watch again, and then realized that she was racing against time. She selected Niko's name and called him again, praying that he would pick up the phone.

*

Just two miles away in the ironbound section of Newark, Niko pulled up in front of a large office building near Market Street. He parked his Audi A8 directly in front of the building. He looked up and read the large chiseled sign on the side of the structure. THE CALL & RESPONSE - REGIONAL HEADQUARTERS. Niko couldn't help but think of all the time he'd spent consulting people from the program. Niko had been visiting this building once a month for the past two years ,but this particular visit was going to be his toughest one yet. Niko was here today to deliver some bad news, and he felt reluctant to go through with it. He had spent most of his morning speaking with his clients and making plans to assign their cases to other defense attorneys. Before the walls were to come tumbling down at the Stanton Law Firm, Niko wanted to make sure all of his clients and old friends were well taken care of.

As Niko got out of his car, he took a deep breath and prepared himself to see one of his favorite clients. But before he could walk into the building, his phone started ringing in his coat pocket. Niko scrambled for the phone and quickly answered the call.

"Hello."

"Baby, it's me," Kimi shouted from the other line. "Where are you?"

"Huh…I'm downtown. I'm about to visit one of my last clients for the day," Niko stuttered.

"Baby, we need to talk," Kimi shouted.

"What happened?" Niko's voice grew high with concern. He pushed the phone closer to his ear. "Are you okay?"

"Baby, I have to show you something, and it can't wait. This is serious." Kimi's tone was fearful, and her voice made Niko's adrenaline kick in.

"What's going on, Kimi?" Niko shouted. "Where are you?"

"I'm headed to Clinton Avenue."

"In Newark?"

"Yes," Kimi responded. "I have to make one more stop, and then we need to talk."

"Okay, let me take care of my last client, and then I can meet you back at the firm."

"No!" Kimi yelled. An image of Raymond's face popped into her mind. "Not at the firm!"

"Huh? Why not?" Niko shouted. He was beyond confused. Kimi's worried voice had him on pins and needles, and he didn't know what to think.

"Baby, just trust me," Kimi said. "Let's meet at the parking garage in twenty minutes. And I will show you everything then."

"No problem, but are you sure you're alright?" Niko quickly asked.

"Yes, baby," Kimi responded. "Just make sure you meet me there in twenty minutes. I got to go."

Before Niko could respond, the phone went dead. Niko dropped his eyebrows. His heart was still racing, and he tried to figure out why Kimi was bouncing off the walls.

Niko turned his attention back to the entrance of the office building, and then tried to calm his nerves. He walked into the lobby, then made his way to his destination. He entered two large double doors and was greeted by a lively receptionist.

"Good morning, Mr. Stanton." The receptionist smiled.

"Good morning," Niko uttered.

"I will buzz Mr. Wakefield for you right away ,sir." The receptionist gave Niko a pleasant gesture and picked up her phone. She buzzed her boss, and then informed him that Niko was waiting for him in the lobby. Niko turned around and was just about to take a seat, when he heard a loud voice call out his name.

"Niko Stanton…!" the male voice yelled. "What are you doing down here today? I thought we meet on the fifth of every month, right?"

Niko turned around and was greeted by the smiling face of Tycen Wakefield. Tycen was the department chief of the Call & Response program, as well as the newly elected West Ward Councilman. After almost ten years of building a career in social work, Tycen decided it was time to expand his scope. The Call & Response program had grown tremendously over the last few years, and Tycen's hard work was rewarded when he decided he wanted to pursue a career in politics. Tycen won the West Ward seat in a landslide, and he was slowly becoming a political star in the city. Despite the fact that his schedule was air tight, Tycen always had time for an old friend. When Niko reached out and requested a meeting, Tycen cleared his scheduled, eager to find out what was on Niko' mind.

"How are you, brother man?" Tycen asked with his signature smile.

"I've seen better days," Niko responded.

"Let's talk in my office." Tycen motioned for Niko to follow him, and the men headed down a short hallway. Tycen walked through a large metal door, and then motioned for Niko to have a seat.

As Tycen walked around to the back of his desk,

Niko looked around the lavish office space. Photos of Tycen's election run to councilman were plastered all over the room with newspaper clippings of his victory. Niko felt proud of his old friend, and looked over to him.

"It's still hard for me to say it out loud." A small grin came to Niko's face. "Councilman…Tycen…Wakefield."

"I still can't believe it myself." Tycen smirked. "I'm waiting for someone to come in here and snap me out of my dream."

"Well, you deserve it brother. You worked hard." Niko nodded as he continued to look around the office. He noticed a picture of Tycen with a tall and very attractive woman. She had both arms wrapped around his waist as they posed for the photo. "So are you still with that insanely beautiful woman you introduced me to last year?"

"I am." Tycen nodded his head with a proud smile.

"What was her name again? Niko asked as he closed his eyes for a moment. "I remember she had a white girl name or something like that."

"Heidi Kachina," Tycen said and let out a small chuckle. "Everybody says the same thing about her name when I say it."

"As they should," Niko joked. "You don't see too many black women in Newark named Heidi."

Both men laughed, and Tycen shook his head. Niko chuckled for another minute, and then reached into his briefcase. He shuffled through some paperwork and handed Tycen a small folder.

"What's this?" Tycen asked as the mood in the room started to shift back to business.

"That is a list of good defense attorneys in Essex County," Niko said, leaning back in his chair. He slowly put his hand on his chin. "I will no longer be available to represent the members of your Call and Response program, Tycen. I'm sorry."

"What's this about, Niko?" Tycen asked as he looked up from the folder. "What happened?"

"Tycen, I'm not going to sit here and paint myself as the victim in all of this," Niko said and let out a loud gasp. He slowly shook his head and gave Tycen a deep stare. "Let's just say that I made some really bad decisions and let power and greed go to my head." Tycen didn't say a word. He listened as his friend continued speaking. "My firm is being investigated, and sooner or later the story is going to break in the paper. I've decided to shut down my firm indefinitely and move on."

"My goodness, Niko. That is….wow…I didn't expect you to say that," Tycen uttered. He was virtually speechless. Tycen looked down at the list of lawyers, then rubbed his forehead. He didn't know what to say.

"It's really for the best," Niko uttered. "I have some money saved, and I'm planning to move to another state and make a fresh start. So who knows, maybe I can be a respectable lawyer again one day." An uneven smile came to Niko's face.

"Damn. I must say that this is really coming at a bad time, Niko," Tycen said.

"Why is that?" Niko questioned.

Tycen looked around for a minute and put the papers down. He folded his arms on his desk and leaned forward as if he was trying to tell Niko a secret. "No one knows about my plans yet, but I am seriously considering making a run at Gary Banks," Tycen revealed.

"For mayor?" Niko gasped and smiled across the table. "You are about to run for mayor?"

"I haven't made a decision yet ,but I am leaning toward a yes." Tycen nodded his head with confidence. "I was writing down a list of people I needed for my campaign, and your name was at the top of my list."

An uncomfortable silence fell over the room. What should have been an exciting announcement for Tycen was short lived by the news of Niko's fall from grace. An ugly feeling came over Niko as the magnitude of his mistakes started to mount in his mind. He felt bad that he wouldn't be able to join the campaign. Niko realized that he would be a political liability to Tycen the minute his investigation was announced. Niko pressed his lips together and forced a smile to come to his face.

"Tycen, you will do just fine without me," Niko uttered. "Trust me, they love you here in Newark. And if there is anything I can do to help you from the sidelines, you just let me know."

"I sure will," Tycen said.

He noticed the uncomfortable look in Niko's eyes, and he decided not to press the issue. Niko stood up and prepared himself to leave. Tycen followed suit and extended his hand to his old friend.

"Life is crazy," Niko uttered. "Just when I was trying to get used to calling you Councilman, now I have to fix my mouth to call you Mayor Wakefield. "

Niko and Tycen exchanged pleasant smiles. Niko gave him a firm handshake and left his office. As Niko headed out of the building, his mind switched to Kimi. Niko checked his watch and noticed that he still had plenty of time to make it to the parking garage to find out what was bothering his friend.

Meanwhile, back on Clinton Avenue, Marcel was standing in the snow next to his truck. He had been staring at his phone for the past five minutes and growing more impatient by the second. Despite the freezing temperature outside, Marcel's body was on fire. He'd spent the past twenty minutes contemplating what he was going to do once he finally made it down to Orchard Street. Before he could think any longer about Khalil, he noticed Kimi's X5 speeding up Clinton Avenue. He watched her as she carefully parked in back of his truck, then jumped out of her vehicle. Marcel couldn't get out two words before Kimi was all over him. She gave him a huge hug and looked at him.

"Marcel, are you okay?" Kimi whined. "You know I am so sorry about Sabrina. I really am. Is there anything you need? Is everybody okay?"

"Everything's cool," Marcel calmly uttered.

Kimi looked at his tired eyes and sensed that Marcel was hurting. He tried to put on a strong face for Kimi, but she could tell that Marcel was going through a lot.

"Are you sure you're okay?" Kimi asked. "If you need to talk, I have a few minutes."

"No everything is fine, Kimi," Marcel lied. "I just wanted you to have this."

Marcel reached into his coat and pulled out the DVD. He slowly handed it to Kimi and gave her a blank stare.

"Why are you giving this to me?" Kimi quietly asked.

"I really don't know." Marcel gave her an honest expression. "I don't care about the money no more. All I know is that my niece died because of that goddamn video, so I figured you would be smart enough to know what to do with it."

"Okay, Marcel," Kimi said, putting the DVD in her jacket pocket. She gave Marcel a deep glance, trying to read him. Marcel looked away, not wanting her to pick up on the evil thoughts that swirled in his mind. "Are you going to be okay, Marcel?" Kimi asked again.

"Yes," Marcel uttered. "I just need to take care of one more thing."

His words were cold as the wind whipping though the neighborhood. Kimi knew better than to believe that everything was fine with Marcel. She knew how his mind worked. Marcel was not going to sit by while somebody got away with murdering his niece. She moved closer to Marcel and gave him a tight hug. She even surprised her old friend with a small kiss on his cheek. Marcel looked at her and she noticed that his eyes were slightly emotional.

"Whatever you are thinking about doing, Marcel, just know that there are people that care for you and depend on you," Kimi tried to appeal to something deeper in her friend.

"I know, Kimi," Marcel continued. "That's why I gotta do what I have gotta do and get this shit over with."

Kimi closed her mouth and nodded toward Marcel.

"Just be careful," Kimi uttered.

"I will."

Marcel turned around and headed back to his truck. Kimi watched him for a moment as he jumped inside the SUV and started his engine. He quickly pulled off, and Kimi strained her eyes trying to get one last look at her friend before he disappeared down the snowy street. Kimi tried to shake the feeling, but something deep inside her revealed to her that there was a strong possibility that she would never see Marcel again.

Twenty-Four

Fifteen minutes later, Marcel found himself on Orchard Street near downtown Newark. His adrenaline was rushing uncontrollably through his body, and his mind was hyped. Marcel was focused on handling his business. He circled the block a few times, taking a mental note of everything that was going on in the quiet neighborhood. There were only three houses on the small street, and Marcel realized why the Marquez boys chose that area for one of their stash houses.

107 Orchard Street almost resembled an abandoned building. The old structure was only two floors and was protected by two vacant lots on both sides of the house. There was limited traffic on the desolate street, and Marcel knew this would be a perfect location to end his drama with Khalil.

Marcel circled the block one last time, and then pulled over near the edge of the street. He made sure to park his truck facing away from the house, and kept an eye on it from the rearview mirror. Marcel reached under his seat and grabbed his gun. He checked the clip and made sure he was fully loaded for the impending battle. He racked his brain for the next few minutes and tried to figure out the best way to get inside. Erick's words echoed in his mind about the guns and drugs that were inside the stash house. Marcel quickly abandoned the idea of an ambush, fearing that he would be cut down the minute he tried to break into the house. Marcel had to come up with something clever if he was going to confront

Khalil. He looked around the quiet street searching for a spark that would open up his mind.

A few minutes later, Marcel heard a slight crash just around the corner. He was clearly jumpy this morning, and felt compelled to investigate the noise. He put his truck in gear and slowly drove around the corner. He noticed a restaurant worker walking out the back of the local pizza shop. The short Italian man tossed a few bags of trash inside of a larger garbage can. Without warning, the worker banged on the side of another trash can with a small stick. The loud banging blared throughout the neighborhood. Marcel dropped his eyebrows as the man continued to bang on the side of the can. *What the hell is he doing?* Marcel thought . The worker angrily knocked on the trashcan again and tipped it over. All of a sudden, a family of rats fled from the garbage can in a rush. The worker scrambled, then grabbed a handful of rocks. He started throwing the stones at the scampering rodents. The worker didn't stop until he hit a few of the rats with the rocks. A devilish smile came to Marcel's face as he looked at the comical scene. An idea lit up in his mind. Marcel twisted his face and knew what he had to do. He slammed his truck back into gear and drove off the block. He was eager to put the impious plan into motion.

*

A few miles away, in the basement of a vacant parking garage, Kimi sped around the corner and looked at her watch. She knew she was running late to meet with Niko, and was hoping he didn't leave. The tires of her X5 came to a screeching halt when Kimi saw her friend's Audi parked in the corner. Niko got out of his car and walked over to her. His face was beyond stressed, and Kimi didn't recognize his body language. She turned off her SUV and got out to greet Niko.

"Kimi, what is going on?" Niko groaned as he

approached her.

There was a mix of anger and concern plastered all over his face. Kimi didn't say a word. She rushed over to her friend and hugged him. Kimi gave Niko a deep kiss on his lips.

"Baby, I need to tell you something," Kimi whispered. She pulled away from his face and looked into his eyes. She felt remorseful for him. Kimi almost felt herself about to boil over with emotion. "Baby, please believe me, I'm not happy about telling you this. I'm so scared ."

"Okay," Niko uttered. He was burning with anticipation.

"Baby, please don't be mad at me for telling you this."

"Telling me what?" Niko snapped. "What the hell is going on?"

Niko's tone made Kimi retreat for a moment. Her mind raced for another second and she slowly wiped her face. Kimi walked back to her car and opened the passenger side door. She reluctantly snatched the black and white photo from the seat, and then walked back to Niko. His face tightened with curiously as he looked at his friend.

"Charlene came by the house today." Kimi tightened her jaw.

"Charlene?" Niko uttered. "Bowser?"

"Yes, baby. She gave me this." Kimi slowly lifted her arm and handed Niko the photo.

"What the hell is this?" Niko blurted. He raised the image to his face, and then took a long and hard look at it.

Niko's entire world came to a violent halt. His face froze like a bronze statue as he stared at the evidence of betrayal. Niko was so stunned. His body felt like somebody had walked up behind him and snatched out his spine. His eyes slowly turned red with fury. Kimi covered her mouth, almost busting into tears as she watched her friend's face turn to sheer hatred.

"Is this real?" Niko grunted like a wounded bear.

"Baby, I'm so sorry," Kimi whined.

"Is this fuckin' real?" Niko shouted. His ferocious voice echoed throughout the vacant parking garage.

"Niko…baby…it's real," Kimi stuttered. She'd never saw him so angry.

"THIS MOTHERFUCKER!" Niko roared and tightly clinched his fist. "I can't believe this fuckin' snake!" Niko turned around and furiously punched the brick wall.

"Niko…!" Kimi screamed and rushed over to him. Niko's body was so enraged that he didn't feel the pain. Kimi grabbed his arms and stopped him before he could do any more damage . "Baby, please calm down," Kimi yelled.

"Fuck that, I'm gonna kill him!" Niko cried out. "That motherfuckin' snake is dead!" Niko pulled away from Kimi and stomped toward his car. Kimi tried to stop him and convince him to calm down ,but her pleading fell on deaf ears.

"Baby, wait a minute, please…!" Kimi shouted.

Niko hurried to his car like a mad man. He'd never felt so jealous in his life. The hot rage rushed through his body, and all Niko could see was red. He didn't know who to confront first; his cheating wife or Raymond Bowser. Niko could barely see straight as he climbed into his car. Kimi continued to yell his name,but his ears were clogged by his fury. He fired up the engine, and Kimi continued to yell.

"Niko, please. Don't leave…!" Kimi shouted as she rushed over to the car.

Niko backed out of his parking space and slammed the car back into gear. He was just about to tear out of the parking garage when Kimi made a desperate move. She jumped in front of the Audi and forced Niko to stop. Her eyes were filled with tears and the look of horror on her face forced him to acknowledge her.

"Niko, I'm not moving....!" Kimi pleaded.

"Get the fuck out the way!" Niko barked.

"No, baby, please don't leave!" She yelled.

"I'm serious! I will run your ass over . Get the fuck out the way!" Niko continued to shout at Kimi ,but she didn't budge. She knew he was uncontrollably livid, and she feared the worse would happen if he left the parking garage.

"Baby, I can't move. You are upset," Kimi yelled. "We need to talk about this. Just calm down."

"There is nothing to talk about," Niko shouted from the car. "That motherfucker is dead!"

"No, Niko." Kimi vehemently shook her head. "Baby, look at me. Please don't leave. I can't lose you, Niko. Please!"

Her words shot through Niko's ears, and hit him directly in his heart. He glanced at Kimi's crying face and his mouth fell open. Her emotional outburst calmed him down just enough to make him aware of his own wrath. Kimi and Niko stared at each other for what seemed to be an emotional hour. Kimi wiped the tears away from her face.

"Baby...let's just talk about this, please," Kimi whispered.

Niko's face momentarily softened as Kimi continued to plead with him. She slowly raised her hands in the air as if to tell Niko to take it easy. He balled up his lips and tried to calm himself down as Kimi slowly walked around to the passenger side of the Audi. She carefully opened the door and sat in the car with Niko as he continued to stare straight ahead. The silence in the car was eerie. The only thing Kimi could hear was the humming of the engine and Niko's uneven breathing. She looked over to her friend and slowly started rubbing his shoulder. Niko was hurting badly. She had never seen her friend this way, and it affected her like never before. She started to feel angry inside as Niko continued to break down next to her. She could read it all over his face. Niko was experiencing a roller coaster ride of emotions.

"That fuckin' bitch!" Niko yelled in the car. He tried to hold back his jealousy ,but he couldn't contain it anymore. He punched the dashboard and yelled again to the top of his lungs. "That fuckin'…BITCH…!" Niko repeated. His anger was contagious as Kimi found herself fuming too. She continued to rub on Niko's shoulder in an effort to calm him.

"I'm gonna fuckin' kill them…!" he announced.

"What?" Kimi uttered and looked away from Niko. There was something very serious about his threat.

"Both of them!" Niko blurted. "They are fuckin' dead!" Kimi never noticed it before, but Niko was crying. His eyes became so flooded with tears that they started to trickle down his face. "How the fuck could Raymond do this to me?" His voice cracked with anger.

"Baby, don't talk like that," Kimi pleaded. "You have to calm down."

"Fuck that…and fuck him!" Niko shouted. "I invited that piece of shit into my house, and he fucking betrays me like this. It's not enough that he wants my fuckin' firm, now he wants my fuckin' wife?"

Kimi raised her eyebrows and turned back to Niko. His revelations were shocking. Niko continued to yell ,but Kimi was stuck on his last statement.

"Wait, baby. What do you mean about Raymond wanting your firm?" Kimi quickly asked.

"He's fucking working with Leon's son to set me up," Niko responded in frustration. "That's why I have to shut my firm down. Raymond is trying to get me out so he can take over."

"Oh shit," Kimi gasped as she finally realized the scope

of Raymond's treachery. Another revelation flashed into her mind and she turned back to Niko. "So it's a possibility that Desiree is helping him?" she asked.

"You fuckin' right, she's helping him!" Niko yelled. "That bitch is probably the one that set the whole shit up from the beginning."

Kimi couldn't believe what she was hearing. The web of lies and deceit was becoming stickier by the second. Niko looked down at the photo again and slowly shook his head.

"I can't believe this shit," Niko whispered.

The car fell silent once again. Kimi's mind was racing out of control and her heart started pounding out of her chest. She looked at Niko again and saw that he was sobbing. Kimi reached over and grabbed him with both arms.

"Baby, look at me," Kimi whispered.

She reached up and kissed his broken face. She hated to see him so weak,but she knew Niko was hurting. "What do you want?" Kimi asked with a stern expression.

Although her eyes were filled with water, Niko could sense something cold emerging in them. "What?" Niko mumbled through his tears.

"Tell me what you want," Kimi repeated. "Niko… what do you want….right now?"

"I…um…I want to fuck Raymond up. That's what I want," Niko uttered. The words caused his face to stiffen with anger.

"How bad?" Kimi whispered. Her cold stare froze Niko for a moment.

"I want to fuck him up real bad," Niko said. He thought about the photo again. The images of Raymond fucking Desiree flashed into his mind. The thought infuriated Niko. "I want to fuck him up until I kill him…!" he soullessly whispered.

"And what about her?" Kimi asked.

She gave Niko another deep glance. Niko looked away from Kimi and tried to avoid the question. Kimi never blinked an eye as she gently grabbed the side of Niko's face.

"Hey...baby, I'm serious," Kimi whispered. "It's just you and me in this car . Nobody else." Kimi looked deeply into his eyes. She was feeling his pain like they were Siamese twins. "Baby, the other night when I told you I would do anything for you, I meant that. I always wanted to be the one to make you happy. And I never wanted to be the one to make you feel any pain." Niko quietly listened as Kimi continued to speak. "I always told myself that if you was ever hurt, I wanted to be the one to take the pain away. No matter who or where that pain came from, I wanted to be the one to take it away. No matter what...!"

Niko didn't know what to say as he looked at Kimi. Her expression was cold and very direct.

"What are you saying, Kimi?" Niko whispered. For the first time since he met her, Kimi had made him nervous. Her eyes cut though him, and her face was almost sinister.

"Baby, it's a simple question. I don't want you to tell me what to do Niko," Kimi responded in a low tone. "Just tell me what you want." Kimi picked up the black and white photo and showed it to Niko. He studied it again like it was his first time seeing it. More images of Desiree's indiscretions flashed into his mind, and Niko felt another shot of rage boil in his stomach. He looked back to Kimi and gave her a cold look.

"I want both of them dead," Niko whispered.

The words slid out of his mouth like hot venom. Even with tears in his eyes, Kimi could see the pain in Niko's face and hear the agony in his voice. She nodded her head and gave Niko a slow kiss on his lips. She rubbed the back of his head and calmed him down. The tense mood in the car started to fade, and Kimi wiped away the tears on his cheek. She gave him another soft kiss, then forced a small smile to her face.

"Don't worry about a thing, baby," Kimi whispered and looked at Niko. "I will make it all better."

*

Back on Orchard Street, Marcel eased his truck down to a slow creep. He kept his eyes fixed on the stash house as he circled the area one last time. The empty street was still quiet, and Marcel knew that now was the time to do what he needed to and handle his business with Khalil. Marcel parked his truck at the end of the block and shut off the engine. His mind was clouded with revenge, and he took a moment to calm his racing heart down. He slowly took a deep breath as images of his niece's face motivated him to carry out his plan. Marcel turned around and stared at six bottles of the 151 Proof Bacardi Rum. He scowled at the sight, and then proceeded to wrap each bottle top with a thick wad of toilet tissue. After wrapping the final bottle, he didn't waste another moment. He jumped out of his truck and stomped through the snow. His face tightened with anger as he got closer to the stash house. He pulled out his cigarette lighter and set fire to the first bottle. There was no turning back now.

Meanwhile, inside the stash house, an eerie feeling came over Khalil as he walked out of the bathroom. He wiped his face and headed into the living room where two men were relaxing on a broken sofa and playing a video game. Khalil looked around the filthy area and shook his head.

"I can't believe you motherfuckers are still at it," Khalil barked as he sat on the sofa next to a brown skinned man with long dreads.

Even though Khalil had been staying with the men for the past few days, he clearly had no love for them. The men lived like slobs, and Khalil hated the fact that he had to stay with them until things calmed down on the streets. The stash house was in bad shape, and neither one of the men made an attempt to keep it clean. Piles of trash and rotting food were

219

scattered everywhere in the house, and it smelled more like a landfill than a residence. Khalil resented the disgusting men, and gave them a hard way to go every chance he could.

Despite the fact that the men were hired by the Marquez boys to protect the stash house, Khalil had no respect for the so-called killers. He even refused to call them by their street names. The brown skinned man with the dreads reminded him of a reggae artist so Khalil called him Bob Marley. The younger man was light skinned and dressed more like a pop singer than a gangster. Khalil couldn't resist the urge to call him Chris Brown. The men hated the nicknames, but they were clearly scared of Khalil. They knew of his reputation and avoided any confrontation with him.

Khalil watched with disgust as the two men engaged in a competitive video game of NBA Live. They were both yelling at the television when Khalil decided to break up the fun. Without warning, he snatched the game controller from Bob, who shot him a rough look.

"What the fuck man?" Bob yelled.

"Shut the hell up, and let me try this shit," Khalil barked. He flicked a few buttons on the controller and shook his head. "I don't see what all the hype is about. This shit is corny," Khalil joked.

Bob looked over to Khalil. He was tempted to snatch the controller back ,but he was too scared. He stood up from the couch, and then walked into the bathroom. Khalil blew him off and turned his concentration to Chris, who was sitting on the other side of the sofa.

"I can't believe y'all play this shit all day. This type of shit is for losers," Khalil said with a crooked smile.

Chris didn't respond to him. He kept his focus on the game, not taking the bait. A few seconds later, Chris put the game on pause. Khalil looked at him and dropped his eyebrows.

"Do you smell that?" Chris quietly asked.

"What?" Khalil blurted. "It's probably all of this trash."

"Nah, my nigga. It smells like smoke," Chris reported.

Both men looked around the room as the house fell silent. They started sniffing around, and the aroma of the smoke started to get stronger. Khalil stood up and looked at Chris.

"What the fuck is that smell?" Khalil asked as he intensified his search.

"Something is definitely burning," Chris uttered and quickly stood to his feet. He rushed into the kitchen and yelled out for help.

Khalil sprung into the action, and then headed to see what was going on. "What the fuck...!" Khalil gasped.

A huge fireball flamed near the rear of the kitchen. The scorching flames were spreading fast, and Chris rushed over to the sink and tried to put out the fire. Khalil started helping him, and, all of a sudden, he heard a window smashing. Khalil ran out of the kitchen. His heart dropped to the floor when he noticed another large fire erupting in the living room. Khalil looked out the broken window and thought he saw someone running away. Before he could focus his eyes, the sound of another breaking window blared from the opposite side of the house. Another huge fireball exploded, and now both sides of the stash house were set ablaze. Khalil tried to stomp out the fire ,but it was spreading too quickly. All of the garbage on the floors only made the flames spread faster, and, before long, the men found themselves in the middle of a fiery inferno. Bob rushed out of the bathroom to investigate the noise. He almost gagged as the heat and smoke engulfed him.

Chris ran out of the kitchen and yelled at the men. "The whole fuckin' house is on fire," Chris panicked. "I'm outta here."

"What?" Bob shouted. "Wait, I gotta get the dope!" Bob rushed upstairs.

"Fuck that dope. I'm outta here, B!" Chris yelled.

The fire was too much to bear, and Chris fearfully headed for the front door. Khalil looked outside again, trying to make sense of everything before he made a move. Chris jumped over the burning furniture and made a break for the exit. He opened the front door and was just about to rush out onto the front porch when a loud gunshot rang out from the street. Khalil looked over to Chris just in time to see a bullet fly through his left arm. Chris yelled in pain ,but another bullet quickly muted him. Chris took three quick shots to his chest, then stumbled onto the porch and died. Khalil ducked behind the wall in the living room and took a deep breath. He realized it was a set up. Bob rushed down the stairs with a black bag strapped over his shoulders and two guns in his hands.

"Give me a burner…!" Khalil yelled.

"What?" Bob shouted as he made it to the first level.

"Give me a gun!" Khalil repeated the order. "I think somebody is out there."

Bob looked at the front of the house, and then tossed Khalil one of his guns. The fire was spreading fast, and Bob started to panic. He tossed the black bag out of the broken window and started to climb out.

"What are you doin'?" Khalil shouted.

"Fuck that!" Bob yelled. "I'm not getting burned alive in this bitch." Bob forced himself out of the tight window and fell to the ground. Khalil's eyes were fixed on him when he heard another round of gunshots. Bob's body was riddled with bullets. He died before he could even make it to his feet.

"Fuck…!" Khalil yelled. His worse fears were confirmed. There was clearly somebody out there, and they were prepared to kill all of them. Khalil looked around in a panic. He didn't have a lot of options left. He looked at the front door and noticed that it was his only way out. Khalil checked the gun to see how many bullets he had. *Four shots*, Khalil thought, dropping his head. The walls and the ceiling began to buckle under the fire, and the house started to collapse. Another bottle flew through the front door, and a huge fireball exploded near Khalil. The rush of flames threw him to the floor. He yelled out in pain. Khalil had to make a move, and he had to do it now. He crawled on the hot floor for a few feet and made it to the front door.

"Who's out there?" Khalil yelled as he took cover behind the door. He looked back into the living room and realized he didn't have much time. The fire seemed to be creeping toward him like it was alive. Khalil yelled out again ,but there was no answer. He decided it was now or never. He had to face whoever was outside or be burned to a crisp. Khalil bravely stood up and cocked the hammer back on the pistol. He blindly rushed outside and made it to the porch.

Boom. Boom. Boom. Boom.

Khalil fired his pistol the whole time, trying to clear a path for himself. A barrage of return-fire quickly met his four shots. Khalil was struck in the chest and leg. His momentum caused him to stumble onto the porch and down the stairs. His face cracked against the payment, and he was almost knocked unconscious. Khalil moaned in pain as he rolled over onto his back and tried to breathe through his damaged lungs. He heard the pattering of slow footsteps creeping toward him. He looked up, focused his eyes, and almost chuckled when he saw the familiar face.

"I got no words for you," Marcel uttered. "Rest in piss...you fuckin' animal!"

Marcel's voice was low and filled with pain. He ruthlessly raised his gun toward Khalil's chest, and then fired three more shots into Khalil's helpless body. Khalil never stood a chance. Marcel's face froze as he coldly watched Khalil take his final breath.

A loud siren blared from the distance and shook Marcel. He looked around the neighborhood. He had to act fast. Rushing away from the house, he stumbled to his car. Marcel started to feel weak and unconsciously held onto his stomach. He climbed into his truck and pulled off of the block. Marcel thought for a moment, then reached for his phone. A few tears started to trickle from his eyes, and Marcel started to feel the chills. His bloody fingers quickly dialed his friend Tricia, and he waited for her to pick up the phone.

"Hello?" Tricia answered from the other line.

Marcel opened his mouth, but nothing came out. He tried to speak to his friend, but he couldn't. He looked down at his stomach and noticed he was bleeding uncontrollably onto the seat. In all the commotion, he never realized that Khalil had shot him with one of the bullets he'd fired as he rushed out of the burning house.

"Baby, are you there?" Tricia yelled through the phone.

Marcel never heard her. He tried to force himself to breath ,but it was too late. He was dying. His truck drifted into the left lane, and then crashed into a fence. Marcel gripped the phone tighter and tried to speak again. He couldn't.

Tricia continued to yell Marcel's name into the phone. She was crying hysterically as she sensed something was wrong.

Marcel faded, then died.

Twenty-Five

Two Days Later

*A*nd *in local news, what began as an orchestrated rally has become what some are calling the largest demonstration of public unrest since the city's big riot in 1967. People have taken to the streets to protest a surge of violence as another woman has been brutally murdered during a carjacking last night. Reports are coming in that indicate the public unrest is increasing across the city and in Essex County. Community leaders are calling for the resignation of Mayor Banks as conditions around Newark continue to deteriorate. A spokesman from the mayor's office has announced a press conference today at noon. Please stay tuned as more details emerge.*

Kimi slowly turned over and peered at the clock radio on the dresser. The loud news story awoke her from a deep slumber, and Kimi reached out and turned off the alarm. A rush of morning air filled her lungs, and Kimi felt alive. She turned over to a sleeping Niko, and looked at his peaceful face. For the past two days, they had been staying in the luxury confines of the Hilton Resorts in Newark. After Niko's emotional outburst in the parking garage, Kimi didn't want to take a chance with him going home and confronting his wife. She'd convinced him to stay in the lavish suite until she was able to put her plan into motion. Niko didn't put up a fight. His mind was consumed with jealousy and resentment, and he realized things would turn ugly if he returned home. Kimi assured him that today would be the day that she would make both Raymond and Desiree pay for betraying him. As Kimi looked at Niko's handsome face, she couldn't resist the urge to kiss his soft lips.

"Baby, it's time to wake up," Kimi whispered to her friend.

Niko groaned and slowly opened his eyes. He was clearly not ready to face the day. He calmly stretched his body, then looked up to Kimi, who gave him a soft smile. She kissed him again and slowly got out of bed.

"What time is it?" Niko uttered.

"It's nine o'clock, baby," Kimi responded. "Today is the big day."

Kimi's words seem to slap Niko with a heavy dose of reality. He knew exactly what she was referring to. For the past two days, the secret lovers had been planning out every detail of their plot to get even with Raymond and Desiree. Niko felt his heart speeding up as he reworked the plan in his mind. He looked over to Kimi, who seemed to be calm as a summer breeze. He watched her as she laid out her outfit and prepared to get dressed.

"How are you feeling?" Kimi uttered as she walked over and grabbed Niko's phone from the nightstand.

"I'm good," Niko responded and closed his eyes. "I could use another hour of sleep."

"No, baby." Kimi shook her head and handed Niko the phone. "Call your wife."

Niko opened his eyes again. The command from Kimi was stern enough to grab his attention.

"This early?" Niko mumbled.

"Yes," Kimi quickly replied. "That's the only way this is going to work. You have to make sure she stays home."

Niko sat up on the edge of the bed and grabbed the phone from Kimi. He looked down at the phone and hesitated for a moment. Kimi walked over to Niko and sat down next to him.

"Baby, look at me," Kimi whispered. Niko turned to her and gave her an uneven expression. "Are you sure you want to go through with this?" Niko didn't answer. "We are almost home, baby. All you have to do is make the call. Believe me, baby, this is going to work."

Niko slowly nodded his head and looked at Kimi. She had a determined look in her eyes. She hadn't told Niko the whole plan, so he had no clue how all of this was going to end.

"Do you trust me, honey?" Kimi quietly asked and touched Niko's hand.

"Yes," Niko whispered.

"Then make the call, baby. Believe me, this is going to work."

Niko looked at his phone again and dialed the number. Kimi stood up and walked to the other side of the hotel suite. Niko took a deep breath and waited for the call to connect.

"Desiree, it's me," Niko uttered as his wife picked up the other line.

"Niko, where have you been? I have been trying to find you," Desire groaned on the other end of the phone. "Where are you?"

"I have a pressing issue at the firm. I had to work late and visit a few clients out of town," Niko lied and tried to keep his voice calm.

"Niko, you have been gone for two days," Desiree snapped. "What could be that important?"

Niko felt himself about to boil over with anger and resisted the urge. He looked over to Kimi and thought about the plan.

"Desiree, it's a serious issue, and it's very important," Niko fired back. "I couldn't call you back because I was busy."

"Okay Niko, whatever," Desiree snapped. She was clearly frustrated. "When are you coming home?"

"I'm meeting with one of Marquez's sons today, so I will be home after that," Niko responded.

"Okay, I might not be here when you get back so just call me," Desiree said.

"Where are you going?" Niko quickly asked.

"I don't know, just out," Desiree uttered. "You haven't been home for two days, and I have been stuck in this house waiting on you. I need to get some air."

"No!" Niko raised his voice. "You have to stay home, Desiree."

"What?" She fired back with frustration. "Why?"

Niko looked over to Kimi, who shot him a hard stare. She waved her hand toward him as if to tell him to proceed with the plan. Niko took another deep breath, and then turned his focus back to the phone call.

"Desiree, I need you to do something for me," Niko whispered. Kimi raised her eyebrows and kept a close eye on Niko. She was hoping he could go through with the plan.

"You need me to do what?" Desiree asked from the other line.

"I'm in a bit of a jam at the firm, and I need to make you Power of Attorney over my affairs in case anything happens to me."

"Are you serious, Niko?" Desiree gasped. "Anything like what? What's going on at the firm, Niko?"

"I can't explain it all, Desiree. But I need you to be around in case I need to take care of this today," Niko's voice sounded plausible.

Desiree was growing more concerned from the other line. "Okay Niko, but what exactly do you want me to do?" she asked.

"I just need you to take charge of the company in case something happens to me. I will explain it later," Niko continued. "Just stay close by the house in case I have to handle this today."

There was a silence on the phone. Desiree thought about Niko's request, but didn't know what to say.

A few thoughts ran through Niko's mind. "Are you still there?"

"Yes, I'm here."

"So, will you be there when I get back?"

"I'll be here, Niko," Desiree uttered. "I don't know why you can't tell me what's going on, but I will be here."

Niko could tell that her mind was racing. He couldn't recognize her tone, but he knew Desiree was very curious about what he was up to. "Okay, I will call you later," Niko mumbled.

"Bye," Desiree uttered and hung up.

Niko looked at his phone and disconnected the call. He glanced over to Kimi, who was wearing an intense look on her face.

"So what do you think?" Kimi asked.

"She's pissed off, but she will be there," Niko uttered.

"Good. Just make sure you handle Raymond, and I will take care of the rest." Kimi looked at her watch and turned away from Niko. She rushed to get dressed and put her things together to leave the hotel room. Niko never moved from the edge of the bed. His mind was still racing about Kimi's plan, and he started to grow nervous. He knew that this was a risky plan, but he decided to go along for the ride no matter where it was going to take him. Kimi walked over to Niko and kissed him on the side of his face. "Baby, just remember," Kimi continued. "I'll be leaving Shady Meadows by eleven, so everything has to go down after that."

"Okay, Kimi. I won't forget," Niko whispered.

He watched as Kimi grabbed her keys and left the hotel room. Niko laid back down on the bed and closed his eyes. Images of Raymond and Desiree entered into his mind, and he started to feel betrayed again. A small grin came to his face as he thought about Kimi's plan. The only thing left to do was handle his part, and all of his enemies would soon get what they deserved.

Twenty-Six

About an hour later, Kimi slowly turned down the long road leading up to Shady Meadows community. She took a look at her watch and nodded her head, knowing she was right on time. She knew her favorite security guard was already on duty, and she continued with her plan. As she approached the guardhouse, she put on her sexiest smile as Christopher opened his window and prepared to flirt.

"Good morning, Ms. Moore," Christopher said as his young face brightened with each word. "I haven't seen you around in a few days."

"I know, sweetie, I was away on business." Kimi gave him a flirtatious look and smiled.

"Well, you know I missed ya," Christopher uttered, trying his best to look smooth.

"Awl. You are sweet," Kimi giggled. "Listen, Christopher, I may need a favor from you."

"Anything you need." Christopher nodded. He was eager to help out Kimi.

"Okay, sweetie. I have to run up to my house for a few, but I will be right back, and I will let you know what I need."

"Sure thing. I will be right here." Christopher licked his lips and smiled.

He nodded toward Kimi and watched her as she

continued through the gate. Kimi made her way to her house and parked directly in the front. She didn't bother to open the garage as she got out of the car. She headed into her house and rushed upstairs to her bedroom. Kimi grabbed a handful of brand new sheets and headed back downstairs into her living room. She proceeded to cover all of her furniture and valuables with the white sheets. She looked around and nodded her head at the sight. Kimi took a look at her watch and realized she still had a few minutes left to kill. She headed upstairs to the linen closet, activated the Big Brother system, and then went back downstairs. Kimi grabbed her phone and her keys, and then left the house.

The cold weather made her move faster as she made her way back to her X5. She reached into the back seat and pulled out a large *For Sale* sign. She placed the real estate marker on her lawn and looked around the neighborhood. Kimi turned her focus to Desiree's house across the street. She was making good time ,but she knew she had to act fast to keep her plan going.

Kimi took a deep breath and dropped her head. She walked through the snow and headed onto Desiree's porch. Although her heart was nervously thumping through her chest, Kimi forced a relaxed expression to come to her face. She rang her neighbor's doorbell and waited. The combination of the cold weather and her adrenaline made Kimi's hands shake. A nervous smile came to her face when Desiree opened the door.

"Good morning, Kimi," Desiree sang with a crooked smile. "How are you?"

"Hey. I'm sorry to come by so early ,but I needed to ask for a huge favor." There was a hint of anxiety in Kimi's tone.

"Okay, neighbor, no problem," Desiree replied. "Come in, let's talk."

"Oh no, Desiree, I can't. I'm in a rush." Kimi shook her head. "I have a huge meeting today to discuss my company and I have to get on the road soon."

"Okay. What do you need?" Desiree asked and tightened her face.

"I'm thinking about selling my house, and I have a few people coming by today to look at it," Kimi said.

"That's funny you said that, Kimi, because I was just about to ask you about that sign on your lawn," Desiree quickly blurted. "So are you moving, Kimi?"

"I don't know yet. I'm just testing the market, really," Kimi lied. "But I really want to show the house today, and I was hoping you could housesit for me."

"Huh?" Desiree looked across the street and turned back to Kimi.

"I know its so last minute ,but I really need this favor, Desiree." Kimi gave her neighbor a humbled expression.

Desiree thought for a moment and scratched the back of her neck. "So what do you want me to do?" she quietly asked.

"The first couple should be showing up around noon," Kimi replied. "They may call my house for directions, so if you could hang out over there until they arrive that would be great. It will only be for an hour or two, Desiree. Please?"

Desiree couldn't help but give her neighbor a suspicious glance. She thought about the request and stared at Kimi for a few seconds. Kimi smiled at her again and softened her expression. Desiree figured she owed her neighbor since Kimi had showed up to dinner and was embarrassed by Charlene. She thought about the request for another moment, and then nodded her head.

"Okay, Kimi," Desiree uttered. "What time do you need me over there?"

"Thank you so much, Desiree." Kimi smiled. "Anytime between eleven thirty and twelve o'clock is good. I left the door open, so don't worry about the alarm or anything."

"Okay," Desiree uttered.

"I also went food shopping this past week, so you can help yourself to whatever is in the kitchen." Kimi gave her neighbor a wide smile.

"That sounds good," Desiree chuckled. "I was going to make lunch over here ,but I guess I can eat up your food instead."

"Help yourself." Kimi smiled. She looked at her watch and nodded toward her neighbor. "Thanks again, Desiree. I have to go now. But don't forget, they may call my house around noon for directions. If you could be there before then, I would appreciate it."

"No problem, I'll be there," Desiree mumbled.

Kimi walked off of her neighbor's porch and headed back to her SUV. She never turned around as she got inside the driver seat and fired up the engine. She politely waved at her neighbor and pulled off down the street. Kimi let out a lung full of air. Another crucial part to her plan was in place. She sped through the neighborhood until she came to the guardhouse near the entrance.

Christopher noticed Kimi's BMW coming down the road and walked outside into the cold. Kimi slowed down in front of him and rolled down the window.

"Hey sweetie, you still want to do that favor for me?" Kimi asked and smiled at the young security guard.

"Absolutely," Christopher responded. He couldn't contain his excitement.

"Okay, here is what I need." Kimi handed the young man a small note and a prepaid cellphone.

Christopher gave Kimi a strange look and took the items. "Ms. Moore...?" he uttered and looked at Kimi. He dropped his eyebrows.

"I know this is not in your job description, Christopher." Kimi smiled at the security guard and gave him a deep glance. "But trust me, sweetie, if you do this for me, I will make it worth all the trouble." Kimi gave Christopher a seductive grin and dropped her voice. She almost laughed as she thought about the old game she was running on the young man.

Christopher almost wet his pants. He was so excited about Kimi's words. He nodded toward her and his mouth fell open. "So...what is the favor, Ms. Moore?" Christopher nervously asked.

"At exactly twelve-thirty, I want you to use that phone and text the message written on the note to that number," Kimi instructed.

"That's it?" Christopher asked.

"That's it," Kimi responded with a serious face. "I gave you a few more instructions in the note, but make sure to text that message at exactly twelve-thirty. Okay, baby?"

Christopher nodded his head toward Kimi. He put the note and the phone in his jacket pocket.

"Okay, sweetie, don't forget. If you do this for me, and do it right, maybe we can talk about how I can repay you for the favor." Kimi smiled at the security guard and winked.

Another wide grin came to Christopher's boyish face and he nodded toward her. "I will do this for you, Kimi. Don't you worry," Christopher responded.

Kimi playfully waved at him and sped away from the guardhouse. She looked at her watch again, and almost felt excited that things were moving along as planned. She grabbed her phone and decided to check on Niko to see if he was still on schedule.

*J*wenty-*S*even

Back in Newark, Niko pulled up in front of 723 Broad Street and parked his vehicle in the front of the building. He checked his watch and realized that he was slightly behind schedule. He didn't bother to grab his briefcase as he quickly jumped out of the Audi and made his way into the building. Niko only got a few feet inside before his phone started buzzing in his hand. Niko looked down and noticed it was Kimi. He quickly answered the phone.

"Baby, are you good?" Kimi quickly asked from the other line.

"Hi, Kimi. I'm running just a few minutes late, but I'm here at the firm now," Niko responded.

"Is everything okay?" Kimi asked with a hint of concern in her voice.

"Everything is fine. I am on my way upstairs now," Niko said as he headed to the elevator.

"Okay, baby, I will be by my phone if you need me," Kimi said. "Remember, tell him to be there by twelve, Niko."

"I will," Niko quickly responded. "I will call you back."

"Okay, sweetie."

"Goodbye."

Niko disconnected the call and entered the elevator. He

checked his watch again and slowly exhaled. Although Niko never had a problem with his poker face, today was going to be a serious test of his patience. The images of Raymond and Desiree flashed in and out of his mind, and Niko knew it was important to Kimi's plan not to blow his cool. As the elevator reached the top floor, Niko found himself trying to remain calm as he made his way to his office.

"Good morning Mr. Stanton," his secretary sang with a polite smile.

"Good morning," Niko responded. "Can you buzz Raymond and let him know that I want to see him in my office."

"Okay, Mr. Stanton."

Niko continued to his office and walked over to his desk. He grabbed a yellow folder out of his drawer and looked through a stack of forms. Niko found the blank form he was searching for, and then sat down in his leather chair. Niko was filling out the paperwork when Raymond walked into his office.

"You wanted to see me, boss?" Raymond asked.

Raymond's choice of words woke up Niko's temper, but he forced himself to remain calm. Niko looked up to Raymond and glared at him for a moment. It was the first time he'd looked into his eyes since seeing the photo of him and his wife together. Niko reminded himself to remain calm. He took another moment to gather his thoughts and nodded toward Raymond.

"We can't meet with Ronald tonight," Niko uttered and turned his focus back to his desk.

"What?" Raymond uttered. "Why not? He's going to be expecting us. He really wants to meet with you, Niko."

"I never said *I* wasn't meeting with him," Niko responded and continued to fill out the form. "I just said I'm not going to meet with him *tonight*. I want to reschedule the meeting up for one o'clock today."

Raymond looked at his watch and looked back to Niko. His mind started racing as he thought about his next words. "Niko," he mumbled. "Why can't we just meet with him tonight? Everything is set up for tonight."

Niko nodded his head and continued to complete the form. "I can't do it tonight. It's either today at one o'clock or never," he sternly said.

"Okay, I will call him and tell him we need to meet with him earlier," Raymond uttered.

"Not you…!" Niko snapped and never raised his head form his desk. "I'm going alone."

"What? Why?" Raymond asked.

"Because, you're going to take this to my wife," Niko replied and handed the form to Raymond. Niko gave him another hard glance, and then pointed to the form. "I need my wife to sign that Power of Attorney today. And I want you to sign on as a witness to her signature."

"I don't understand, boss," Raymond quietly uttered. Niko sensed that Raymond was growing slightly nervous.

"I don't know what's going to happen when I meet with Ronald today," Niko said. "I know he's not wrapped too tight and he has a problem with me. So I want my wife to sign that form before I meet with him."

Raymond looked over the form and then he looked back to Niko. He couldn't believe his boss' request. "Niko, you do realize this form gives your wife total control over the firm?" Raymond asked.

"Raymond, I'm a fucking attorney," Niko blurted. He was clearly frustrated. "I know exactly what that form means. Just get your ass up to my house, and have my wife sign that form before twelve. I have some more work to do here, and

I'll meet with Ronald at the restaurant. Don't forget to call me when you get there."

Raymond didn't say another word. He thought about asking Niko another question, but he decided against it. Raymond turned around and headed to his office. A devious smile came to his face as he looked down at the Power of Attorney form. Raymond couldn't help but think that having Desiree take over the firm was the next best thing to taking over the business himself. He looked at his watch and grabbed his things. He was more than happy to head up to Shady Meadows to see Desiree.

*T*wenty-*E*ight

The cold wind danced around the quiet neighborhood in Shady Meadows. Desiree tightened up her jacket as she rushed to make it across the street to Kimi's house. She took one look at the *For Sale* sign on Kimi's lawn and shook her head. She had no clue why Kimi would want to leave the beautiful community. Desiree shook the thought and walked up to Kimi's front door. She remembered her neighbor mentioning that the lock was open and she didn't hesitate to go in from the cold.

Desiree's mouth fell open when she entered Kimi's home. She was impressed with the stunning layout, starting with the hardwood floors and deep rich colors of her walls. Desiree slowly walked into the living room and marveled at Kimi's taste. She recognized that Kimi was serious about selling her house. Desiree stepped over the moving boxes on the floor, and made her way to the kitchen. She noticed all of the white sheets covering the furniture and assumed that Kimi was looking to move very soon. Desiree walked past the dining room and almost scoffed at the sight of more white sheets covering the table and chairs.

"This chick is serious about her furniture," Desiree uttered with a slight chuckle.

She walked into the kitchen and grabbed a glass of juice. Desiree went back into the living room and took a seat on the sofa. She made sure not to move the sheets, fearing that Kimi wanted to keep her furniture covered. Desiree decided to watch a little television before the first couple came to view the house. She grabbed the remote and flipped through the channels until she found something good to help her pass the time.

A few minutes later, Desiree sat back and started to relax into the soft sofa. She felt her body getting warm, and started to slowly rub on her neck. Desiree readjusted her body as a strange feeling started coming over her. Desiree's hands moved from her neck down to her legs. Before long, Desiree started to feel frisky. She looked around Kimi's house and almost felt embarrassed that she was feeling horny. She sat back against the sofa and stretched out her body. She turned to the side and found herself sniffing the white sheets. The aroma was intoxicating, and her body seemed to be awakened by the scent. Desiree was just about to massage herself when her phone started buzzing in her pocket. The sound brought her back to reality, and Desiree quickly answered the phone.

"Hello," Desiree answered with a soft tone.

"Baby, it's me, Raymond."

Desiree sat up on the couch and looked at the phone. "Hey Raymond. How are you?" Desiree uttered. She was still trying to come down from her momentary high.

"Where are you? Are you home?" Raymond quickly asked.

"Yes…I mean…no," Desiree stuttered. "I mean…I am home, but I am at my neighbor's house across the street."

"Oh okay. I am about fifteen minutes from you," Raymond announced.

"What?" Desiree quickly asked. "What's going on? Are you with Niko?"

"No, baby. I'm by myself." Raymond smiled. "You will never believe what I have next to me."

"What's that?" Desiree asked.

"Niko asked me to get you to sign a Power of Attorney today." Raymond was beyond excited about the news. "Baby, he wants you to take over the firm."

"Damn, so he was actually serious," Desiree gasped.

"Serious about what?"

"He asked me about that this morning, but I thought he was losing his mind."

"No, he was serious. I have the form right here. And if everything goes right, he will be losing more than his mind in a couple of hours."

"Damn Raymond, so everything is falling into place," Desiree whispered.

"I told you it would, baby," Raymond bragged. "Listen, I have to get off this phone, but I will be up there in a couple of minutes."

"Okay, Raymond, but meet me at my neighbor's house across the street," Desiree continued. "I have to stay here for another hour or so. I will see you when you get here."

"Okay, no problem."

"See you soon."

Desiree hung up the phone and thought about Raymond's news. Although her mind was curious to find out more about the Power of Attorney, her body was craving to see Raymond. Desiree leaned back into the sofa and quietly anticipated his arrival.

About twenty miles away, at the Stanton Law Firm, Niko turned off his computer and stood up from his desk. He checked the time on his clock and realized he had to make his move. He grabbed his mobile phone, dialed Marquez's son, and waited for him to pick up. Niko started to feel nervous about his meeting with Rojo ,but he knew he had to follow through in order to end the drama with the Marquez boys. As Rojo picked up the other line, Niko felt a shot of fear rising in his stomach.

"Ronald, this is Niko Stanton," he announced with a professional tone.

"How many times I gotta tell ya retarded ass that my name is not Ronald?" Rojo yelled through the phone.

"Okay, Rojo. There is no need to get hostile," Niko uttered. "I was calling because-"

"I know why you callin'!" Rojo barked as he cut Niko short. "I already got the call from Raymond."

Niko shook his head and almost yelled into the phone. He was sure that Raymond and Rojo were making plans for him not to leave the restaurant in one piece.

"So you gonna be at the restaurant by one o'clock, right?" Rojo asked with a bitter tone.

"Yes, I will be there at one," Niko nervously responded. "I will bring your father's case files, and we can discuss everything there. "

"Yea, whatever man," Rojo snapped. "You just make sure you there by one. I don't have all fuckin' day to be playin' around with you. You just get your ass down to the restaurant, and don't be fuckin' late."

The fear in Niko's stomach was now in full swing. Rojo's tone was cold as an icicle. Niko looked at his phone and kept his cool. He knew the drama with Rojo would all be over soon. He looked at the clock on the wall and realized he had more than enough time to make it to the restaurant.

"Okay, Rojo. I'm leaving now," Niko continued. "I will be there by one."

"Lata," Rojo snapped and abruptly hung up the phone.

Niko gritted his teeth and shook his head again. He grabbed the Marquez case file from his desk, and then headed out of his office. Niko was walking to the elevator when his phone started buzzing again. He was expecting to see Rojo's name ,but he smiled when he noticed it was Kimi calling his phone

"Hey," Niko quickly answered.

"Hey, baby," Kimi greeted her friend. "How are things looking over there?"

"Everything is on schedule," Niko quietly responded. "I'm on my way to my meeting, and I will be there by one."

"Good." Kimi smiled. "I just wanted to make sure you were okay. I will check on you in a few hours."

"Okay, baby," Niko whispered.

"Niko, please be careful."

"I will," he responded. "You be safe too."

"For sure. I will call you later."

Niko disconnected the call and entered the elevator. He took a few deep breaths and tried to get his nerves under control. He was clearly shaken by Rojo's violent nature. But he realized that if he wanted to end the drama with the Marquez family, he needed to push all of his fear to the side and follow through with the plan.

Back in Shady Meadows Raymond pulled up in front of Desiree's house and looked around. He was so excited about the Power of Attorney that he couldn't contain himself. Since his first day working at the law office, Raymond dreamed of becoming a partner for the powerful firm. Raymond couldn't believe that with one stroke of the pen, he was now going to have the firm all to himself. And with Niko being pushed out of the way, Raymond would now be the star attorney in the limelight. Raymond smiled as he dwelled on the fantasy. He snatched his phone and dialed Desiree, who quickly picked up on the other line.

"Baby, where are you?" Desiree groaned. Her tone

stunned Raymond for a minute.

"I'm outside of your house," he replied.

"Ok honey, I am right across the street. It's the only other house over here," Desiree said. "The door is open."

Raymond looked across the street and disconnected the call. He grabbed the paperwork and headed over to Kimi's house. Raymond knocked on the door and twisted the doorknob. A wide smile came to his face as he slowly walked into the living room and noticed a sexy Desiree sitting seductively on the sofa. She had obviously made herself comfortable in her neighbor's house. By the look on her face Raymond could tell that she was feeling some kind of way. Before he could greet her, Desiree stood up and walked over to him. Her bare feet slowly pressed up against the hardwood floors, and turned Raymond on with each step. A nervous smile came to his face and he looked into her warming eyes.

"What took you so long?" Desiree groaned and wrapped her arms around Raymond's neck.

She kissed him on the lips and started rubbing on his back. Raymond was clearly shaken by Desiree's fire and dropped the Power of Attorney. She kissed Raymond with such fervor that he instantly became aroused. Desiree moaned and pulled Raymond back toward the sofa. The lovers fell onto the white sheets, and things quickly escalated. Desiree was hornier than she had ever been. Raymond started to flow with her and forgot about Niko, the Stanton Firm, and the Power of Attorney. Desiree moaned out loud and was ready for action. She quickly took off her clothes, and the two made love on the sofa right in the middle of Kimi's living room.

Back at the guardhouse, Christopher looked at his watch and noticed that it was twelve-thirty. He reached into his pocket, pulled out the phone and the note that Kimi gave to him earlier in the day. He thought about Kimi's beautiful face and followed the instructions on the note. He could only imagine how Kimi was going to repay him for the favor, and he wanted to make sure he did everything to perfection. Christopher looked down at the message and read it out loud a few times to make sure he got it right.

You should keep better tabs on your husband. He's at Kimi's house right now, and I don't think they are discussing business.

Christopher twisted his face as he tried to decipher the note. He decided not to pry, but just do what was asked of him. He entered the message into the phone, then sent it. He had no clue that his action was about to set off a huge war at Shady Meadows.

Twenty-Nine

"That will be twenty-eight dollars, ma'am," a soft voice spoke to Charlene Bowser as she stood in the line at the Macy's department store. Like the majority of mornings in her life, she found herself at the mall shopping for anything she could afford. Because she didn't have a full time job, she was overloaded with time to spend her husband's money and live the life of a kept housewife. Today, she'd decided to buy a few items for her home. As she reached into her bag to grab her money, she heard her phone chirping from her purse. Charlene pulled the phone out and saw she had a text message. She handed the clerk the money for the items, and then turned her attention to the message. Charlene clicked on the *read* button and froze. He face turned to stone as the words hit her like a ton of bricks.

"What the fuck...?" Charlene yelled like a mad woman.

The sudden outburst startled the cashier, and she backed away from the register. Charlene yelled again, and almost slammed her phone to the ground. She furiously turned around and rushed out of the department store. She dialed Raymond's cellphone, but there was answer. She bolted to her car and continued to try Raymond, but he refused to pick up. She nearly lost her mind as she fired up the engine to her car, then sped out of the parking lot.

"I'm going to kill this bitch!" Charlene yelled to the

top of her lungs.

Her tires sped down the highway, and Charlene was so upset that she was near tears. She tried Raymond again ,but she was having no luck reaching him. She headed straight for Shady Meadows, deciding that it was finally time to handle her business.

*

Back in Newark, Niko slowed down his engine as he approached Albert's Soul Food Restaurant on South Orange Avenue. He looked around the busy street and decided to park his car directly in front of the restaurant. He had no clue what was going to happen at his meeting with Rojo, so he decided to take every possible precaution. Niko grabbed the Marquez file from the passenger seat and got out of the car. The cold air seemed to be stiffer on this part of town. Niko tightened his jacket and walked toward the entrance of the restaurant. Before he could enter the establishment, a homeless man asking for spare change confronted Niko. Niko thought about ignoring the bum ,but something told Niko to help the man get a meal. He slowly reached into his pocket and gave the man a five-dollar bill. The homeless man looked at Niko and a wide smile came to his face. Niko dropped his eyebrows when he noticed a strange sight. The bum had the whitest teeth Niko had ever seen in his life. Niko ignored his suspicions, and then continued into the restaurant.

"You are fuckin' five minutes late!" a burley voice yelled from the back of the dining area.

Niko quickly looked around. The voice was coming from Rojo Marquez. With the exception of Rojo and two other men sitting at his table, the restaurant was totally empty. Niko slowly walked over to the table and took a seat directly across from Rojo. Niko's back was to the door, and he was shaken by the mood at the table.

"I'm sorry I'm late. I had to make another stop." Niko looked at the other men. All three men shot Niko a hard stare, and Niko felt like a midget amongst giants. He slowly put the Marquez file on the table and began to speak. "Now, Rojo, I know you said you didn't want to discuss a plea deal," he nervously uttered. "But after careful consideration, I found-"

"Shut the fuck up Niko…!" Rojo coldly blurted from the other side of the table.

He leaned back in his chair and took a hard and long look at Niko's tense face. The two men flanking Rojo readjusted themselves in their chairs, and Niko became increasingly nervous. He didn't know what to say. His heart raced out of control as he tried to prepare himself for the worse.

"You know why you're sitting on that side of the table and why I'm on this side of the table?" Rojo smoothly asked.

Niko dropped his eyebrows and nervously blinked his eyes. He was baffled by the question. "I don't know," he nervously responded. His hand started to tremble as a heavy rush of fear came over him.

"You're sittin' over there because you're weak, Niko," Rojo said with a grim tone. "That's your life. A fuckin' weak existence. And I'm sittin' over here 'cause I'm strong."

Niko didn't say a word. He looked at the other two men and decided to see where Rojo was going with his conversation.

"You ever heard that sayin' that only the strong survive?" Rojo coldly asked.

"Yes," Niko uttered like a child being scolded by his parents.

"Do you know why…only the strong survive?"

Niko didn't answer the question. He slowly shook his head and continued to nervously stare into Rojo's eyes.

"Because the strong…eat…the weak!" Rojo

whispered.

His words seemed to electrify Rojo's crew. The men quickly stood up, and then grabbed Niko by the arms. They ruthlessly slammed him face-first down onto the table. Niko screamed in pain.

"Wait…Ronald…what are you doing?" Niko yelled as the men held him down.

"Something that should've been done a long time ago," Rojo yelled out. He grabbed a pistol from his waist and pointed it directly at Niko's back.

"Wait, Raymond told us to make him suffer," one of the men shouted out.

"Fuck Raymond ," Rojo barked. "This is my show!"

"Please God…no, Ronald!" Niko loudly pleaded.

A loud bang came from the front entrance of the restaurant. Rojo looked up and noticed a homeless man stumbling into the dining area near the bar.

"Get the fuck out of here, old man," Rojo yelled as he watched the bum try to regain his balance.

The homeless man finally stood up straight and looked at Rojo. He suddenly pulled out a shiny badge and quickly showed it to the men.

"Police! Put the fuckin' gun down and step away. You're under arrest," the man yelled out.

Before Rojo could make a move, an army of officers rushed through the door and apprehended the three men. Niko tried to catch his breath as the commotion intensified in the small restaurant.

"Get the fuck off of me!" Rojo shouted as three officers wrestled him to the ground.

More officers hustled the other two men out of the restaurant. Niko grabbed his chest as a female officer rushed over and stood him up.

"Are you okay, Mr. Stanton?" the officer quickly asked.

"I'll be alright. Thanks," Niko gasped.

Rojo heard the exchange and looked over to Niko. As the two traded hard stares, Rojo realized that Niko had set him up. An officer abrasively brought Rojo to his feet and started to read the Miranda Rights to him. Rojo never took his eyes off of Niko. A shot of adrenaline rushed through Rojo's body, and his temper exploded. He tried to break free from the officer and rush over to Niko. More cops converged on him and held him back.

"You can't fuckin' hide from me, Niko. I'm gonna find you," Rojo yelled.

"Fuck you, Ronald…!" Niko yelled back, knowing Rojo would never be able to touch him again. "Who's the fuckin' weak one now?"

"I got you motherfucka!" Rojo shouted and bobbed his head. "This won't be the last time you see me. I promise you!"

The officers rushed Rojo out of the door, kicking and screaming. Niko shook his head and let out a sigh of relief as he thought about how close he came to dying at the hands of Marquez's son. The officer who was dressed as a homeless man walked over to Niko and shook his hand.

"Good job, Mr. Stanton," the policeman smiled. "We would have never got this guy without you."

"No problem," Niko whispered as he continued to catch his breath.

The front door to the restaurant opened again and a woman walked through the door. It was Niko's friend, Laura Sanchez. She walked right over to Niko and gave him a firm handshake.

"Counselor, I have to say, I didn't think you had it in you." Laura smiled. "How are you feeling? Do you need medical attention?"

"I'm fine, Laura." Niko nodded toward the prosecutor.

"I had to take the trip down here to see this for myself." Laura pursed her lips together and gave Niko a proud look. "Thanks for doing this for us. We finally have a leg to stand on to cage these animals." Niko took a deep breath and gave Laura a calming expression. "Don't worry about a thing, Niko," Laura continued. "I will take care of everything with the judge and make sure you don't face a single charge."

"Thanks, Laura." Niko nodded. "What about the envelope I got from Ronald Marquez? I still have the money."

"Don't worry about that." Laura waved it off. "Give it to charity or something. I don't want to muddy up this investigation at all. We got him for a thousand other charges. Believe me, its game over for him."

Laura's words took a huge weight off of Niko's shoulders. He took another deep breath and closed his eyes for a moment. He was relieved that his problems with the Marquez bunch were over. He gave Laura another handshake and headed out the restaurant. He quickly got into his car and fired up the engine. Niko took one look at his watch and realized that there was only one more problem that was about to be erased from his life. He sped off the block and made his way back to his house.

Thirty

"I swear I'm going to kill this bitch!" Charlene repeated as she sped up the winding road leading to the Shady Meadows community. Charlene was in a jealous rage and couldn't contain her emotions as she blazed passed the guardhouse near the entrance.

Christopher almost choked on his own air as he watched the angry lady speed through the checkpoint and tear into the complex. His heart nearly jumped out of his chest, and he rushed to the phone to call the police.

Charlene whipped her car around the tight corners and nearly crashed her vehicle as she turned on Victoria Way. She couldn't make it to Kimi's house fast enough. Her mind flashed with a thousand morbid images, and she was itching to confront her husband. She pulled up in front of Kimi's house right behind Raymond's car.

"This fuckin' bastard...!" Charlene yelled.

Before her car could come to a complete stop, Charlene slammed the gear into park and jumped out of the car. She rushed to Kimi's front porch and banged on the door. Without another thought, Charlene twisted the knob and the door surprisingly flew open. Charlene barged into the house like she paid the mortgage. She quickly scanned the area and noticed Raymond's shoes and jacket on the floor. Charlene clinched her fist and continued to look around the living room. She dropped her eyebrows at the sight of all the white sheets covering the furniture in the room.

A giggle coming from the second floor pulled her attention, and she rushed upstairs to investigate the noise. Her mind tried to brace for the worse, but her heart was pumping with so much rage that she had no time to think rational. The female voice became louder, and Charlene realized the noise was coming from the master bedroom. She didn't hesitate for another second. She rushed to the room and pushed open the door.

"Oh my God!" a female voice screamed as Charlene barged into the room. Raymond's face was priceless. He couldn't believe his wife was standing only a few feet from the bed. Charlene's mouth fell open, and she froze for a chilling moment. Her entire world was shattering again, right in front of her very eyes.

"Desiree, what the fuck are you doing?" Charlene cried out like a wounded animal.

A hurricane of emotions rushed through Charlene's body and her eyes became flooded with tears. Desiree reached for her clothes and tried to cover her half naked body. Charlene couldn't figure out if they were just finishing having sex, or if they were getting ready to go at it again. Either way, the graphic scene forced Charlene's soul to leave her body. She instantly became an animal. Charlene rushed to Desiree's side of the bed, then went into attack mode.

"Wait, Charlene, you don't understand…!" Desiree tried to explain, but it was too late.

Before she could say another word, Charlene was all over here. Charlene grabbed her by the neck with both hands and started choking Desiree.

"I'm gonna kill you….you fuckin' slut!" Charlene yelled and tried to squeeze the life out of her.

Desiree fought back and punched Charlene in the

face. She tried to pull Charlene's hands from her neck ,but Charlene was too strong. She smacked Desiree in the face and made her nose bleed. Raymond jumped over the bed and grabbed his wife. He pulled her off Desiree, and the heroic move gave Desiree a chance to run to the other side of the bedroom. Desire wrapped the white sheets around her body, then tried to find her clothes.

"What the fuck is wrong with you?" Raymond yelled.

"What the fuck is wrong with *me*?" Charlene fired back. "You fuckin' my friend, you asshole!"

"It's not like that," Raymond tried to calm his wife down.

"Get the fuck off of me!" Charlene yelled and pulled away from him. She rushed back to Desiree, and the two entangled again. Desiree yelled as Charlene continued to punish her. She proceeded to punch, scratch, claw and pull at Desiree's pretty face. With every pull and tug, Charlene caused more bloody damage. Raymond tried to pull his wife off Desiree again, but her fury was too intense. Charlene started banging Desiree's head up against the wall. The pain was too much to bear, and Desiree aggressively pulled away from Charlene in terror. A disheveled Desiree fell against the wall, and she ran to the other side of the room. Charlene pursued her like a hawk, and Raymond tried to keep up with his angry wife. Before Desiree could make it to her clothes, Charlene lunged at her. The impact forced Desiree into the adjacent wall. Desiree screamed to the top of her lungs as her body crashed into the huge window near the bed.

"DESIREE...!" Raymond yelled and reached out to her, but it was too late. Desiree's body awkwardly toppled through the broken window, and she dreadfully fell to her death.

"DESIREE...OH MY GOD NO....PLEASE... NOOOO!" Raymond yelled and rushed over to the window.

255

He looked beyond the broken glass and screamed in pain as he spotted Desiree's lifeless body on the ground below.

"Oh my God, no Desiree. No!" Raymond put his hand on his head and stared down to the ground. His world started to spin like crazy, and Raymond felt dizzy. He couldn't believe what was happening. He turned back to Charlene and noticed she was frozen stiff. Her face was emotionless, and she couldn't believe what had just happened.

"What did you do, Charlene?" Raymond angrily yelled. Charlene didn't respond. "What did you do?" Raymond repeated.

Charlene didn't say a word. She slowly sat down on the edge of the bed. Her eyes stared into eternity as a cold chill rushed though her body. She didn't know how to feel. Everything had happened so fast, and Charlene never weighed the consequences of her anger.

Raymond continued to pace back and forth in the room. He looked around and realized they both were going to jail if he didn't act fast. He looked over to his wife as she sat silently on the edge of the bed. She was clearly out of it. He continued to pace, trying to find a way out of this deadly dilemma. All of his experience as a defense attorney had never prepared him for this day. He started to push his mind to think a way out of this jam. The sound of police sirens caused him to panic. He rushed to the window again and noticed a half dozen police cruisers were making their way up the winding road. He ran back over to Charlene as she sat on the side of the bed.

"Charlene look at me," Raymond shouted and grabbed her hands. Charlene slowly looked up. Her eyes were distant, and Raymond realized she was beyond the point of no return. "Baby, listen, when the cops ask you what happened tell them that she jumped out the window, okay?" Raymond instructed with a stiff tone. Charlene never responded. A small grin came to her face as she started to grow delusional.

"Charlene, I'm serious…!" Raymond yelled and tried to pull her back to reality. "When the cops ask you what happened. Tell them that you caught me cheating, and Desiree panicked and jumped out of the window. Okay?"

"Okay," Charlene nodded with a nonchalant tone.

"CHARLENE, LISTEN TO ME DAMMIT!" Raymond yelled in frustration. "You want to spend the rest of your life in jail? Do you?"

"No," Charlene quietly answered. She was almost in tears.

"Then say it with me," Raymond nodded. "Desiree jumped out the window."

Charlene looked at Raymond and slowly nodded toward him. She swallowed the lump in her throat and decided to cooperate. "Desiree jumped out the window," she whispered through her pain. She looked at Raymond and said it again. "Desiree jumped out the window."

"Good girl," Raymond gave her an uneven expression. He was clearly worried for them. "Just stick to the story, and we will be fine, okay."

"Okay," Charlene mumbled.

Raymond hugged his wife as the sirens became louder. He sat on the bed with Charlene and held her in his arms. They sat in silence as the police barged into the house and, eventually, made their way to the master bedroom.

*

An hour later, Kimi pulled up to her street in Shady Meadows. The large scene of police cars, fire trucks and EMS units caused her heart to race out of control. Kimi thought about turning around and leaving the scene, but she didn't want to attract any suspicions in her direction. She pulled her

BMW over to the side of the road and decided to walk the one block up to her house. She navigated her way through the maze of police tape, law officers and news crews. Kimi was a few yards away from her front door when a uniformed policeman approached her.

"I'm sorry, ma'am. Authorized personnel only," the cop warned.

"I do apologize, sir. But I live here," Kimi humbly whispered. She pulled out her driver's license and showed it to the officer. "What happened? Did somebody break into my house?" Kimi played her role as the helpless homeowner to perfection. She looked around the scene, and her worried face was worthy of an Academy Award. The officer took one look at Kimi and called over a detective to assist her. Kimi forced another painful expression to come to her face as a female detective walked over.

"How can I help you? I'm Detective Reynolds."

"Hi. I'm Kimi Moore, and this is my home," Kimi quickly responded. "What happened?"

"There was an accident, Ms. Moore," Detective Reynolds replied. "We have identified the victim as Desiree West. I'm guessing she was a neighbor of yours?"

"Oh my God." Kimi covered her mouth and looked across the street. "Desiree? Oh yes…that was my neighbor. Oh my goodness. What happened?"

Detective Reynolds took a deep breath and looked around the scene. "Somehow she was in your house with a Raymond Bowser, and his wife caught them in bed together. Now according to their story, they are saying Desiree West panicked when she saw Raymond's wife and jumped out the bedroom window."

"Jumped?" Kimi whispered in horror.

"Yes, that is the story we've gathered." The detective

gave Kimi a slightly suspicious glance. "Any idea why Ms. West was in your house?"

"She was house-sitting for me today," Kimi answered, trying to clear the cobwebs from the news. "I'm selling my home, and I asked her to show it today to a few potential buyers."

"Okay, thanks for the information," the detective said. "We may need you to answer more questions as we wrap up here."

"Yes, of course. Anything I can do to help." Kimi nodded her head. "Have you checked the camera system?"

"Camera system?" Detective Reynolds uttered.

"Yes, I have a Big Brother camera system in my house." Kimi gave the detective a serious glance.

"Show me." Detective Reynolds raised her eyebrows.

Kimi lead the detective into the house. As Kimi walked into the living room, she saw Raymond and Charlene being questioned by a group of officers as they sat on her sofa. Charlene gave Kimi a hard stare and tried to read her body language. Kimi kept her cool and led the detective to the second floor. She opened up her linen closet and showed the detective the intricate camera system.

"I'll be damned," the detective blurted. "Can you show me the video of today?"

"I sure can," Kimi responded.

Kimi cued the video and showed the detective the images of the house from just about an hour ago. Both women covered their mouths as the video of Charlene pushing Desiree out the bedroom window flashed across the screen.

"Goddamn," the detective gasped. "I need to seize this video ."

"No problem," Kimi uttered.

The detective rushed back down to the living room

with Kimi following close behind. Detective Reynolds walked right over to Charlene and Raymond and stood over them.

"You both are under arrest," the detective yelled. Her words caused the other officers to quickly handcuff the married couple, then bring them to their feet.

"Under arrest for what?" Raymond yelled.

"The murder of Desiree West," the detective shouted.

Charlene didn't put up a fuss. She simply looked at Kimi and realized that she was caught red handed. Charlene never blinked an eye as she gave Kimi a cold stare. Charlene knew Kimi was hiding something, but it was too late to try to figure it out now. Charlene's anger had gotten the best of her, and she had ruthlessly murdered her friend Desiree. Kimi felt an eerie chill rush through her body as Charlene gave her one last look. Kimi didn't know for sure, but, for a slight moment, she thought Charlene flashed a devilish smile in her direction.

The police walked Raymond and Charlene Bowser out of the house and placed them in the first available police cruiser. Kimi walked to the front door and looked outside just in time to see the cop car speeding off Victoria Way. As she looked around the neighborhood, Kimi couldn't help but think of how her plan worked to perfection. Desiree was being tagged on her lawn, and Charlene and Raymond Bowser were heading to prison for her murder. A small grin came to Kimi's face, and a rush of relief flushed her body as Kimi thought about how this dramatic chapter to her life was finally coming to a close.

Epilogue
One Month Later

And in other news...the city of Newark can breathe a collective sigh of relief as one of the largest criminal cases has finally ended with a guilty verdict. Local businessman-turned-convicted-felon, Leon Marquez, was found guilty of six counts of fraud and two counts of money laundering. Marquez is due back in court to face additional charges along with his son Ronald Marquez, who is currently out on bail. The new charges were levied after evidence surfaced that linked the one-time philanthropist and his son to several violent crimes, including murder and assault. Mayor Gary Banks has referred to this case as a victory for the citizens of Newark, who have been crippled by the outbreak of violence. A press conference is scheduled for noon today.

An icy grin came to Kimi's face as she turned off the car radio and continued to cruise down Broad Street. Things were finally calming down after an explosive month in the cold city of Newark. Kimi looked at her watch and realized she was running slightly behind schedule. She only had a few minutes to make it to the train station and pick up Niko. Kimi couldn't help but feel excited about the new chapter she was about to write in her life. Desiree was finally out of the picture, Kimi finally had Niko all to herself, and Charlene and Raymond Bowser were both behind bars, facing a mountain of charges. Kimi wanted to keep it that way, and made sure she turned over all of the video evidence from her Big Brother system to the police. Her brilliant plan worked to perfection, and there was only one thing left to do before Kimi and Niko left New Jersey for good. She reached over in her purse and grabbed her phone. She quickly dialed a number and waited for the call to connect.

"Vanguard Enterprises," a male voice politely answered from the other line.

"Hello this is, Kimi Moore. I was told to call this number today."

"Yes, Kimi how are you?" the man politely asked. "My name is Keith Robinson, and I'm in the acquisitions department with Vanguard. I just wanted to give you the great news that everything has been cleared for the purchase of your Messy Sheets Company. The acquisition has been approved, and the funds are waiting for you at MLT Escrow Company."

"Wow," she uttered. A rush of emotions came over her. "Thank you very much, Mr. Robinson. I do appreciate all of your help in this."

"No problem, Ms. Moore. Please reach out if you have any issues accessing the funds," he said.

"I will do that," Kimi uttered. "You have a great day."

Kimi disconnected the call and shouted praises to the top of her lungs. She couldn't believe her company had finally sold. As she continued to the train station, her face was bright enough to light up an entire city. She was excited and couldn't wait to tell Niko the great news.

Niko stepped off the curb and flagged down Kimi when he saw her BMW whip around the corner near the train station. He took one look at her smiling face and nodded his head toward her.

"Hey, baby, need a ride?" Kimi joked as she pulled up alongside Niko. He put his bags in the back seat and climbed into the passenger seat. Kimi reached over and gave him a deep kiss. It felt good to finally kiss him in public with no worries. Niko smiled at Kimi as she pulled away from the train station.

"Kimi, I have one stop to make and then we can hit the road." Niko pointed to the corner as they approached a traffic light. "Make this left here, and you can pull over right in front of the Call & Response Building up the street."

"Okay, baby." Kimi smiled. "Guess what..."

"What?" Niko asked and turned to Kimi, who couldn't wipe the smile from her face. She was clearly excited.

"They sold my company, baby," Kimi announced. "It's official."

"That is wonderful Kimi," Niko gasped. "Damn, that is actually great news. No wonder you are grinning from ear to ear."

"I know, can you believe it, baby?" Kimi asked and giggled with glee. "They said the money is available, so I can transfer it at any time. We are going to be fine ,baby."

"Wow….congratulations." Niko smiled.

He looked at Kimi as the two exchanged a deep stare. A huge air of reality filled the car as Niko realized for the first time that he was saying goodbye to his old life and today was the beginning of his journey with Kimi. The Stanton Firm was now on the auction block, and there was no reason for Niko to stay in the state. He couldn't wait to get as far away from New Jersey and bury the memories of Desiree, Raymond Bowser and the Marquez Boys. As Kimi approached the Call & Response building, Niko motioned for her to pull over.

"This will only take a second," Niko said. He reached for the back seat and pulled out a white envelope from his bag. "I just need to drop this off to Tycen before we leave."

"That's fine, baby." Kimi smiled. "I waited this long for you. What's a few more minutes, right?"

Niko chuckled and gave his friend another quick kiss.

"So where are all of your things? You only have one bag?" Niko asked as he looked in the back seat.

"I left my stuff at the hotel," Kimi responded.

"Hotel?"

"Yes, baby." Kimi grabbed Niko's shoulders and began to slowly massage him. She gave him an all too familiar look of seduction. "I rented a hotel room for us. I hope you don't mind. I figured since this is our last day in Jersey, we can say goodbye the right way."

"Is that right?" Niko smiled.

"Yes, baby," Kimi responded.

Niko gave her a look of approval. Kimi licked on her bottom lip, and Niko knew exactly what was on her mind. She reached over and kissed Niko again. This time she started touching on Niko's chest and caressing him. Niko moaned and slightly jumped as Kimi started moving her hand lower.

"Whoa, baby," Niko chuckled. "Let me handle this really quick, and I will be right back."

Kimi smiled at Niko and nodded her head. She watched him as he got out the car and headed into the building. He was moving like a man on a mission. He looked at his watch and couldn't help but smile as he thought about getting Kimi back to the hotel room. He put a tighter grip on the white envelope, then walked right into the office of Tycen Wakefield.

"Niko, how are you?" Tycen asked and stood up from behind his desk.

Niko put a quick smile on his face when he noticed that Tycen was not alone. A tall and sexy woman stood up from the leather sofa. Niko took one look at her familiar face, mesmerized.

"Tycen, this is your girlfriend, right?" Niko blurted. He pulled his face back for a moment, clearly taken with her stunning beauty. He reached out to shake the young lady's hand.

"Actually, this is my fiancée," Tycen proudly announced and walked over to Niko. "I would like for you to meet Heidi Kachina."

"It's nice to meet you Ms. Kachina," Niko said. He gave Tycen's fiancée a charming look. "I've heard a lot about you."

"Thank you. But you can call me Heidi." The sexy woman gave Niko a calm expression.

"So Niko, what brings you by?" Tycen asked as he tried to move the focus off of his fiancée and back to business.

"I just wanted to make good on a promise before I left," Niko said.

"Wow, so you are really going to leave New Jersey?" Tycen uttered. He gave Niko a concerned look.

"Yes, it's time to say goodbye to all of this." Niko slowly nodded his head and looked around. "But just remember the list I gave you in case you or anyone from your program needs a lawyer. Or even Ms. Kachina here," Niko joked.

"Not my baby," Tycen chuckled and gave Heidi a sweet kiss on the face. "She would never need a defense attorney. My baby wouldn't hurt a fly. She's an angel."

Heidi gave Tycen a crooked grin. She covered her smile and waved off her fiancé.

"Well, I just wanted to stop by and make my official campaign contribution to you." Niko handed Tycen the white envelope he'd gotten from Rojo. "I know I can't be here to help out with your campaign, but I figure I can become your first donor."

Tycen took the envelope and quickly glanced at the money. He looked up to Niko and gave him a confused look.

"Damn, Counselor. What can I say?" Tycen reached out and gave Niko a firm handshake.

"I don't want you to say a thing. Just win that election next year." Niko smiled. "This city needs an honest man on Broad Street."

Tycen didn't respond. Niko's choice of words touched him, and he began to feel more confident about his decision to run for office. Tycen looked over to his fiancée, Heidi. He handed her the envelope, and then turned back to Niko.

"Speaking of honesty, I also wanted to give you this." Niko reached into his pocket and gave Tycen an all white DVD.

"What's this?" Tycen asked.

"I don't know what's on the video," Niko responded. "I never got a chance to watch it. But my friend, Kimi, told me to give you that. She said it should help out with the election. I'm not sure what that means, but she was pretty serious about me getting this to you."

"Okay, I will check it out." Niko gave Heidi the video, and she put it in her purse. Tycen turned back to Niko and gave him a reassuring look. "So what's next for you, Niko?"

"Well, I plan to start from scratch, and see if I can get it right this time." Niko slowly nodded his head and closed his mouth. "I don't know if I will ever come back to New Jersey, but, if I do, I will look you up."

"Okay, Niko, I'm going to hold you to that." Tycen smiled.

"No problem, Mayor Wakefield." Niko nodded his head and gave Tycen a confident gesture.

Tycen reached out and shook Niko's hand again. He watched as Niko turned around and headed out of the office. Niko felt another weight lift off of his shoulders as he strolled out the front door to the building. Although he wouldn't be around to help out with the campaign, Niko knew, with the right strategy, Tycen had a good chance of becoming Mayor of Newark. He was hoping the money would help Tycen get his campaign kicked off with a positive start.

Niko walked out of the building and headed straight to the car. He looked up to the sky and noticed that a few snow showers were starting to fall. He jumped back into Kimi's BMW and nodded to her. She smiled at him and pulled off from in front of the building.

"Is everything okay?" Kimi quietly asked.

"Everything's fine, baby," Niko calmly responded.

The car fell silent as Kimi pushed her X5 through the snow. Niko looked out the window as an emotional feeling came over him. Images of his past started to swirl in his head and he tried to shake the ugly feeling. Starting a new life with Kimi in another state was not going to be an easy transition, but he was beyond ready to start a new chapter in his life.

Kimi looked over to her friend and noticed that he was deep in thought. She reached over to him and started rubbing on his inner thighs. Niko looked at Kimi, and she gave him another suggestive glance. Kimi's beautiful face was like kryptonite to his heart. She didn't have to do much to get his attention, just a simple look into her captivating eyes would engage him. She started to nervously nibble on her lips again, and then smiled like a schoolgirl.

"You know what I'm thinking ?" Kimi whispered.

"What's that, baby?" Niko responded.

"I'm ready to play," Kimi quietly stated with a slight moan.

A smooth grin came to Niko's face as Kimi's request danced around in his mind. He looked over to his friend and slowly shook his head.

"Right now?" Niko calmly asked.

"Right now, baby." Kimi smiled. "Can we?"

Niko didn't say a word. He looked outside at the snowy

ground and turned back to Kimi. He slowly nodded his head and almost laughed at her face lighting up like a Christmas tree. Niko's body started to grow excited as Kimi turned down a side street and parked the X5 near an abandoned warehouse. She put the SUV in park and popped open the hatch back. Niko dropped his eyebrows and started rubbing on his chin like a pimp. He watched as Kimi got out of the car and walked around to the passenger side of the BMW. She opened Niko's door and pulled him out of the car by his right arm.

"You're coming with me," Kimi sternly ordered as she playfully jumped into character.

"Where are you taking me?" Niko asked lightheartedly, standing in front of Kimi.

She moved closer to him and pinned him against the SUV. A slightly nervous grin came to Niko's face when Kimi reached up and kissed him on the lips. She moaned and started to rub her body against his. The snowfall became heavier, and the cold flakes started to cover their faces. Kimi continued to kiss Niko as the snow instantly melted the second it touched their hot lips. Kimi paused for a moment and passionately touched Niko's face. She looked into his eyes and gave him the look he loved to see.

"Don't worry about where we're going," Kimi whispered and kissed him again. "You just be ready to please me when we get there."

Niko closed his eyes and smiled. He loved it when Kimi spoke forcefully to him. She grabbed him by the arm again and led him to the rear of her BMW. She watched him closely as he got inside the trunk and made himself comfortable. Kimi took one look at his excited face and knew that she was in for a very explosive episode with her friend. She reached down and gave him one last sexy kiss before she closed the back of the trunk.

Kimi looked around the quiet street and rushed back to the driver side door. She jumped in the X5 and sped off down the street. Kimi was growing more excited with each passing second. She looked at her watch and yelled to the back of the vehicle.

"We should be there in less than fifteen minutes, baby," Kimi yelled.

The snowy downtown streets started to fill up with drivers and pedestrians. Kimi found herself taking a few detours as she tried to make it back to the highway. She took a look at her clock and noticed that rush hour was only a few minutes away. The thick snow started to fall faster. Kimi pushed the SUV though the storm and decided to avoid the busy downtown traffic. She turned up Clinton Avenue and drove though the neighborhoods to make it to the highway. An eerie feeling came over Kimi as she cruised through the broken down streets she hadn't seen since she was a child. Her old neighborhood hadn't changed at all, only the faces were different. Kimi felt herself reminiscing as she turned onto Avon Avenue. She pushed the BMW through the rising snow and made it up the hill. Kimi stopped at a traffic light and looked around. She felt an urge to blow through the red light ,but she decided against it. She waited impatiently and looked at her clock again. She realized the time was getting away from her.

"Come on," Kimi quietly whispered as she looked up to the long red light.

A black SUV slowly crept up behind her, and Kimi took a mental note of the vehicle in her rearview mirror. She turned her attention back to the traffic light, and then nervously started to tap on the steering wheel. A few more cars started to build a line behind her. Kimi couldn't believe how long the light was. Before she could curse the traffic light again, the signal changed to green.

Kimi punched the gas and continued up the street. She looked in the rearview mirror and noticed that the black SUV was still behind her. It was moving closer to her, and Kimi sped up. Her heart started to grow nervous. She continued to speed up the car despite the snowy conditions. She heard the engine of the black SUV revving behind her, and she sped up the X5 again. Kimi dropped her eyebrows when she noticed that the SUV was flashing its headlights. Her adrenaline kicked in as a rush of fear consumed her. The black SUV was close enough to kiss her rear bumper. The lights continued to flash, and Kimi's eyes were fixed on the rearview mirror. A loud car horn abruptly pulled Kimi out of her trance. She turned her eyes back to the road just in time to see another black SUV flying down the street, coming directly toward her. Kimi screamed in shock as the second SUV made a sharp turn and cut her off. Kimi slammed on the brakes just in time to avoid the collision.

"What the hell!" Kimi yelled and quickly put the BMW in park.

Before she could gather herself, she heard the loud sound of a few cars screeching to a halt. She looked out her front windshield and watched in horror as two armed men jumped out of the second SUV. Kimi froze like a Polaroid. She turned around and thought about putting her BMW in reverse ,but more armed men were quickly approaching her vehicle from the rear. Kimi screamed Niko's name ,but it was too late. Kimi soon realized she was getting carjacked. One man rushed to the driver-side door and tried to open it. Kimi quickly locked the door and looked around.

"Open this fuckin' door!" the man viciously yelled.

Kimi ignored him and reached for her phone. The angry man didn't hesitate for another second. He pointed the gun at the X5 and fired a single shot into the corner of the window.

"Oh my God, please no!" Kimi screamed as the gunshot shattered the glass.

Kimi dropped the phone and a rush of tears exploded from her eyes. The man opened the door and grabbed Kimi by her hair. He violently pulled her out of the BMW and smacked her flush across the face with the pistol. The heavy metal crushed her jaw like a ton of bricks. Kimi crumbled to the concrete as the impact knocked her half unconscious.

"Open the fuckin' back…!" the man yelled to his crew.

As the armed man walked to the rear of the BMW, one of his partners reached behind the steering wheel and popped open the trunk. The armed man cocked the hammer on his pistol and quickly raised the hatch. Niko put his hands up. He'd heard the commotion from the trunk and realized they were being carjacked. Niko took one look at the armed man and his heart dropped to the floor.

"I told you motherfucka!" the man barked. "You was gonna see me again."

Niko couldn't believe his eyes. The man's familiar face haunted him like a ghost. The angry scowl belonged to Rojo Marquez. Niko opened his mouth to speak ,but he never got a word out. Rojo quickly swung the gun at Niko's head and connected with a heavy blow. Niko flew back as the impact knocked him out. Rojo continued to brutally punch Niko in the face until he was sure Niko was out cold. Rojo looked around the icy street, and then slammed the hatch shut. He calmly walked to the front of the BMW and climbed into the driver seat. He fired up the engine to the X5 as his partners returned to their black SUVs. Kimi heard the engine to her vehicle and slowly opened her eyes. She was too weak to make a move. She laid on the ground in pain and slowly turned her head. One by one, she watched as the trucks sped down the street. She looked at the rear of her BMW and a dark feeling of dread fell over her. The back of the X5 started to disappear as it drove into the midst of the thick snowfall. The last thought that ran through her mind was the image of a helpless Niko in the trunk. Kimi whispered his name just before she slipped into a state of unconsciousness. And everything faded to black.

Read the conclusion of
Messy Sheets
in
Dashawn Taylor's
next highly anticipated novel,

THE FINAL KISS

Coming soon!

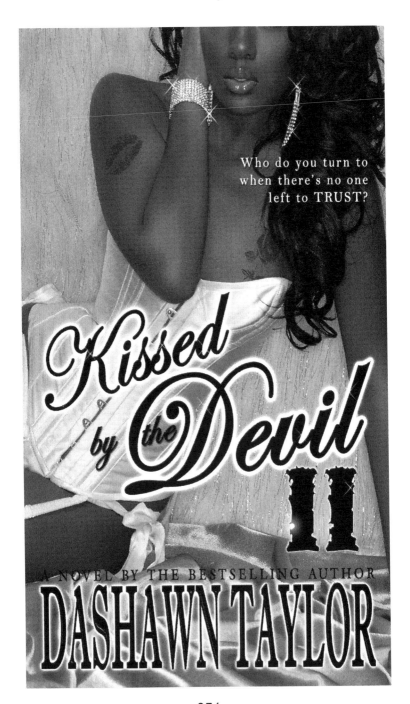

Who do you turn to when there's no one left to TRUST?

Kissed *by the* *Devil*
II

A NOVEL BY THE BESTSELLING AUTHOR
DASHAWN TAYLOR

FROM POVERTY TO
POWER MOVES
THE TRUE STORY
Second Edition
As Seen On BET's ULTIMATE HUSTLER SHOW
Inspiration comes to us all in many forms. With his back against the wall, this entrepreneur finds the WILL to do better deep within his past.
This is his journey!
DASHAWN TAYLOR
WITH STEPHANIE JOHNSON

DASHAWN TAYLOR

QTY	TITLE	PRICE
	From Poverty To Power Moves ISBN-10: 0-9800154-1-3 ISBN-13: 978-0-9800154-1-6	$15 USD $19 Canada
	Kissed By The Devil ISBN #: 0-9800154-0-5 EAN #: 978-0-9800154-0-9	$15 USD $19 Canada
	Kissed By The Devil II ISBN #: 0-98001-5421 EAN #: 978-09800-1542-3	$15 USD $19 Canada
	Messy Sheets ISBN #: 0-9800154-8-0 EAN #: 978-0-9800154-8-5	$15 USD $19 Canada
	*Shipping & Handling (2.95 per book)	

Name: _____

Address: _____

City/State: _____

Zip: _____

Institution info* _____

TOTAL $ _____

Send check or money order to:
Next Level Publishing
PO Box 83
Newark, NJ 07111

Wholesalers and Credit Card Orders, please call 973.634.8421
or email info@nextlevelpublishing.com

*Please allow 5-7 Business Days for Shipping and
2-3 Weeks for All Institution Orders.

276

Thank You For
Your Support!

www.NextLevelPublishing.com

10817866R00160

Made in the USA
Lexington, KY
01 October 2018